The DROWNED VILLAGE

NORMA CURTIS

The

DROWNED VILLAGE

Bookouture

Published by Bookouture in 2022

An imprint of Storyfire Ltd.
Carmelite House
50 Victoria Embankment
London EC4Y 0DZ

www.bookouture.com

ISBN: 978-1-80019-859-3
eBook ISBN: 978-1-80019-858-6

This book is a work of fiction. Whilst some characters and
circumstances portrayed by the author are based on real people
and historical fact, references to real people, events, establishments,
organizations or locales are intended only to provide a sense of
authenticity and are used fictitiously. All other characters and all
incidents and dialogue are drawn from the author's
imagination and are not to be construed as real.

For
Jane Tilbrook
Louise Grewal
Charlie Frampton
Those happy days!

PROLOGUE
Night thoughts

During the long, troubled nights when Virginia groans restlessly next to him and Al can't sleep, he keeps his heavy eyelids shut and returns secretly to the tiny village of Capel Celyn, nestled snugly in the green foothills of North Wales.

In his drowsy imagination he drives up the steep lane, his car popping stones under the tyres, until he reaches the quarrymen's stone cottages at the side of a scarred hill, grandly named The Mountain Ash Guest House.

Before entering, he stops and turns around to look at the endless, gentle mountains smudged with green trees, chequered with hedges and stone walls, flecked with wandering sheep.

Waiting inside the guest house to welcome him are the young proprietors, Jane and Eric Oswald Hughes, standing by a flickering fire that smells of wood and coal dust.

He sees their faces clearly. In their late twenties, they are trying to make a go of the place by letting out rooms to climbers and walkers. Eric is a thin, grim-looking man with a dark widow's peak and the expression of someone about to deliver bad news. Jane is eager and welcoming.

Al is smiling at them now in the comfort of his bed.

He is young and wearing his navy blues. All he wants is to see Elin and drive her somewhere secluded – *very secluded* – but after unpacking his kitbag, just as he is leaving the guest house to walk down to the village to meet her, Jane Oswald Hughes calls him back.

'Captain! Could I have a word, please?'

He turns reluctantly.

'Now then.' She looks at him keenly, folding her arms. Jane prides herself on knowing everyone there is to know, and not only them but their cousins, their second cousins, and all their distant relatives. 'I know you from somewhere.'

He doubts that very much, but her eager expression makes him go along with it. 'You do? Maybe you saw me in Liverpool Port,' he suggests.

'Now what would I be doing in Liverpool Port?' she asks sharply, as if he has accused her. 'Are you related to William Jenkins from Ruabon, to the east?'

'No,' he replies firmly.

'Evan from Cefn? Mrs Sarah Moses? Jones she was, before she married—'

'Take my word for it, I'm a stranger to the area,' he says, hoping to put an end to it, hearing the time ticking by on the slate clock on the mantelpiece.

Suddenly the door opens, and joy! It's Elin, come to find him. She enters the guest house in a shaft of sunlight, her dark hair gleaming, happy to see him.

Jane Oswald Hughes jumps to her feet, saying, 'Just the person!' and she grabs Elin by her shoulders to view him as if he is an exhibit. 'Now! Who does he remind you of?'

Elin stifles a giggle and holds his gaze. 'Well, let's see,' she says, joining her friend in studying him. 'He's got a bit of Richard Burton around the eyes.'

'Nonsense!' Jane Oswald Hughes says firmly and shakes her head. 'Richard Burton's from Glamorgan.'

'Oh well, I'm sure you'll work it out, Jane. I came to find Al because tea's nearly ready up in the village.'

But Jane is not ready to give up and she follows them to the door. In a last desperate stab in the dark she says, 'Mr Locke, let me ask you. Where in America do you come from?'

'Philadelphia, Pennsylvania.'

'Well, that's it!' Mrs Oswald Hughes claps her hands joyfully, satisfied he is one of their own. 'Pennsylvania! Why didn't you say? You're one of us! You'll be from Fron Goch originally, same as Abraham Lincoln's ancestors. There we are then!'

In his bed, Al stuffs the duvet into his mouth and laughs out loud at the happy memory. *There we are then!*

'Al?' Virginia whimpers.

He has disturbed his sorrowing wife from the safe refuge of her sleep. 'I'm sorry, darling,' he says softly, and she mumbles a reply and then falls silent.

Quietly, stealthily, so as not to disturb her again in any way, Al retreats back into the past, leaving his grief behind him. He takes Elin's hand and they walk down the leafy, curving, overgrown track that leads to the village. It brings them out near a bridge over a river, and along the road, past the stone houses, past the chapel, and the school, is her parents' farm. The farm is set back off the road and up a gentle hill.

One of us. After tea, Elin takes him to see Abraham Lincoln's great-great-great grandmother's grave. 'Seeing as you're related.'

Al turns onto his back and stares at the ceiling, letting the tears leak back into his eyes again. The ceiling fan is grey in the dark; it looks like a helicopter rotor.

He walks with Elin through the village in the evening sun, and everything is golden, the long shadows are golden, the hills are golden and the people are gilded with welcome.

Captain, they call him, and Al feels the tears roll down his creased cheek onto the pillow because tonight those days are in his grasp again – he can reach out and touch them.

CHAPTER ONE

Present day

Sophie Rodale was sitting outside the Mountain Ash Bunkhouse with a mug of coffee, tanning her legs in her red dress. The sun lit the foothills of Snowdonia green and gold beneath the wispy sky; the sounds of birdsong and the tetchy bleating of sheep filled the air.

The last two ramblers left the bunkhouse bent under their packs, their lunches swinging from the straps, blue windbreakers tied round their waists, rustling with every step. Sophie watched them until they were out of sight, but they never looked back. Mountain Ash was just a place to rest up for the night before moving on.

Now, in the warm stillness of late morning, her mind came back to something she'd heard once and had been obsessing about lately: that in times of danger, female polar bears eat their young.

She wasn't clear whether this was about saving them from a worse fate, or whether the polar bear mother was being pragmatic and ensuring she could live to breed another day, but either way, it had a nightmarish quality to it that Sophie couldn't shake off. The bottom line was, when bad things happen, the female polar bear goes and makes it worse; Sophie could relate to that.

The air was warm and gentle as breath, and a breeze lifted her hair from around her face and then dropped it again. The sensation was familiar. Max used to do that: lift her hair and drop it. He used to love her hair. When they had first met Max had told Sophie her hair was the colour of warm sand, but by the time he dumped her he'd downgraded it to dirty blonde. After seven years, he'd taken their future away in three words, with no discussion: *It's not working*. After he'd gone she'd given up her job, and in a rare case of perfect timing, bought the bunkhouse from her uncle and aunt who were selling up. She said goodbye to her friends, left London, and here she was – living and working in the middle of absolutely nowhere. Like the polar bear, she'd gone and made everything worse.

Sophie sat back against the grey stone walls and lifted her gaze to the hills. The mountains had been part of the appeal. During the summers of her childhood, they were part of a great adventure, constant and unchanging, except now she was living here she could see she'd got it wrong – they changed all the time. At this moment, in the late morning sun, they were velvety and lavish, but when they darkened and glowered, she longed again for streets lit with neon.

She heard the popping and crackling of car tyres along the gravel track kicking up a plume of dust. Sophie stood up, frowning, smoothing down her dress.

A taxi drove into the car park, its black shine dulled as the dust settled on it. It pulled up right next to her, and an elderly, white-haired man opened the door and gripped onto it as he got out stiffly. 'Um, hi,' she said quickly. 'Can I help you?'

He didn't seem to hear. He was smart, polished, in a dark blue blazer, khaki trousers and tan deck shoes, the kind of guy who was used to the best things in life, like a pillow menu and an en suite.

He let go of the car door and looked at the cottages, shielding his eyes from the sun. He straightened up slowly, squaring his shoulders as if he was absorbing the strength of the old stone walls. 'This is the place, all right.'

American, Sophie thought. The driver was dragging a kitbag with an airline baggage label on it out of the back of the cab.

'Hang on a minute,' she said to the driver. She turned to the American. 'This is just a bunkhouse,' she said quickly, apologetically. 'There's a hotel back in Bala that might suit you better. We're pretty basic.'

The old man's smile faded, and he turned his blue eyes on her, lively and intense in his tired face. 'I know that. It says so on your website. I'm used to a bunk. I'm ex-US Navy. Used to vault into my rack like a letter in a mailbox. My name's Al Locke – I've got a booking.'

'Oh!' she said, surprised. 'Okay!'

When she'd accepted the booking, she'd had a mental image of Al Locke as a lone rugged climber, bearded, lean, ticking challenges off his climber's log and doing yoga at sunset to keep himself spiritually and physically supple. Climbers were an obsessive bunch, they had goals to achieve, and she had imagined this guy, this American, working through a list of rock faces in six days, clinging onto the smooth cool of granite or the rough heat of sandstone, living on the edge. *Don't look down! Definitely do not look down at the rocks, trees, cars far down below, tiny, when your muscles are quivering with pain and your heart pounds with effort and solid ground is down there, look, only a swift and effortless drop away.* This imposter was nothing like what she had expected.

'Welcome to Mountain Ash, Mr Locke!' she said warmly. 'I'm Sophie. You've booked in for six nights.' Nobody ever stayed that long.

'That is correct.'

The driver carried the kitbag to the porch and Al Locke got his wallet out of his jacket and settled up with him.

'Good luck, mate,' the driver said out of the corner of his mouth in a way that suggested he'd need it. 'See you next week.' He got back in the taxi and slammed the door.

'Come on in, Mr Locke,' Sophie said, 'it's cooler inside.'

The new guest followed her into the shadowy reception. She passed him a form, and he put on his glasses and filled in his details.

Sophie reached under the desk and unhooked a blue fob with a couple of keys. 'Here. The small one's for your locker and the big one is for the main door.'

Al Locke hoisted his kitbag over his shoulder and followed her past the birch-wood screen into the dining room, walking between the large farmhouse table and the honesty bar glinting with spirit bottles against one wall.

'The common room is down that way and through here is the drying room,' Sophie said, pushing open the door. A lone pair of thick brown socks steamed on a heated rail. She turned to the bank of blue lockers, pointing to one. 'This is yours. Number eight.'

Next to the drying room was the bathroom, white, functional, with a full-length mirror and three shower cubicles. Beyond that were the sleeping quarters, with red-steel bunks. The room was warm and sunlit.

Al Locke nodded, dropped the kitbag on his bunk and turned to look at her. He hadn't said a word since he'd come inside; now he had his head tilted slightly, narrowing his eyes as if he was expecting her to carry on talking.

'Okay! That's the end of orienteering,' Sophie said brightly. 'Can I get you a tea, coffee, sandwich?'

He reached for his bag and took out an empty water bottle. 'Perhaps you could fill this,' he said, handing it to her. 'I'm going to freshen up and then take a stroll while the weather is fine.'

She looked towards the window, stretched out her arms and yawned happily. 'Gorgeous, isn't it? It's been like this for weeks. Relentless sunshine.'

'Good for business?' he asked astutely.

'Absolutely!'

She left him to it and went to the kitchen to fill the water bottle. Coming back with it, she could hear him talking against the hiss of the shower.

'Hello, Elin,' he was saying in a deep, seductive voice. 'Remember me?'

Embarrassed, Sophie quickly turned round and took the bottle back to reception. She'd started talking to herself too, since she lived here, having conversations out loud, just a sentence sometimes to break the silence. She wouldn't want anyone catching her at it.

She sat at her desk, switched the fan on and checked her emails. She had a booking for three coming up in a few days. She liked groups. People didn't usually come by themselves, but when they did she liked to think they had an interesting story to tell. Didn't necessarily follow, though. She'd actually said that to a guest one night when she was feeling deep and insightful: *you look like a man who's had an interesting life.*

He'd looked almost offended. *I haven't,* he replied.

She looked up as Al Locke came back towards reception. He was wearing a crisp blue shirt with dark trousers, his white hair still damp and grooved by his comb. He smelled of cologne. 'See you later,' he said cheerfully, grabbing his water bottle.

'Have a good day,' she replied, glancing at his shoes as he left. They were black brogues, highly polished. She was intrigued. Al Locke was all dressed up, in the middle of nowhere.

Obviously, that wasn't literally true. They were in the middle of *somewhere*; you could find the bunkhouse on an Ordnance Survey Explorer Map, situated on the side of a hill called Moel Phylip, close to a dam, and just off the main road to the town of Bala, five miles away. But even so, it was somewhere in the middle of nowhere.

She went to the door to see where he was heading. He was striding purposefully across the car park to an overgrown track that led down to the road, arms swinging, one hand gripping his water bottle. He seemed to know where he was going.

She went back indoors, picked up a broom and swept the dust from the tiles, and then went to clean the bathroom. She put the used towels in the washing machine and wiped the surfaces. She liked this time in the middle of the day when she got the place straight. She put her hands behind her head and stretched. Feeling restless, she went to check the state of the common room, the one room she hadn't shown to Al Locke.

You have got to be joking…

It was a mess, beer bottles everywhere and an empty bottle of Penderyn whisky lying on its side on the hearth. The smell of stale beer turned her stomach. No wonder today's ramblers had got off to a late start. She could still hear the whisper of their windbreakers as they walked through reception earlier, stooped, with expressions of depressed resignation. They were three days into a six-day circular walk and had been debating last night over supper whether to go on or go back when it was the same distance either way. *Never again*, the woman kept saying. *Never again.*

Sophie smiled to herself. The mountains attracted four types of people: amblers, ramblers, scramblers and danglers. There were those practical hikers who'd planned ahead and carried full gear, water, food, a compass, maps; and others that turned up on the spur of the moment and headed blithely out in shorts and flip flips, holding their phones to navigate nature's playground.

Never again.

She was dumping the bottles in the recycling outside when Owen Evans drove up in his green van with the vegetable delivery.

'You look busy, girl,' he said mildly, opening the door of his van. He was wearing a red T-shirt, the same clear red as the red dragon tattoo on his left bicep. He had short, wiry fair hair and a face cracked and reddened by the outdoors, half hidden by his wild beard. He wasn't much older than she was: early forties, at a guess. He was passionately proud of his Welsh origins. 'Don't get him started,' someone had warned her in The Lamb, and she had taken their advice.

Sophie moved back into the shade. Her hands were damp from the beer bottles and she could smell them as she shielded her eyes.

The mountains in the distance had now turned mustard yellow. The mornings were usually cool and misty, but with the heat, the ground had dried out and hardened, so that the lower hills looked smooth and brown, like prehistoric creatures. 'Warm, isn't it?'

Owen looked up at the blue sky, as if it was the first time he'd noticed it. 'Not a cloud in sight. Good climbing weather.'

'Yeah.'

'Fair play,' he added with a dry laugh, carrying the vegetable box into the kitchen and making room for it on the table. He picked up a saucepan. 'Bloody hell, Sophie, what happened here?' He scraped half-heartedly at the baked beans burnt on the bottom. 'I don't know why the hostel doesn't go self-catering,' he said, 'you'd save yourself a lot of work.'

'I'd have to put another kitchen in, though, wouldn't I?' she said, washing her hands. 'And anyway, I like cooking. Breakfasts are easy. And people want drinks and a hot meal after a strenuous day.' She unhooked a towel. 'The truth is, we make more from the food than from accommodation.'

Owen stirred some green sludge in a bowl, scooped it up and let it drip. 'The laver bread's not too popular, is it?'

Sophie snapped him with the cloth. 'It might be a Welsh tradition, but come on, who really wants seaweed for breakfast?' Her mind went back to Al Locke, striding across the yard in his highly polished shoes, all dressed up. 'A guy checked in earlier. He's here for six days. American.'

Owen looked surprised. 'What's he going to do here for six days?'

'I don't know,' she shrugged, 'I was wondering that, too. Have you got time for a coffee?'

'No, I'd better get going.' Owen worked hard. He had his vegetable business and spent some weekends helping at the white-water rafting centre and doing bar work for Dai at The

Lamb – scraping a living, really, with his kids to support. 'Are you happy with the veg?'

'Sure.' Sophie looked in the vegetable box. 'What have we got?'

'Peas, onions, peppers, spring onions, lettuce, gooseberries.'

The contents of the box were bright, and the sun was bouncing the colours off Owen's face. He looked wholesome, healthy. A brown earwig was making its way up the side of the box and he held out his broad hand. The earwig crawled onto it, glossy, lithe, antennae twitching. He carried it outside to the yard and came back in saying, 'There might be a few more in the lettuces.'

She smiled at him, liking him for being kind to the earwig. 'You picked it up like the hand of God.'

He laughed. 'There's a comparison I've never heard before.' He put his hands back in the pockets of his shorts and jingled his keys, looking suddenly awkward. 'Okay, then.' He looked at her directly as if there was more to say, but whatever it was, he decided against it.

She was curious, but she hardly knew him. *If it's important*, she told herself as he said goodbye, *he knows where I am.*

CHAPTER TWO

Al was taking the shortcut down to the village, along a steep, overgrown track flattened by tyre marks and with a tall ridge of grasses growing down the centre of it.

The track was bordered by hedgerows and the grass was sprinkled with wildflowers. The trees fluttered with birdsong. The wild hedges bordering the track smelled of honeysuckle and dog roses, and the branches laid quivering stripes of shadow on the sunlit grass. The air was clean and chilled on Al's face.

I'm happy, he thought, *as happy as I've ever been.*

His happiness took him by surprise. For a moment, he stopped walking so as to savour it.

But as soon as he stopped, he became aware of the smell of death nudging him, poking at him, filling his nasal cavities as it often did lately, a reminder of his mortality.

He wasn't sure if it was real or an illusion, and he sniffed the air cautiously and looked around. A bloated badger was lying under a tree, still as a rock, its jaw agape and sorrowful, lively with blowflies, inflated as tight as a bladder and giving off the depressing stench of decay.

He tore up a handful of sweet grass and rubbed it in his hands, inhaling the freshness of it, and let the blades scatter. He stared at the dead badger for a few moments, swatting away the flies, and wondered what might have killed it. He opened his water bottle, rinsed out his mouth and put death out of his mind, as he did so often, and thought instead of his reunion with Elin.

It wasn't an arranged meeting, nothing like that. Al hadn't spoken to her for over sixty years. He had never thought of himself as a superstitious man, or particularly prescient, he had no time for that kind of thing, but he had no doubt at all that he was going to meet Elin in the village today.

He had thought about Elin on and off throughout his life, but lately she had been in his dreams more or less constantly until it seemed as if there was no room in his head for anyone else. He could almost hear her calling his name, and he couldn't disappoint her. Her voice blocked out everything else, including his darling, grieving wife. His absent-mindedness made Virginia impatient. She told him he needed hearing aids.

Elin would have a husband, of course; he knew there was bound to be a husband in the picture. He imagined this man, this stranger, as a dark storm cloud that would eventually pass by. Although, as Al walked, scattering stones under the rhythm of his steps, he considered optimistically, ruthlessly, that she might be a widow by now. Not that he was wishing widowhood on her, but it was quite possible, nevertheless, or even probable.

Well, he could only hope.

Ahead, the track curved to the right. Beyond the curve should be Elin's village. However, once he got there it turned out to be a kind of false dawn, because beyond the first curve he could see the track led to another bend further on.

In the heat of the day, Al stood under a leafy canopy of shade to catch his breath, took out his handkerchief and dabbed the sweat from his face. Happiness flooded through him again. It was like being on liberty again, that same surging freedom of leaving the ship and coming home to this place he revisited in his dreams.

He imagined crossing the stone bridge over the clear river and seeing the chapel, and the school, and then catching Elin in the village as she left the post office, just by chance. He imagined it as vividly as if he was praying for it, as if he could influence her into appearing in that doorway through the intensity of his hopes. He imagined her doing a double take, stopping still in disbelief, and then running to him, into his arms. Maybe not running. *She'll be in her eighties, don't forget*, he reminded himself.

The incline was levelling out and he could hear the rumble of a truck. Rounding the bend and coming out of the lane, he found himself by the edge of a main road that he had no memory of. Across the road, through a dense line of trees, where the village should have been, a startling brightness drew him to it like a vision.

He squeezed the bridge of his nose to blink it away, but it persisted, shimmering, a mirage. He crossed the road, feeling the heat of the asphalt, and entered the line of trees. He found himself at the top of a grassy bank studded with rocks, staring at the glittering lake that filled the valley.

He stared at it in dismay, filled with the uncertainty of old age. *It's been over sixty years*, he thought. *I've taken a wrong turning somewhere.*

Confused, Al looked back towards the road and attempted to get his bearings. For a moment he considered the possibility that he had remembered the route wrongly, and yet he recognised the familiar curving profile of the brown hills in the distance. There was no mistake, and he knew it.

He stumbled down to the water's edge, steadying himself against embedded mossy rocks, and stood on the shore, the clear water lapping at his polished shoes. Looking out across the water, he felt the pain of devastation tear through him.

'Elin!' he roared, and his voice echoed across the water.

There was nothing left now.

The road, the bridge, the railway, the stone houses, the chapel, the school, Elin's farm; they were all gone… drowned beneath the shimmering water cupped in the palm of the valley.

CHAPTER THREE

Sophie cleared the kitchen and took the fan from reception to the common room where she switched it on again as she vacuumed. Despite weeks of good weather, she still wasn't used to the heat.

Her phone rang, making her jump. She switched the vacuum off, saw the number and answered it with a half-smile. One of her guests was attempting an ascent of Shaft of a Dead Man – *nice name, right?* she thought ruefully – where the rock was like glass and the climbers' chattering bounced off it into emptiness, reminding them that they were interlopers in the great ringing silence of the mountains.

She liked her guests back in one piece, always greeting them with drinks, a tradition she'd started when she took over. There was nothing quite as good as beer after a long day.

'Greg. How was it?'

'Awesome,' he said, sounding a million miles away. 'Just to let you know, we're on our way back.'

'Great! See you soon.'

Greg was a regular and, like Owen, seemed to scrape a living one way or another – he lived for climbing, he told her, and the bunkhouse was cheap.

He was lean, tanned, broad-shouldered, with dark hair in need of a trim and a nose that was slightly too big for his face. It made him approachable. She had always been wary of good-looking men.

Max had been good-looking. Out of her league, really. *It's not working*, he'd said. Max didn't bother to try to fix things that didn't work; he binned them and got new stuff.

Greg, on the other hand, was the kind of man who would try to fix something. And she didn't mean herself.

Sophie went into the dining room and took a cold bottle out of the beer fridge for herself while she waited. She uncapped it, took a mouthful and went outside to sit on the slate doorstep which held the sun's heat. Right now, under the clear blue sky, looking over the scrubbed hills with a beer in her hand, there was no other place she'd rather be. On days like this, she could almost forget the troubles that had brought her here.

A noise disturbed her, a low cry of pain. She got to her feet and saw Al Locke emerging from the lane, banging his chest with his fist as if he was trying to kick-start his heart.

Alarmed, she ran over to him. 'Al! What's wrong? Are you ill?'

'Capel Celyn is under water,' he said hoarsely, wiping his face with his shirtsleeve. 'The whole village has gone.'

Her relief was immediate. 'Yeah, Al, I know.' It wasn't exactly news. It had happened a long time ago. 'It's a reservoir now.' *So that's where he was going so purposefully, all dressed up – to visit a village that was no longer there.*

He looked at her with sharp, grief-stricken eyes. 'But where did everyone go?'

Sophie shrugged. 'I don't know. I suppose they kind of – relocated.' She shook her head, but she understood. It might have happened a long time ago but to Al, it had happened today. 'Come on out of the sun and I'll get you a…' she was going to say tea, but changed her mind, '…a beer.'

She picked up her own bottle and took Al inside, into the shady dining room, pulled out a chair and got him a beer from the fridge, and then reached for a glass, because he looked like a man who would appreciate a glass. She popped the cap off, poured it in at an angle and set it down in front of him with a thud. 'Here you go.'

'It's come as a shock,' he confessed. He looked up at her fiercely, his blue eyes narrow, sharply focused on hers. 'I was searching for someone.'

'Were you? Who were you searching for?'

He frowned and clenched his fist. His knuckles bleached white and he studied his gold wedding band, dulled by years of wear. When he looked up at her, his face was pained. 'I was looking for... for... an old Quaker burial ground behind a farm in the village.'

Really? she thought. *Who gets showered and dressed up to visit a graveyard?*

None of her business.

'Yeah, that's right,' she said. 'You're talking about Hafod Fadog burial ground. There's a memorial to it on a boulder at the side of the road.' She took a swig from the bottle and watched the sunlight hit it, throwing an amber glow on the table. 'To be honest, Al, if it's any consolation, you're not missing anything. There wasn't much to see, by all accounts.'

'There was to me!' he said with a sudden rush of emotion. 'It's one of the reasons I'm here. Elin Jenkins showed it to me.' He looked at her hopefully. 'You know Elin Jenkins?'

Sophie shook her head. 'No, I'm sorry. I've never heard of her. Who is she?'

Al took a deep breath and let it out in a sigh. 'Someone I knew once, a long time ago. All this time – I never imagined I wouldn't find her.' He rubbed his fingers over his mouth and his eyes came back to hers. 'She showed me a grave – a relative of Abraham Lincoln's mother. I came back to see it again. Lincoln's mother, Nancy, had a bad press and, if I can, I'd like to put the record straight. It's an ambition of mine. I want people to know that she came from decent Welsh stock, that she had a pedigree, and she wasn't just the rootless, illiterate woman that some people claim,' he said heatedly.

Sophie raised her eyebrows. 'Abraham Lincoln's family came from around here? I've never heard that. Have you searched for them on the internet?'

Al stared at her reproachfully.

'Sorry, Al. Course you have,' she said, answering her own question.

'Over the years, seeing that grave again has become important to me,' he said. 'Some things have become more important as I've gotten older.'

Sophie sat back in the wooden chair and freed her hair out of the way, holding it up to cool the nape of her neck. 'I suppose.'

'I've left it too late,' he said bitterly to himself. 'I should have listened to my instincts and come years ago, but I kept putting it off, there was always something else to do. My wife was intending to come with me. It was the trip of a lifetime that we promised ourselves.' Al shook his head and then, leaning over the wooden table towards her, his weathered eyes intense, he said, 'Let me tell you something, always go with your instincts, Sophie, because if you don't, if you leave it too late, you'll regret it.'

Sophie rested her cheek on her hand. She knew what he meant. She felt as if ten years ago, life had been hers for the taking and she'd let it go, wasted it, just like that.

'It feels nice, though, being here again,' Al said softly, looking round. 'I remember it being small and pokey, a lot of small, dark rooms leading through from one cottage to another. We had to duck through the low doorways and I always forgot. Left with a head full of lumps. It smells the same. Woodsmoke and fresh air. A couple called Jane and Eric Oswald Hughes were running it then.'

Sophie laughed. 'Jane and Eric are my aunt and uncle.'

'They are?' he asked in astonishment.

'Yeah – when they retired, they were going to sell up. I bought the place. They were pleased to keep it in the family and I wanted to be able to come back, you know? I've spent such happy times here over the years. It's good to come back, right?' That was something she and Al had in common, and she smiled at him. 'So, when were you here last?'

'Nineteen fifty-six.'

'Really? Soon after they opened up then.'

'I used to stay here when I was visiting Elin. I couldn't stay at the farm – her parents were moral people and mindful of her reputation, and their own. They entrusted Eric to keep an eye on us, and let me tell you, he took his duties very seriously.' Al grinned. 'Different times.' He sat back and shook his head. 'It's strange. Being here now feels no different from sixty-odd years ago. It's taken me back to emotions that I thought had gone forever; surges of happiness, a sense of purpose, big things to look forward to, life being full of wonderful possibilities.' He laughed ruefully and looked at the bottle in his hand. 'Could be the beer talking,' he added dryly.

'So, this Elin…' Suddenly Sophie was distracted by the engine of an approaching car and she glanced towards the door. 'Excuse me. Greg's back,' she said. She got up, took three cold bottles out of the fridge, put them on the table with a basket of snacks and went to the door.

Greg was parking up in a spiral of dust. He pulled on the brake and grinned up at her through the open window, buzzing with accomplishment, his face tanned and stubbled, his hair wild and dark, his teeth white, happy to see her, or maybe just happy in general.

'Hullo,' he said cheerfully.

'Hi, Greg.'

Climbers are all the same, she thought, watching him get out of the car; she noticed his wind-chapped face, strong shoulders, lean legs. She stood there breathing him in, sweat and testosterone.

Greg took his kit out of the boot and dumped his pack on the floor, stamping the dust off his boots, hanging his primary-coloured jacket up on the coat hooks, high on adrenaline. Al came out of the dining room to see what the noise was.

'This is Al,' Sophie said. She gave Greg his beer. 'Al, this is Greg – he's been climbing. Al is from Philadelphia.'

Greg nodded at him cheerfully. 'Welcome to Wales,' he said.

'Thanks. Have you had a successful day?' Al asked politely.

'No one fell off,' Greg said, rubbing his hand across his stubble. 'Well, not too far, anyway.' He chinked his bottle against Al's. 'Oh, man, that last bit was hairy, though,' he said. 'I was closer to that wall than I have been to most of the women I've slept with.'

'Greg…' Sophie said quickly.

He laughed, so she pulled a face and changed the subject. 'Al came here to visit Capel Celyn.'

Greg whistled. 'Mate, the village was lost in the drowning.'

Al winced, as if the words caused him physical pain. 'So I've discovered. It was a shock, I can tell you. The place seemed timeless. Indestructible. I can't believe it's gone.'

Greg gave him a wry smile. 'Gone? It hasn't gone. It's still there, under the water.' He tore open a packet of crisps. 'How come you know Capel Celyn? What's your connection?'

Al stared into his beer, considering his reply, and then he looked up at Greg intently. 'I was dating a girl from the village,' he said. 'It was a long time ago. I've never forgotten her. I stayed here when Eric and Jane Oswald Hughes ran the place.'

Greg gave an appreciative whistle. 'And you couldn't keep away! You must have Welsh blood in you somewhere.'

'That's exactly what Jane Oswald Hughes said.'

Greg was watching him thoughtfully through the collection of beer bottles on the table. 'How come your girl didn't tell you about the drowning? It was a big deal at the time.'

Al shrugged. 'She didn't get the chance, I guess. We broke up in 1956.'

'That's the year it all started,' Greg said.

'No,' Al said firmly, shaking his head, 'that can't be right.'

'Trust me. Google it. The surveying began late in 1955 and the dam opened in 1965 – the destruction and construction took ten years from start to finish.'

'But… that makes no sense.' Al looked troubled. He was about to say something else, but he changed his mind, and instead rubbed his thumb absently over his wedding ring.

'Jane will be surprised to see you,' Sophie said. 'She's sure to have all the answers you want. She knows everything about everyone.'

Al's features softened. 'Doesn't sound as if she's changed much. How can I get hold of her?'

'At The Lamb,' Greg said.

'The pub,' Sophie added, in case it wasn't clear. 'We could go there after supper if you want?' She checked the time and stood up. 'Excuse me, I'll get the food on.' She had a stir-fry prepped in the fridge and she went to the kitchen, took out the chicken, put oil in the pan.

Sophie rubbed her tongue against her lower lip, tingling from the sun. She gave the chicken a stir and went over the conversation with Al in her mind, remembering the desperate hope in his eyes when he'd asked her about Elin.

She felt a rush of sympathy towards him, the pain of his disappointment. Despite the Quaker grave excuse, Elin was the reason he'd showered, changed and left, trailing the scent of cologne through the lobby.

But it was something that could easily be put right.

She made a phone call.

CHAPTER FOUR

Jane Oswald Hughes was in her sitting room knitting yarn she'd spun from the hair of Hywel Jones's dog. She was making a hat for Hywel. Hats made from dog hair had a unique quality which was invaluable in the mountains; they didn't freeze in winter.

Eric Oswald Hughes, her thin, bald husband of seventy years was in the comfy armchair, his chin resting on his chest, nodding off to *Antiques Road Trip*. The phone rang and jerked him awake. Still dozy from sleep, he heaved himself upright with the grim reluctance of a vulture leaving a kill and made his way to the phone with deep suspicion, sure it was going to be bad news; a legacy from the days when they still had elderly parents to worry about.

Now, they had no one at all to worry about, only people to worry.

As he took his time answering, the phone rang and rang.

'Pick it up, Eric, it might be spam,' Jane said, to encourage him. 'It might be George Watson.'

George Watson was his favourite spammer. Eric had enjoyed conversing with him very much. He had allowed him to lead him a long way down the route of a con to encourage him to transfer all his money into a new account that he, George Watson, had thoughtfully set up for him.

Eric had gone along with it for eighty minutes before announcing biblically in his deep, Welsh voice, 'Be sure your sins will find you out! George Watson, you fraudster! The Lord will send against you curses, confusion and rebuke in everything you do until you are destroyed and quickly perish, because of the wickedness of your actions.' Then he added, unbiblically, 'So bugger off,' and put the phone down.

Moments later, George Watson had called him back full of righteous indignation. 'You want to watch your attitude, mate!' he'd said, and hung up.

Encouraged by the memory, Eric picked up. 'Hullo? Oh, hullo, Sophie.'

Jane stopped knitting so that she could listen to Eric's half of the conversation.

'Do we remember who?' Eric was asking. 'Locke?' He looked pointedly at his wife. 'Jane, do we know an American called Al Locke?'

She knew what that look meant, and she felt her heart quickening. 'Why?' she asked cautiously.

'Jane wants to know why,' Eric said into the phone.

Jane shut her eyes so as to focus her attention on Sophie's reply, but all she could make out was a staccato of top notes, so she widened them again and looked at her husband, eyebrows raised in query.

'Because he's staying at the hostel,' Eric told her, passing on the message. 'Dew,' he marvelled, 'I can't believe he's still alive, he must be as old as the mountains by now.'

'What do you mean? He's younger than us. What's he come back for?' Jane asked. She saw she'd dropped a stitch and she poked the knitting needles into the ball of yarn and laid it on the arm of her chair.

'She wants to know what he's coming back for. Sophie, tell you what, I'll cut out the middleman and hand you over,' Eric said. 'Here you go.'

'Sophie?'

'Hullo, Jane.' Sophie was speaking softly, as if she had a sore throat or a hangover and didn't want to rouse it. 'He's doing some research about Hafod Fadog. He's booked in for six days.'

'Is he now? What research?'

'It's about an American president's Welsh ancestors. Anyway, he hoped you might remember him.'

Jane got to her feet and carried the phone over to the window. Outside, the sky was blue and the hills were spotted with walkers. She thought of Al as she'd seen him last: tall; his thick dark hair brushed back from his forehead; spotless in his naval uniform – navy blue wool trousers, sweater… Oh, he was a fine-looking lad and in love, too, and every word that came out of his mouth sounded like Hollywood. 'How does he seem?' she asked cautiously.

'What do you mean?' Sophie asked.

'How does he seem in himself?'

'Fine. Friendly. Why?'

There was now a keen edge of interest to Sophie's voice, and Jane wanted to shut the door on it as quickly as possible, so she said, 'Only that it's a long way to come for an elderly man. Travelling all that way at his age! I don't know how he can afford the insurance.'

'Tell her to find out who he's insured with, Jane,' Eric said eagerly.

Jane waved her hand to hush him because Sophie was speaking again.

'We're going to The Lamb tonight, so if you come along you can have a get-together and reminisce. We'll be there about eight. I've got to go! I'm just making supper. Stir-fry.'

'See you later!' Jane pressed the red button on the phone and left it on the windowsill. 'Al Locke,' she said, feeling the name on her tongue. 'After all these years.'

'Captain Locke, you mean,' Eric said, folding himself back in his chair. 'Funny, isn't it? I thought he'd be at least an admiral by now. He had that look about him.'

'Aye, he did, I know what you mean.' She frowned at the knitting.

'What if he asks about Elin?' Eric said, trying to read her face.

'It's none of his business, now.'

It was guilt that made her say it like that, sharply. They had wronged Elin many years ago; and because of that, they'd also wronged Al. Not deliberately, but more – she tapped her chin lightly, trying to find the right words – in the way of doing the wrong thing for the right reason. Jane and Eric had gone from one bad idea to the next, trying to focus their anger through action, having a plan which hadn't even worked in the end, despite everything.

It had ended badly, and it was worse for Elin than it was for them.

She and Elin had never spoken about it; and because they'd never spoken about it, Elin had never confronted her, and Jane had never apologised for coming up with the plan in the first place.

Over the decades, Jane had managed to screen off the past so that she didn't have to look at it. But she got the feeling that Elin was still on the other side of the screen, where the past was still in full view.

And now the Captain was back.

Be sure your sins will find you out, she thought.

Eric was looking at her steadily, waiting for her to go on.

Jane picked up her knitting to divert him, because after all these years her husband had become quite good at reading her mind, at least when he was motivated to.

Eric finally spoke, 'Al Locke,' he marvelled after a few minutes. 'Fancy him coming back after all these years! And staying at the hostel again!'

So that was the line they were going to take. She looked at him gratefully. 'Yes! Fancy! Sophie wants us to join them at The Lamb tonight.'

'Just like old times,' Eric said.

CHAPTER FIVE

Al and Sophie walked to The Lamb after supper. It was a mile away, along the road that ran past the dam, the verge bordered by ferns and cow parsley. They walked in silence, caught up in their own thoughts.

In the clean evening light, Al could see the majestic water tower with its five flood gates rising out of the lake, and then the solid dam itself, with a service road across it.

On the other side of the dam, like a before-and-after shot, the untouched continuation of the green valley stretched before them, lush fields bordered by trees, the silver line of the River Tryweryn scribbling through it.

The Lamb was set back from the road, festooned with coloured lights and chalked-up blackboard signs: HOT FOOD! SUNDAY LUNCH! CURRY NIGHT TUESDAYS!

They went in through the open door and exchanged the bright summer evening for the intimate yeasty dark of the pub.

Sophie headed straight for a large table boxed in by wooden benches where an elderly couple were sitting surrounded by white cushions, like two people trapped in a snowdrift. The man was completely bald and the woman had a head of white curls, like pensioners from Central Casting.

Al looked around for Eric and Jane Oswald Hughes.

He couldn't see them.

When he turned back to Sophie, the two old people were looking at him expectantly and he realised with a grim jerk of reality who they must be.

'Here he is!' Jane Oswald Hughes said, and got to her feet to greet him. 'Hello, stranger!'

As Al's eyes adjusted, he thought he could recognise the girl in her. 'Mrs Oswald Hughes! My word!' he said formally, reaching for her hand across the table. Her face was as open, bland and friendly as he remembered it. 'You haven't changed a bit!' he lied.

'Oh, there's a charmer! Call me Jane,' Mrs Oswald Hughes said, squeezing his hand and blushing in the dark. 'You remember Eric?' she asked.

'I do! How are you?'

Eric nodded a brisk hello. 'Home is the sailor, home from the sea,' he observed dryly.

'Good to meet you again!' Al recalled the man's widow's peak and his thick black hair. Now he was completely bald, haggard, with only his dark bushy eyebrows left to preserve his scowl.

'What will you have to drink?' Eric asked, getting to his feet, and the white cushions tumbled to the ground like snow falling off the shingles.

Al glanced at his watch, although it was too dark to see the time on it without his glasses. 'I'll have a cocktail,' he declared, adjusting his cuff.

'A cocktail, is it?' Eric raised his eyebrows briefly at this unusual request. 'You'd better specify the ingredients, or you'll end up with alcohol soup.'

'Vodka and tomato juice, plenty of spice.' Al turned to look for Sophie, but she was leaning on the bar and talking to Dai, the landlord.

Eric went and stood next to her. 'What are you having, *bach*?'

'I'll have a half pint of beer, please, Eric.'

'Good girl,' he said with relief. 'I thought you might have been corrupted into American ways.' He jerked his head towards Al. 'He's having a cocktail, he is. A half, Dai, and a vodka and tomato juice, plenty of spice.'

Dai was an ex-rugby player with a flat nose, curly red hair and a sturdy build – in his heyday he was so broad he had to go through doorways sideways. Even now it was a bit of a squeeze. 'Sorry, Eric, we don't do tomato juice. There's no call for it.'

'No call for it? I've just called for it now, haven't I?'

'Yes, but it's taken me by surprise. Next time, call for it in advance and I'll get some in.'

Eric turned to break the news to their guest, but he was leaning across the table, deep in conversation with Jane, and he didn't care to interrupt. 'Tell you what, make it a vodka and tonic,' he decided. 'Plenty of ice, mind. Americans are partial to ice. I've never understood why. It takes up space in the glass that could be put to better use.'

'Get with it, Eric, it's trendy,' Dai said, reaching for a glass. 'I wish we could charge for it; I'd make a fortune. Friend of yours, is he?' he asked curiously, jerking his head towards Al.

Eric looked at him, too. He took his time in answering. 'No, I wouldn't say that. He stayed with us a few times when he was visiting Capel Celyn as a young man.'

'He didn't know it had been drowned,' Sophie said wryly. 'Hadn't a clue. The lake has put a bit of a dampener on his reunion plans.'

'Seventy-one million litres of water is a hell of a dampener,' Dai agreed. He turned from the optics. 'Single or double vodka, Eric?'

'Make it a double, in the circumstances,' Eric said.

The barman popped open a can of Fever-Tree, poured it into the glass, filled the glass with ice and dropped a slice of lime into it, pierced by a bamboo stirrer. 'On the slate?'

'Yes please, Dai.'

Eric carried the drinks over just as Jane was saying, 'Lincoln's family came from Fron Goch. Quakers, they were, and persecuted something awful, and that's why they left.'

Leaving them to it, Eric returned to the bar.

Dai pulled a pint for him. 'So, what's he doing here?' he asked Sophie.

'Something to do with Abraham Lincoln's family tree, on his mother's side,' she said vaguely.

'Why?'

'Because Abraham Lincoln's mother has had a bit of a bad press, by all accounts.'

'Still, it's not likely to bother her now, is it?' Dai leant on the counter to get a better look at Al. 'He's got a good head of hair, I'll say that for him,' he observed.

Eric ran his hand over his bald head. 'Don't rub it in, man,' he said.

'Nothing personal. You know, big drinkers all have a good head of hair. It's the alcohol, see? It dampens the testosterone.'

Eric stroked his baby-smooth scalp. 'I can see what you're doing, Dai. Don't try your marketing campaigns out on me. I spend enough money here as it is,' he said, picking up his pint.

Dai continued his previous argument where he'd left off. 'And,' he pointed out, 'ancestry's all on the internet. You can find out about Abraham Lincoln's family with a click of a mouse. You don't have to come and visit a place in person.'

'It's not on the internet. He's looked,' Sophie said.

'That's what he's told you,' Dai said sceptically, sticking firmly to his opinion. 'I bet there's a woman involved.'

Sophie smiled. 'Actually, Dai, you might be right.'

'There's no need to sound so surprised about it. Who is she?' At that moment, Jane laughed. She had a musical laugh that was very distinctive. 'Don't tell me it's Jane,' Dai continued, deadpan.

Eric turned to look at his wife with interest, considering the possibility. He was beginning to feel warm and philosophical. Beer always made him that way.

'No, her name's Elin Jenkins,' Sophie said. 'You must know her, Eric.'

'You're talking a long time ago. We haven't seen her in years. You're right, though. That's who he was visiting when he stayed with us. It was before your time, Dai, but, dew…' he lowered his voice, 'Elin was a handful. She didn't like to toe the line, if you know what I mean.' He beckoned Sophie closer and Dai leaned over the bar so as not to miss anything.

First, Eric swiftly glanced over his shoulder to check that Al was not sneaking up on them and catching him engaging in impolite gossip. 'Listen,' he said softly, 'I've never told anyone this, but one winter, I saw him and Elin Jenkins together,' he jerked his head towards Al, 'in the old Quaker burial ground once. I was climbing over the stile coming back from my mam's house and I had a look out for Dafydd Jones while I was there, you know, as I went by, because he used to walk the dog about that time. And I saw them…' He paused to drink his beer because storytelling was thirsty work.

'Go on, Eric. You saw them?'

'I did,' he confirmed, putting his glass down. 'I don't want this to sound as if I was looking, because as I've explained, I only expected I might see Dafydd.'

'Get on with it, man, don't keep us in suspense, I've got customers waiting,' Dai said.

'Well, I didn't see Dafydd, as it goes, because it was pension day and he'd gone into Bala. What I saw was Elin dancing around in the Quaker burial ground. And, would you believe it, she was as naked as the day she was born.'

'No!' Dai was impressed. 'And on consecrated ground, too!'

'Blimey,' Sophie said.

'And the American?'

'No,' Eric said firmly. 'He was there but, fair play to him, he remained as fully clothed as I am now, and he covered her up again sharpish.'

'Get away with you,' Dai said, disappointed.

The three of them looked furtively over at Al and, just at that moment, sensing their gaze, he turned to them, and they all found themselves in a triangle of intense focus and looked away sharply.

'He heard you,' Dai said reproachfully.

Eric picked up his beer and drank it down to settle his thoughts. Licking the foam from his lips, he put the glass back down carefully, positioning it on the damp ring it had left behind on the wood. 'It's nothing he doesn't know, is it? He's probably been thinking about Elin dancing naked in that burial ground all his life. It's the kind of behaviour that can leave an impression on a man.'

'It's certainly left an impression on me,' Dai admitted, keeping his voice low. 'What was she like, this girl?'

'Lively.'

'Forget her energy levels. What did she look like? You can't tell me half a story without giving me a context for my imagination,' Dai protested.

'Oh, right. Slim. Short black hair. Al had black hair then too, and they made a good couple, I'll say that for them. Straight out of Hollywood, Jane said.' He put his pint down. 'By the way, I've never mentioned the, you know, nudity, to Jane. You know what she's like. No mute button.'

Sophie nodded. *Couldn't argue with that.* 'So, what happened with Al and Elin?' she asked. 'Why did they break up?'

Eric was silent for a moment. The dim overhead light flared on his smooth scalp. He sunk his chin on his chest and sighed.

'She died?'

'Worse than that,' Eric said. He lifted up his foam-laced glass and saw that it was empty.

The door of the pub opened at that moment and Greg and Owen came in, bringing with them a wave of summer heat. Eric waved his empty glass at them and said, 'Just in time!'

'Same again all round?' Greg asked, joining them at the bar. 'Four pints here, please, Dai. What's Al having?'

'Cocktails,' Eric said gloomily.

They scraped up some chairs and they all went to join Jane and Al at the table.

Now that there were newcomers, Jane became more familiar with Al, and she rested her hand on his arm. 'Beautiful, he was, in his uniform,' she told them breathlessly with a quiver in her voice. 'Handsome.' She patted his hand. 'Still are! Fancy!'

Al looked very pleased.

Sophie was feeling pleased, too, and slightly light-headed. She tried to work out the amount she had drunk, starting from the beer she'd had when Greg called after the climb. Losing count, she looked at Al. He was once more the happy man who had arrived at the bunkhouse that day. She rested her chin on her fist and thought of Eric's story about Al and Elin in the Quaker burial ground. Al still had Elin on his mind after all these years. She wasn't dead, but *worse than that*, Eric said. What did that even mean?

Greg swapped seats to sit next to her. Sophie shifted up to make room for him. She could feel the heat of him against her arm.

'Owen told me you used to climb.'

'He's right. I did.'

'But you don't any more?'

'No.'

His gaze roamed her face. 'Pity,' he said.

She shrugged good-naturedly, but she didn't feel the need to explain why she'd stopped. Max breaking up with her had been the worst thing that could happen, and after the worst thing happened, nothing had mattered anymore. It had made her reckless.

*

Sophie realised this one day when she was free climbing Gogarth, a sunny stretch of pre-Cambrian sea cliff on the western edge of the island of Anglesey, just after Max had left and she'd taken over the bunkhouse.

She had been scaling it alone, which reflected her frame of mind at the time. Some way into the climb, as her muscles began trembling with exertion, she'd noticed dispassionately that the rock was unstable in parts, crumbling beneath her fingertips. She put her weight on a stone the size of her fist, and felt it break off, and as she clung on, she'd looked down and watched it falling into the tumbling sea far below. The shale she'd climbed up from was completely covered over now. The tide had come in.

Instead of her usual intense engagement with the ascent, looking for holds, or searching for screws placed there conveniently by other climbers, she had become mesmerised by the drop.

The glossy green water beneath her hit the cliffs in a froth of white lace. It looked inviting that day, even welcoming. Sophie imagined what it would feel like if she relaxed and let go; she wondered whether time really would slow down, or whether there would be no discernible pause between letting go and hitting the water, which from that height would be hard as concrete.

It was oddly seductive, like a dream, the idea of giving up on the sheer effort of keeping on going.

Climbers had a death wish; she'd always known that. Not all of them, but some. Maybe she was no different. She'd never understood it until that day though – the way they kept climbing, challenging themselves over and over until one day they tumbled into the sea below as hopelessly dead as a spider in a bath.

Suddenly, to get rid of the image, she had opened her eyes. As she stared at the rock face, her mind had cleared, as if she'd just woken up.

Instead of improving matters, the burst of clarity had made her fearful. Her body was weakening, her muscles jerking. She was unable to climb up or down. She was trapped.

'Move!' she said aloud to herself. The voice was stern. It seemed to come from some separate part of her; the sensible part.

I can't.

'Yes, you can,' the voice, *her* voice, ordered her. 'Or else you'll die. Reach left!'

She looked up. There was a handhold to her left. She wasn't aware she'd seen it, but moving again felt good, the right thing to do.

'You're doing fine! You're nearly there!'

She kept going until she could see the fringe of grass growing on the top of the cliff.

Once she reached safety, she lay on the rough, springy turf for a while, staring at the clouds, before heading back to her car the easy way, along the cliff path. What she learnt that day was that to be safe on a mountain you needed someone to live for.

*

Wrenching her mind back to the present, Sophie realised that Greg was looking deep into her eyes as though he was reading her thoughts.

Suddenly his elbow slipped on the polished table and she laughed, because she suspected he was drunk.

He grinned and straightened up, his tanned face close to hers, his eyes dark and gleaming.

Jane called from across the table, 'Sophie, listen, I'll come and do the dusting this week.' Jane was saying it as if she needed rescuing. 'Keep my hand in.'

'Okay, great.'

Al tapped his glass for attention and asked whether any of them knew the US Navy hymn 'For those in peril on the sea' by the Reverend William Whiting.

'It's not called "For those in peril on the sea",' Eric argued, 'it's called "Eternal Father, strong to save".'

Eternal Father strong to save
whose arm does rule the restless wave…

Oh hear us when we pray to thee
for those in peril on the sea.

'No it's not,' Al said. 'It's called "The Navy Hymn".'

'Whatever it's called, we can sing it!' Eric said, and he got to his feet to demonstrate.

Al got to his feet too, and as it was a navy hymn he saluted automatically and tipped over his glass which he'd forgotten he was holding. They all jumped away from the foaming table and Dai came over with a cloth and a fresh drink, and said if there was going to be any more rowdiness he'd be forced to join in.

They made a good loud noise with their singing. Eventually Al sat back down and conversed with Eric across the table about presidents via shouting and sign language, and Sophie was laughing so hard she got hiccups.

Dai rang the bell for last orders and Al started singing again, and after that, they drunkenly made their way home.

CHAPTER SIX

Breakfast the following morning was somewhat subdued. Sophie was cooking in the kitchen when Al tapped on the door. His face was puffy from sleep.

'Do you have any painkillers?' he asked hoarsely. 'Got a pounding headache.'

'You're not the only one.'

'It's jet lag,' he said.

'Who knew jet lag was contagious?' she asked, handing him a pack of paracetamol out of the pocket of her shorts.

She plated up Greg's order and took it through. He had the pallor of a man needing more sleep. His brown hair was ruffled and his eyes were tired. Sophie put the plate of sausage, bacon and eggs in front of him.

'Al, would you like a traditional Welsh breakfast?'

'Yes please,' he said, but Greg looked up sharply from his plate, caught his eye and shook his head.

'And, er… what would that consist of?' Al asked Sophie.

'Fried bacon, cockles and laver bread,' she replied.

He considered this for a moment. 'What type of bread is laver bread?'

'It's not bread at all, it's a sort of pureed seaweed,' Sophie replied brightly. 'It's delicious.'

Al thought it over and pointed at Greg's plate. 'Can I have what he's having?'

'Of course,' she said. *Fair play, laver bread was an acquired taste.* 'Help yourself to orange juice.' She went back into the kitchen and put the sausages under the grill, thinking about Eric's reply when she'd asked him if Elin had died. What had made her ask him that question in the first place? It was the guilty look that came over him, the way he lowered his head, shifting his gaze from hers as if he was searching for an escape route, as if there was something he didn't want to face.

She hadn't died, it was *even worse than that.*

Whatever that was supposed to mean.

After breakfast, Sophie called Eric to find out more about Elin Jenkins.

Eric seemed to be regretting his openness in the pub. He told her rather sharply that they'd lost touch with Elin years ago and he had no idea where she was now, and neither did Jane, and that was that, end of conversation.

Sophie went outside and found Al sitting alone on the bench in the sun. He looked tired. His blue shirtsleeves were rolled up his forearms and he was looking across the yard towards the track, deep in thought.

The bunkhouse was a long way to come just to sit on a bench in the sun.

As her shadow fell over him, Al raised his sunglasses and looked at her with his sorrowful blue eyes.

'Sorry,' she said, 'I didn't mean to disturb you.'

'That's fine. I was thinking about the past, about wanting to go back. Do you ever feel like that?'

'Sometimes.'

'What if you can't go back?' he asked intently, as if he was expecting her to have the answer.

Sophie shrugged and sat on the warm bench next to him. *You couldn't. It was impossible to go back. It didn't stop you wanting to, though.*

She started thinking of the things she would have done differently if she had her chance with Max all over again, if she could go back to those early days of their relationship. *Time pushes us onward, whether we like it or not,* she thought. 'What are your plans for today, Al?'

'I'm at a dead end,' he said.

'I could take you to the Memorial Hall in Llanfair Ceiriog down the road. It's got a memorial honouring an American president.'

'Lincoln?'

'Probably. I went there with my parents once, on a rainy day when I was young and the past was completely irrelevant.'

He got to his feet. 'Let me get my phone and I'll be right with you.'

Sophie's car was an old blue Peugeot convertible that she'd bought cheap from Owen. It had peeling bodywork and the rumble of a tractor. She got her keys and her sunglasses and opened the car door for Al. 'Jump in.'

The car was stifling, and he tried to open the window.

'Don't bother. The windows don't work,' Sophie said.

'Is that legal?'

'It must be, it passed its MOT – don't ask how. Owen's going to fix them. I'm looking on eBay for the parts. I'll open the top. You'll have to help me though,' she said. 'It's a bit stiff. I don't use it much, it's a two-person job.'

Al looked at the console and helpfully pointed out the controls that open the roof.

'They haven't worked for years,' she said. 'Got to do it manually.' They got out of the car and she opened the back and found a spanner.

It was a slow step-by-step process and the mossy roof was stiff with age, but between them they eventually opened it, folded it up and by putting their body weights on the panel, managed to shut it away.

They got back into the car.

They were now sitting, hung-over, in the full remorseless glare of the morning sun. Sophie tied her hair back and drove towards the A5.

They passed through a place called Corwen. Sophie told Al it meant white dwarf. She pointed out a passing blur, a statue of Owain Glyndwr, the last true Welsh prince, who fought the English in 1400. She glanced at Al sideways, ponytail flying.

'But you have a Prince of Wales now,' he pointed out.

'Yes, and he speaks Welsh very well.'

Al told her that Elin had taught him four things in Welsh, two of them unrepeatable. He tried the others out on her: '*wmbarel*', meaning umbrella, and '*mwnci*', meaning monkey.

Sophie laughed. 'Very good,' she said encouragingly, 'you never know when those might come in handy.'

He cheered up enormously and he said he was looking forward to seeing the memorial.

Llanfair Ceiriog Memorial Hall was an impressively ancient-looking building right on the high street with gables and stained-glass windows, and the quiet authority of a place full of answers.

A man came out of the office and looked surprised to see them. Sophie explained that Al was a visitor and that he'd come to see the memorial to the president.

'Welcome,' he said, shaking Al's hand vigorously. 'We're always happy to greet our guests from the New World.' He led them over to the plaque. It gleamed like a revelation in the light.

'Here it is!'

Al put his glasses on. He read aloud:

To the memory of a great Welshman, Thomas Jefferson

He rubbed his temples. 'Wrong president,' he stated crossly, taking his glasses off. 'I'm looking for the memorial to Abraham Lincoln.'

'Abraham Lincoln? Well, there have been several presidents with Welsh roots. John Adams from Penybanc Farm, John Quincy Adams, William Henry Harrison – his great grandfather was from Llanfyllin. James Abram Garfield's father came from Caerphilly, and Richard Nixon, well, the less said about him, the better. Barack Obama's people came from Anglesey of course, but I didn't know Abraham Lincoln was from around here,' the guide said doubtfully. 'Are you sure about that?'

'I'm certain. I have it on good authority.'

'I'll take your word for it. You learn something new every day!'

Al wasn't hiding his disappointment well at all; he looked mightily pissed off, in fact.

'Sorry, Al,' Sophie said.

'I know what will cheer you up,' the guide said. 'Come and see the memorial to Ceiriog, while you're here.' He spoke in a hushed and wondrous tone, his enthusiasm restored. 'So you'll have something good to take away with you. You'll be especially interested in this, Mr Locke, because Ceiriog's pen name was Syr Meurig Grynswth.'

Al looked at him blankly.

'Meurig?' the guide prompted, rubbing his hands with the patience of a teacher. 'After Richard ap Meurig, the Welshman who named America.'

'A Welshman named America?'

'Not only that, but it was also a Welshman who discovered America!'

Al looked sceptical as he attempted to take on board this unlikely fact. 'Christopher Columbus was Welsh?'

'No, of course not.' The guide patted his pockets for his phone. 'Columbus was Italian, everyone knows that. I'm talking about

Prince Madoc ab Owain Gwynedd. He set sail for a country he was convinced lay to the west of Ireland, and he found it too, although to be honest it was quite a bit further west than he'd imagined. There is a commemorative plaque in Mobile, Alabama – I've seen it with my own eyes.' He took out his mobile phone and scrolled through it. After a few moments, he showed Al a photograph.

The first line of the sign read:

IN MEMORY OF PRINCE MADOC, A WELSH EXPLORER, WHO LANDED ON THE SHORES OF MOBILE BAY IN 1170 AND LEFT BEHIND, WITH THE INDIANS, THE WELSH LANGUAGE.

'See? There it is, the proof, in black and white. And colour.' He showed it to Al, and then to Sophie before tucking the mobile phone back in his jacket.

'Who knew?' Sophie said, impressed. 'So, the New World was first discovered by a Welshman, three hundred years before Columbus, and a Native American tribe spoke Welsh.'

'Surreal,' Al agreed without enthusiasm.

'Now, this is the memorial to Ceiriog.'

The guide described Ceiriog's many talents at great length, with the enthusiastic manner of a proud son boasting about his father. 'Ceiriog was a musicologist, a poet, and a collector of old Welsh folk songs, a great writer and a great man.' He ended his address by saying to Al, 'Good luck in your quest. Let me know what you find out, won't you? There's always room here for another memorial to a good Welshman.'

'Will do,' Al replied, mollified.

Back in the car, Al was quiet.

'Maybe only Elin knows about it,' he said after a while. His voice was full of loss, almost panic. 'But no one seems to know where she is now, not even Jane – I asked her last night. Don't you think that's strange?'

Sophie glanced at him quickly, the sunlight flashing on her dark lenses. It really was strange. She thought again about her conversation with Eric that morning. Some people could tell you they'd lost touch and you'd take it as fact, because, let's face it, people lose touch all the time. But the odd thing was that Jane hadn't dominated the call as she normally would have. Knowledge was Jane's thing; she knew everyone. It was her superpower. She was always keen to show it off.

She prided herself on knowing everyone there was to know locally, and not just them but their family history, their good deeds and their scandals. People had long memories in a small community and if it had been a simple matter of drifting apart, in ordinary circumstances Jane would have been the first to speculate and theorise – *I'll tell you who she used to be friendly with…*

It was as if something had happened between them, some kind of rift that her aunt and uncle didn't want to talk about. Sophie was about to suggest this to Al, but his head was resting against the window. He was fast asleep.

CHAPTER SEVEN

Late that afternoon, Sophie was taking crumbs out for the sparrows when Al came outside, his face creased from the pillow, his blue shirt dark with sweat.

'I must apologise for my grumpiness earlier,' he said.

'No need.' She went round the side of the house where the sparrows were chirruping in two elder trees, their fluttering wings scattering the elder blossom and releasing its pungent sweetness. Shaking the crumbs out of a napkin, she leant on the ivy-covered stone wall to watch them. The wall was wobbly; the ivy was holding the whole thing together.

A sparrow hopped to the ground and flew back into the tree again.

Al chuckled softly, so as not to scare them.

Sophie liked him, and she was sorry that he hadn't found what he was looking for.

She turned to face him, holding her hair back, seeing her own reflection in his sunglasses. The way he came alive when he talked about the past, she wondered how Abraham Lincoln fit into this story. And what he'd told his wife, his family, and maybe even himself about why he was here. 'Was it Elin who got you interested in Abraham Lincoln?' she asked.

'In his roots, yes, for sure. But it was a mutual interest. She took me to see the grave of his great-great-great-grandmother in Capel Celyn. It took some finding, as I remember. It was sunk into the earth, more like a stepping stone than a grave. You had to know it was there.' He rubbed his jaw. 'I've wanted to make this trip for a long time. Well, I'm eighty-five now and my time's running out. I've come here while I can still make it. As my son said: *Just do it.*'

'What will you do with the information if you find it?' she asked him curiously.

'I'm not sure.'

'You should put it on YouTube,' Sophie said. 'You should share it with the world. There's absolutely nothing as interesting as an obsession.'

Al lifted his sunglasses to look at her, his eyes creased against the light. He grinned suddenly. 'That's an opinion that I've never heard before.' His eyes held hers and he seemed to come to a decision. 'Sophie, I want to show you something,' he said. 'Wait here.' The sparrows retreated into the tree in a flurry.

A few minutes later, he was back with his laptop. He rested it on the tangle of ivy and opened it up. 'This is it,' he said. 'My labour of love.'

On the screen was an image of a room with a cluttered desk in the foreground and a wall of graffiti behind it. 'What am I looking at?'

'It's my basement. Check out the wall, see? That's Lincoln's family tree, right there.'

Sophie zoomed in on it. 'Wow.'

The names were written with a black Sharpie, patched up here and there with additions and corrections on sticky labels. She scrolled up slowly. Abe's father was Thomas Lincoln, his grandfather was Abraham Lincoln, his grandmother was Bathsheba; his great-grandfather was John and his great-grandmother was Rebekah; good Biblical names for a good God-fearing family. The pattern of names on the Lincoln side climbed right to the top of the wall, where the writing touched the ceiling: starting with 'Samuel Lincoln, born 1622', the family tree cascaded all the way down to President Abraham Lincoln's great-grandchildren, Mary and Robert Beckwith. *Crazy*.

'These names along Abraham Lincoln's father's line are easy to find,' Al said, running his hand over the screen. 'I know them better than my own family, that's the truth. But Nancy here,' he continued, pointing to the parallel side of the family tree, 'is the problem.'

The bloodline of Abe's mother, Nancy Hank, on the other side of the tree, occupied a pristine blank space that, on the screen, gave a ghostly glow in the basement light, begging to be filled. It had no branches. It was, Sophie thought, like the victim of a rogue tree surgeon, struck off for malpractice.

'It's my duty to fill it in, a duty I've taken upon myself, because Nancy's had a bad press. She was said to be "physically unappealing, with dark brown hair, small grey eyes, a thin, angular face, stoop-shouldered, thin-breasted, sad". Her ancestry is, by all accounts, a mystery. But I have reason to believe her family originated from this part of the world.'

A fly settled on the screen and Al waved it away. 'Lincoln was only nine years of age when she died.' He was silent for a moment. 'I lost my mother young, too.'

Sophie looked again at the names on his basement wall, *a labour of love*, as he called it. She was starting to understand. That wall linked the present and the past for Al, she realised, with the compelling power of a holy relic.

She sometimes watched a TV programme about a workshop where people brought in old broken things to be fixed, and the things that they brought always had a sentimental story attached to them. The people wanted their things working perfectly once again and looking as good today as they had in the past.

But it seemed to Sophie that what they really wanted was not to remember the past but to actually return there. They didn't just want the feelings that they had then; they wanted to revert to being young, to being the people that they used to be, reliving the joy that they felt when these things were wonderful, new, pristine.

And she couldn't help wondering what happened when they carried these things home, and the excitement wore off, and the owners found that they weren't young again after all; the dead hadn't returned, nothing had changed. Did their prized possessions once more gather dust or were they put away in a box in a wardrobe or on a shelf in the shed to continue ageing inexorably along with their owners?

'So, what are you going to do next?'

Al closed his laptop, took a deep breath, raised his head and stared across the ageless hills spotlit with brilliant sunlight.

He was silent for so long that Sophie gave up waiting for a reply. She rested her chin in her hand and went back to watching the lively sparrows hop out of the bushes on the ground, picking up a crumb on the way and fluttering back again, gaining confidence in the spirit of competition.

When Al finally spoke, it was like a declaration. 'I'm going to find Elin,' he said.

His eyes were very blue, intensely alive in his creased face. He seemed, at that moment, heartbreakingly brave and indomitable. He added, 'She was going to be my bride.'

CHAPTER EIGHT
Liverpool, 1955

In December 1955, the streets were twinkling with Christmas lights, and the pavements glittered with frost in the chill winter air. Al's ship was docked in Liverpool for repairs and an invitation had been extended to a few suitable, decent young seamen to attend a supervised Christmas dance at the nurses' home.

Al and his buddy, Parks, punched each other in excitement, astonished at this unexpected turn of events.

'Nurses!' Al repeated in disbelief. 'Somebody up there loves us.'

The hall was warm, music was playing, and the nurses had been waiting restlessly for the sailors to turn up, only half-believing the rumour. There was this buzz of high spirits that you only feel when you've been cooped up and your life hasn't been your own for some time; this was a chance to let off steam, to enjoy yourself. When they came in through the doors, the air shimmered; the nurses watching the sailors and the sailors watching the nurses.

Al saw the dark-haired girl straight away. He ran the palm of his hand over his face. He had dry shaved and combed his dark hair in preparation for the night ahead, but now he wished that he had taken one last look at himself before coming out.

The girl was slim with short dark hair, blue eyes and sharply angled, dark eyebrows. She was wearing a cream dress, something silky that caught the light like the moon on water. She was talking to her friend, one hand on her hip.

Al nudged Parks. 'See the tall, dark-haired girl? I'm going to ask her to dance.' Really it was a warning to Parks to keep away, because there was something about her that stood out, that spoke to Al, and he was worried his friend might ask her first.

The girl was looking directly across at him now. Meeting his eyes. *Yes, it's me,* her look said; she gave Al a smile as if she knew something that he didn't and she was waiting for him to catch up.

Parks said to him out of the corner of his mouth, 'The one next to the blonde, right?'

'Yeah,' Al said, although he hadn't noticed the blonde.

The band started to play.

When Parks approached the blonde girl, the dark girl laughed. 'You're in, Andrews,' she said to her friend.

Al asked her if she'd care to dance.

The blonde girl said over her shoulder, 'You too, Jenkins.'

Jenkins she became, in Al's mind, and he took her hand with its warm, fragile bones. He held her with a sense of elation; he could feel the heat of her back through her slithery, silky dress; he inhaled her scent, something light and flowery; and as they danced she half-closed her knowing eyes and he couldn't think of anything to say to her that wasn't corny or lame or a chat-up line.

He span her round past three older women who were standing together, keeping a stern eye on the proceedings. He could smell the pine resin of the Christmas tree and the girl's skin was so smooth, so fine within its frame of dark hair that the fairy lights tinted her cheekbones blue, pink, red as they glided past it. 'Jenkins,' he said, and already he loved the name.

'Yes?'

'I'm Al, Al Locke.'

'What's Al short for?'

'Albert.'

'Albert Locke,' she said, giving him a sudden, happy smile as if she had discovered the key to something good. 'I'm Elin. In the hospital they call us by our surnames.'

'Eileen?'

She raised her face to his, mouthing her name at him. 'Elin.'

That mouth! Small pillowy lips, pink lipstick; he could feel her breath on his skin. Without thinking, he moved in to kiss her and she stiffened her arms to keep him away.

'Not here.' She jerked her head towards the three older women. 'That's Matron, making sure we don't enjoy ourselves too much. It's her job and she's very diligent about it.'

Not here. *Somewhere, though.*

Parks passed him, gave him a wink, and twirled Andrews around. She caught Elin's eye and laughed.

Elin entwined her fingers in his, and it felt unexpectedly intimate. Everybody was dancing, and in the crowd it was easier to hide from Matron's sharp gaze.

At the end of the third set the four of them sat breathlessly at a table drinking something that tasted so watered down it was impossible to tell its origins. The blonde girl, Rose Andrews, took a compact out of her bag and at the same time she surreptitiously slipped Parks a pewter hip flask under the table.

'Don't be too mean with it,' she said to his reflection in her compact mirror.

'Yes, ma'am.'

Al was dismayed to find they had a 10 o'clock curfew. 'You're kidding!'

Elin laughed. 'I know! You think that's bad – it's normally nine,' she said. 'But it's Christmas.'

Al couldn't bring himself to laugh with her. He could feel her slipping away from him and he felt something approaching panic. 'But I… when can we… when can you—'

Elin took the hip flask from her friend, surreptitiously topped up her drink and said comfortingly, 'Don't worry, Al, we've got a plan.'

Later that night, Al and Parks stood in the cold outside the nurses' house, hiding in the shadows of the building, breath fogging, shoulders hunched, their hands in their pockets for warmth. The frost was crisping on the grass and the sky above them was clear and dark, with one bright star directly above. All was quiet.

'You think they were serious?' Parks asked, stamping his feet, looking doubtfully at the darkened windows.

Earlier, Al would have sworn on his life that they were, but now he wasn't so sure. They'd been waiting a while in the freezing cold, watching the lights go out in the rooms. The whole building looked asleep. He checked the time again. 'Let's say we give them another few minutes, and then we'll head back.'

They let the minutes go by and at last they heard the rattling slide of a sash window and looked up hopefully. Elin's head appeared out of the window. 'Hey! Boys!' she said in a loud whisper. 'We're coming down!' She ducked out of sight again and then came out of the window legs first, found a foothold, reached for the drainpipe, stretched across, lowered herself down onto the adjacent wall and then jumped to the ground, looking up and beckoning Rose.

Al and Parks grinned at each other – it was an impressive, well-practised manoeuvre.

'We've got to keep quiet, the warden is on the lookout,' Elin whispered.

'Where are we going?'

'For cocktails,' she said, and Al could see the curve of her lips in the dark.

They walked arm in arm to a hotel a couple of streets away. It was lit up by the rainbow crystals of a large dusty chandelier, vibrating with laughter and music. Couples were hurrying past them, incongruously wearing togas – where they were going, Al wasn't sure, because once they were inside in the glittering warmth, he didn't see them again.

The four of them sat at a table by a log fire. Al was hungry to know Elin, he wanted to swallow up everything he could about her. Elin had one hand on the curve of her glass, and under the table her fingertips touched his. He curled his fingers around them and held on tight.

'How long are you here for?' she asked him.

'Could be a couple of months.' *Hopefully*, he thought. 'The ship's under repair. She took a hammering in a hurricane.' He grinned suddenly. 'I never thought any good would come of it, until now.'

She gave him a smile that creased a dimple in one cheek.

'How long have you been nursing?' he asked her.

'Since the summer. I started my general training when I turned eighteen.'

She was a couple of years younger than him, younger than he'd thought. 'What's your accent?'

'Welsh. I'm from Wales.'

'Yeah? Whereabouts in England is that?'

'It's not in England. Different country, with its own language.'

'Is that so? Say something in Welsh.'

Elin leant towards him intimately, her eyes holding his, and softly recited what could have been a poem in a language that sounded a cross between Finnish and Arabic.

When she finished, he said, 'It's a love poem, right?'

'It's about death, actually. Where are you from, Al?'

'Philadelphia, Pennsylvania,' he said.

'That's a coincidence. A family from my village moved to Pennsylvania,' she said.

'Is that so?' he asked hopefully. 'Maybe I know them.' It was unlikely, although he desperately wanted to say he did. 'When did they move?'

'In 1698,' she said, teasing him, her eyes creasing up in a smile. 'They did all right for themselves, too, because a few generations later one of their descendants gave birth to Abraham Lincoln.'

Al felt his heart beating hard, as if someone was tapping on his chest. It was as if she'd looked straight into his soul. 'My mother was a great admirer of Lincoln,' he told her. 'We have a memento that my family claims belonged to the president's mother.'

Elin laughed. 'Really? I could show you his great-great-great grandmother's grave one day. It's on a hill above a farm where they used to hold Quaker meetings,' she added quickly. 'It's nothing much to look at, just a stone with initials and a date. It's pretty worn.' She sounded apologetic, as if she'd over-promised.

'I would love to see it,' he said with sincerity, staring at her lovely face, barely able to concentrate on anything else.

Blankly, he noticed Parks get to his feet, saw him helping Rose into her coat. 'Where are you two going?'

Parks tapped his watch. 'Come on, Locke, the fun's over. We've got to get back to the ship,' he said.

Al was dismayed. He couldn't believe how quickly the time had gone. 'Already? We'll see you home,' he said to Elin. 'Can I see you again?' He had to see her again; it felt as if his whole future depended on it.

'Of course,' she said, nodding. And then she laughed.

CHAPTER NINE

Safely back in their room, Elin and Rose crouched in the chill draught of the window until the two men were out of sight. They kept on watching until their long shadows were gone, too.

Rose turned around to check that their roommate, Smith, was still asleep under the bed clothes.

'Elin, did he try anything?' she asked softly.

Elin shook her head. 'No. Well, just at the dance. Did Parks?'

'Wandering hands,' Rose said, rolling her eyes.

'Al's hands were perfectly well behaved, worse luck.' Elin felt euphoric. 'He's gorgeous looking, isn't he?' She closed the window as gently as she could. 'He was so nice,' she said wistfully.

Rose sighed happily. 'Fun, wasn't it?'

'The best fun! Did you see Al's eyes? He's got lovely eyes, like they've absorbed all the blue of the sea.'

'Parks says he works in the engine room. He never sees the sea at all.'

They'd forgotten to whisper.

'Shut up, you two,' Smith said irritably, 'and go to sleep.'

'Sorry, Smith. Good night.'

Elin got ready for bed and closed her eyes. She thought of the serious way Al had looked at her, and his smell of cologne and tobacco, and how she didn't want to look away. If they kept looking at each other like that, it was a shortcut to knowing each other, and all the other bits were just extra knowledge stuck on afterwards.

*

A few days later, in the early hours of Christmas morning, Elin was woken the by the sound of stones rattling against the window. She got out of bed, peered through the curtains and saw Al standing in the glow of the street light, looking up at her, snow falling on him like glitter. She opened the window as quietly as she could and leaned out.

Al called up, 'Merry Christmas, Elin!'

She laughed. 'Merry Christmas, Al!'

'Will you come out with me on Monday?'

She felt a delightful thrill of excitement. 'Yes!'

'Great!' He grinned up at her and tucked his hands into his pockets. 'Night, Elin!'

'Goodnight, Al!'

She got back into bed, hugging herself. It was the nicest and most unexpected Christmas present she could ever hope for.

Elin had been looking forward to their date the following week, but it turned out be a tough day. A patient in her late twenties who she'd grown fond of, Mrs Metcalfe, had died quietly sometime in the afternoon.

Elin had checked on her a few times as she passed by. She seemed comfortable enough. Restful. Elin had thought she was sleeping and didn't like to disturb her.

Later that afternoon Miss Wilson in the next bed rather pointedly got up and covered Mrs Metcalfe's face with the sheet.

'Just a minute!' Elin said, rushing over and pulling the sheet back again. 'What are you *doing*?'

'Some nurse you are,' Miss Wilson said, and got back into her bed, her lips tight with disapproval.

'Oh!' Elin felt for Mrs Metcalfe's pulse. She was cool to the touch. There was no heartbeat and her colour was different, her face was no longer pale but slightly yellow. Elin looked around for help. Apart from Miss Wilson, nobody else seemed to have noticed. She pulled the screens around the bed, distressed. It didn't seem fair at all, Mrs Metcalfe of all people, who was kind, friendly and fun.

Mrs Metcalfe never judged, or complained, not even about the consultant who slapped nurses' bottoms and who was rough with the patients and turned out to be wrong with his prognosis; not even when Elin was clumsy in finding a vein. Her illness hadn't made her self-absorbed and she remained curious and outward looking.

Elin asked her once what the secret to her patience was, hoping she could spread the word to Mr Jackson in orthopaedics who constantly and querulously called for attention, and complained about his pillows and his sheets and the sunlight, and the nurses' attitudes. It was sad, really, and when she was off duty Elin promised herself to be nice to him, but when she was on duty with other patients to attend to he drove her mad.

'There's no secret,' Mrs Metcalfe had said, and she seemed amused at the idea. 'Help yourself to a chocolate.'

They were still there on the locker now. Elin's eyes burned with tears.

Sister came over and opened the screens. 'Jenkins, what are you doing?'

Elin quickly wiped her nose and waved her hand towards the bed. 'Sister, I think Mrs Metcalfe's died.'

'You *think?*' Sister felt for her pulse. 'Mmm.' She straightened up and looked at Elin, registering her tears for the first time. 'It's not your job to cry, nurse,' she said briskly.

*

When Elin met Al that evening, she still carried the weight of her sadness for Mrs Metcalfe. She thought about Al all the time and just wanted to be close to him, safe in his arms. The days that had passed without him just seemed colourless. But everything brightened when she saw him again.

Elin loved his dark hair, his straight dark eyebrows that shaded his serious eyes, his smile when he saw her. She ran to him and as he caught her, he felt solid, a man you could lean on. He hugged her tight and she breathed in his smell of cologne and cigarettes. He put his arm around her and walking in step with him they headed towards the cocktail bar again. It was already 'their place'.

'One of my favourite patients died today,' she said.

'That's rough,' he replied softly.

'I'm not going to think about it, though.'

They had reached the cocktail bar and stopped at the bottom of the steps. The roar of conversation and music poured out heartlessly, indecently raucous and loud. Al turned to face Elin and took her gloved hands in his and pulled her close.

'Would you rather we went walking, instead?' he asked her, as if the warm, noisy club and the cold deserted streets were all the same to him.

Elin nodded.

They carried on past a drunk who said, 'Gissa kiss, darlin',' then backed down as he spotted Al. It occurred to Elin with a sudden tearful realisation that Al had that same quality of spirit as Mrs Metcalfe, the blessing of a calm and generous personality.

She wasn't calm herself. That's why she admired calmness in others. She had a tendency to be passionate about things, fly off the handle, have a short fuse, no matter how hard she tried to control it. Al was the kind of person she would like to be, happy, easy-going, warm. They walked as far as the park and sat on a frosty bench under a street lamp. The grass sparkled in the circle of light.

He put his arm around her, and she rested her head on his shoulder.

A dog barked in the distance, and the sound echoed off the houses in the empty streets.

'Penny for them,' Al said, his breath warm in her hair.

Elin lifted her head from his shoulder and looked into his eyes. Since she'd stopped him from kissing her at the dance, he hadn't tried again, and she was regretting not taking the risk of Matron seeing. For the first time since she'd met him, she felt insecure. 'Aren't you ever going to kiss me?' she asked in a small voice.

Al was silent for a moment.

Elin felt herself grow cold with embarrassment. 'Sorry, forget I said that.'

'Listen, Elin,' Al said softly, 'do you believe in love at first sight?'

The question took her breath away. Wasn't that always the dream? To fall in love with a handsome stranger? 'Yes,' she whispered.

'Me too. Elin, I want to talk to you about something. There's a girl at home I've been seeing.'

His words hit her like a blow. 'Right. Of course there is,' she said miserably, pulling away. In a way, she wasn't even surprised. It had been that kind of day. 'A girl in every port.' She stood up and Al caught her arm and pulled her back down.

'Elin, it's not like that. I just want to be straight with you.'

'Great. Okay then, be straight. What's her name?'

'Virginia Delman.'

'What's she like?'

'She's… nice. Ordinary.'

'Not like me then,' Elin said flippantly.

'No,' he agreed. 'Not like you at all.'

Elin moved to the far edge of the frosty bench, leaving space between them, and folded her arms. 'What does Virginia Delman do?' She put as much sarcasm as she could into the name.

'She's at Bryn Mawr.'

Elin was confused. 'Bryn Mawr in Dolgellau?'

'Bryn Mawr in Pennsylvania. The college.'

'Oh. There's a Bryn Mawr in Wales, too. It's a house.'

'Small world.'

'Yeah.'

They'd wandered up a different route in the conversation, off the beaten track to somewhere easier to talk about. Elin slumped back and exhaled a plume of her breath, making a fog of the street light. 'She's nice, ordinary and clever, then,' she said. She didn't really know Al at all. 'You should have told me about her straight away, Al,' she said. 'That first night at the dance.'

'I had you down as the kind of girl that would walk away right there and then if I had.'

'I *am* that kind of girl.'

'That's why I couldn't tell you.'

Despite wearing gloves, Elin's hands were freezing, and she pulled her sleeves over them. She could feel the tears freeze on her cold cheeks. 'So that's it.'

'Don't say that. Hear me out, Elin,' he said. 'I've written to her. I'm breaking up with her. She deserves better. See, our parents have always assumed we were a match, but I've never felt about her the way I feel about you.' His eyes gleamed in the dark. 'And I figure that even if it all goes wrong and you never want to see me again after this, I know for sure now what love looks like.'

Elin looked away anxiously, biting the inside of her cheek. She felt a dizzying rush of emotion. She wanted to believe him – she did believe him – that he felt like that about her, and she felt like sobbing with relief. 'You wrote to break up with her?'

'Yeah.'

'At Christmas?' Elin started to feel a bit sorry for the girl who Al said deserved better than him.

'Wrote to my parents, too. You know, they're going to find out because her family and mine are close and I thought they should hear it from me first.'

'You've told your parents about us?' She hadn't realised he was serious about her until now.

'Yes. Have you told yours?'

'No.' She hadn't known there was anything to tell. Her feelings for him were intense, but she didn't trust them that much. She reasoned that Al wasn't going to be here for long and she would only worry her parents for nothing. But it was different now that they were talking about the future. 'I'm going to, though.'

'I'll meet them when you take me to see that grave.'

'Yes, you will.' She was surprised he'd remembered, or that he even cared. She looked into his eyes. 'I'm sorry I made a fuss.'

She saw him smile. In the street light his face looked perfect, flawless, as if he was made of silver.

'That's okay.'

Elin moved along the bench to be close to him again. She'd never felt this close to anyone in her life before. She suddenly felt entirely different and she was just about to tell him so, when he brought his face close to hers and for a moment he was a silhou-etted shadow against the street light, and then her lips touched his in a kiss which was a delirious sensation of warm breath and ice-cold noses.

CHAPTER TEN

Going to Capel Celyn with Al at the beginning of the new year, Elin felt the pure excitement of coming home.

They drove in and out of wintry shade, under bare branches, past hedges, telegraph poles and barns, watching buzzards swoop over conifers crowding on hills, glimpsing bright holly bushes and ivy clinging to tree trunks, until they were in the foothills, looking up at the snow-covered hills above the tree-smudged valley.

Elin's mother hadn't said much about her bringing Al home to meet them. She hoped she would be happy for her, and impressed, because he was an American and very good-looking, but that was because of her own pride in him.

Looking back, her mother must have known that if it got serious Elin would leave the village for good, and not just the village but the country, because it was unlikely that a man in the US Navy would want to settle in a small Welsh village so far from the sea with nothing but a river running through it.

But she didn't say anything to Elin, and maybe she wasn't thinking those things at all. She kept her own counsel. If Elin had to describe her mother in one word, she'd say she was stoical.

Ahead of them along a dirt road were the quarrymen's cottages belonging to her friends Jane and Eric Oswald Hughes. They had knocked them into one solid, low grey stone building with blue slate roofs, and grandly called it The Mountain Ash Guest House.

Al would be staying here because Elin's mother had worried that he and Elin being under the same roof together might lead to temptation and the neighbours would talk.

Jane came out to greet them, her curly brown hair pinned back from her wholesome, bare face, her smile warm and sweet. She was wearing slacks and a blouse, with a navy cardigan on top, and spread her arms out for a hug. 'Happy New Year! Oh, Elin, you're looking well,' she said breathlessly.

'You, too,' Elin said. 'This is Al,' she added, once Jane let her go.

Jane's eyes widened in appreciation. 'Well! You're a good-looker, fair play,' she said, shaking his hand. 'Eric! Come out here! They've arrived! Come on in,' she said, 'Eric's got the kettle on.'

Eric came out radiating disapproval and disappointment, but he was quite cheerful really. He had very black hair, and thick black eyebrows, dark eyes and a mouth that was permanently downturned.

'Afternoon, Captain,' he said, giving Al a sharp salute. 'Welcome to Mountain Ash.'

Al looked disconcerted and he glanced at Elin. 'I'm not a captain,' he protested.

'That accent!' Jane said. 'You're straight out of Hollywood, that's what you are!' She took them into a room with faded Axminster carpets, brass fenders, copper saucepans and china ornaments. Distracted, Al banged his head on the door lintel.

'Tea?'

'Yes please,' he said, rubbing his bruise.

'Not for me,' Elin said. 'I'll just run home and say hello to Mum and Dad and let you settle in, Al.'

'I'll drive you,' he said quickly.

'No need, I'll take the shortcut down the lane.' She kissed him on the lips. 'It's not far. I won't be long.'

The village was only a mile down the track. It had started reverting to nature and Elin walked along the frosty strip of grass growing up the middle of it to avoid the mud.

Coming out of the leafy lane, the bridge, the clear river, the stone houses, the post office, the school and the chapel in the village were all spread out along one road. She had lived in the village all her life and it was home, comfortingly familiar to her, even though it seemed to change colour day by day. Now, as she walked in the afternoon sun, she tried to see it through Al's eyes. Everything looked golden and sparkling and welcoming.

*

After drinking his tea and eating biscuits and answering Jane's many questions about his ancestry, Al unpacked his kitbag in the small cosy bedroom and sat on the bed, feeling restless until, to his joy, Elin came back to fetch him. Al took her arm and they walked down the leafy, curving, overgrown track that led to her village.

They crossed the bridge over the river, and she took him along the road past the post office and the chapel and the school to her parents' farm. The farm was set back off the road and up a gentle hill. On the stone gatepost was a purple slate sign with the name of the farm carved on it: PEN Y BRYN.

Elin took Al into the sitting room where her father was crouching by the fireplace, pushing balls of newspaper into a small pyramid of kindling in the grate.

'Make yourself comfortable, Al,' he said over his shoulder. He took a fresh sheet of newspaper and held the sheet tightly over the fireplace. 'It's chilly in here, but it will soon warm up.'

'Don't set the chimney on fire now, Thomas, will you?' his wife warned him sternly, standing in the doorway. 'Hullo, Al. We've heard plenty about you. Make yourself at home. Tea's nearly ready. Mind what I said, Tom.'

Elin's father had his back to them, and he didn't answer. He'd worked with farm machinery since he was a boy, and it had made him half deaf, although he denied it. He was holding the paper tight over the fireplace, watching it burn.

They were all watching the paper burn. The fire, desperate for oxygen, sucked at the newspaper and roared, but Elin's father held it there firmly, man versus fire, taming it, until the centre of it began to smoulder and blacken, and the black turned into a hole which burned red around the edges and blazed into flame. Mrs Jenkins shrieked, 'Tom!' as the room turned bright orange, and just when Al thought he'd left it too late and they were going to have to save themselves and run out into the road, Elin's father bundled the newspaper up the chimney where it set fire to the soot.

A few minutes after this excitement, there was a knock at the front door, and a small energetic girl with copper hair dashed in, about six years old.

'Elin, there's black paper flying round like rooks,' she said excitedly, and then she saw Al in his uniform and forgot all about the roaring fire. She looked at him with wide blue eyes and dashed back out again.

Another girl came in almost immediately, a dark-haired adolescent with a familiar widow's peak.

'Mr Jenkins, your house is on fire, by the way,' she said cheerfully. She looked at Al. 'I'm Mary Oswald Hughes. Eric's my brother. You're the captain who's staying at his hotel.'

'I'm not a captain.'

'My brother says you are.' *So there*, her attitude implied.

As they were having tea, Al's eyes were drawn to a row of ornately carved wooden spoons hanging on the wall behind Elin's mother. He was surprised to see an object so familiar to him in this unfamiliar place.

'Excuse me, those spoons that you've got,' he said, pointing to them when the meal was over. 'I have one very similar to that first one on the left. It's the same shape.'

Mrs Jenkins turned to look at them. When she turned back, she was smiling. 'That first one is the oldest one.'

'They're for loose tea, is that right?' he asked her. 'It's a caddy spoon, my father says.'

'I'm sure you could use them for tea,' she said kindly. 'They're Welsh love spoons. How did you come by yours, Al?'

He hesitated awkwardly for a moment. 'My mother inherited it from a great-uncle. She gave it to me before she passed. She believed it had a history.'

Elin's mother seemed to understand perfectly. 'It's a love token,' she said. 'A boy would carve one for someone he adored, and the more ornate ones were as good as an engagement ring is now. He could both declare his intentions and show off his carpentry skills at the same time.'

'A love token,' Al repeated. 'Yes, that makes sense. It's got a heart on it, with the initials CE, and a chain, and a cross, and a ball in a cage, and a boat. I used to make up stories about it when I was a kid.'

'That's right, Al. They each tell their own story,' she said, as if she understood.

Elin got up from the table and unhooked the most ornate spoon to show to Al. 'My father made this when Mum and Dad were courting, didn't you, Dad? It's why Mum married him, actually.'

Her mother laughed and spread her hands. 'How could I say no?'

Al turned it over in his hand, admiring the skill that had gone into it. It was very elaborate, a fine work of art, really – three-dimensional, highly polished, with two hearts entwined. He looked at Elin's father with renewed interest. 'It must have taken you ages to craft this.'

'Ah, it was something to do on icy winter evenings,' Mr Jenkins said modestly, swatting away the praise and getting to his feet. He rested his hand on Al's shoulder for a moment. 'Sycamore, it is,' he added softly.

And just like that, Al felt a warm feeling of relief as Elin's parents' approval washed over him.

After tea, Al and Elin walked through the village in the evening sun.

She took him past a large house, up and over a stone wall and into a field on a slope on the side of the valley.

'It's here,' she said, padding ahead of him through the deep grass. 'This is where the early Quakers were buried.'

'In this field?' Al asked, looking around uncertainly.

'Yes. And the stone I was telling you about, it's somewhere around here, by this wall. It's a bit overgrown.' She walked up and down and then stopped and pushed the grass aside, crispy with frost under her foot. Crouching on the frozen ground, she cleared the stone to show him. 'Look! Here it is. See? Margaret Evans. Lincoln's ancestor.'

Al crouched next to her. The marker was small, simple, more like a stepping stone than a memorial. Al felt along the markings with his fingertips. He was silent and respectful. After a few moments he said, 'Just think, Elin, if it hadn't been for her, Lincoln would never have been born.'

This of all things melted Elin's heart and convinced her they were made for each other. There was no one else she had ever met who would marvel at the grave like Al did and respect its significance. She had shared this amazing knowledge without having to explain why it was amazing or say anything at all.

Al laid both his hands on the stone, his tanned neck bent, his hair like black velvet above his collar. 'You know, I can't wait to tell my father about this,' he said.

'Aw, Al.' Elin stood up and she cast her evening shadow over him, her stomach somersaulting in a wild combination of affection and lust. Her hands on her hips, she felt at that moment like she ruled the world. She looked down at Hafod Fadog farmhouse, and then scanned the timeless hills with a beginning of a smile. The sky was turning rose. There was no one around. Smoke was rising from chimney pots, and the lights were going on in the little windows of the houses. She felt a rush of love for him, she wanted him, and she wanted him to know it. Impulsively she took her coat off, threw it on the wall, unbuttoned her dress and let it fall to the ground, her skin prickling with excitement and the cold. She twirled around, laughing, her arms outstretched as if the whole world was hers for the taking.

Al stared up at her for a moment. His eyes darkened and he groaned softly. Then he got to his feet and picked the dress up, covering her up again, buttoning her into it carefully, his fingers trembling at her throat. He picked up her coat from the wall and eased her arms into the sleeves.

Once he'd finished, she hugged him tight and felt his heartbeat reverberate through her ribs. 'Why did you do that?' she asked him curiously.

'Because I'm crazy. And you've got to live here, Elin,' he said into the warm curve of her neck.

Elin pushed away a little, to look at him. 'Do you like me, though?'

'You know I do,' he said. 'I really do. I can't help it.'

CHAPTER ELEVEN

When they got back to Liverpool a few days later, Al booked them a room in the Sunrise Hotel.

Elin borrowed Rose's fake gold wedding ring from Woolworths and admired it on her finger. 'It suits me, don't you think?'

'Definitely, Mrs Smith.'

Elin looked up at Rose. 'Isn't that a bit of a giveaway, calling myself Smith?'

'Let's face it, Elin, they'll know you're not really married. You're just giving them a reason to pretend they think you are.'

Elin met up with Al one street away, furtive as fugitives, and they greeted each other briefly, like strangers, searching each other's faces as if they were preparing to jump off a cliff hand-in-hand.

'Don't look so worried. We don't have to do anything,' Al said.

Elin laughed nervously. 'Isn't that the point, though? Doing something?'

'So what? We'll have a soft bed and you and me. We can just talk.'

'Talk. Do you want to just talk?' She kissed him. Her lips were swollen from last night's kissing; she was addicted to kissing him.

She was scared, though. She imagined them having sex. She'd seen enough of it on the farm – the pursuit, the pounce, and then it was all fast and furious, bulls servicing cows, dogs humping bitches, the cockerel pinning down hens. She wondered if it would change things between them, and how she would feel afterwards, if it would change her or damage her morally forever. 'Oh, I love you, Al,' she said painfully, looking into his blue eyes. 'You're so lovely.' She said it without thinking, and then she remembered: *Never be the first one to say it*, Rose had warned her, *because he'll run a mile.*

Too late.

Al didn't run a mile. He pulled her to him and leaned on a lamp post and held her face in his warm hands. 'I love you, too,' he said.

She'd never been looked at before the way Al looked at her, with a combination of intense gentleness and reckless energy. Elin could smell Old Spice on his hands. She put her hands over his. She loved him for being clean and healthy and fit and strong.

The hotel was painted sunrise orange. The name had been written in such elaborate lettering it was hard to read, and as if the signwriter had realised his mistake, he had added a small illustration of the sun appearing on the horizon.

They walked into the hotel and went up to the reception desk. The manager gave them the cursory, bored look of someone who had seen it all before. He handed Al a pen and a book to write their details in.

Elin watched over Al's shoulder as he signed their names.

He didn't sign in as Mr and Mrs Smith, he wrote Mr and Mrs Locke.

As they walked up the narrow stairs to their room, Elin asked him why.

'Because, Elin, writing Mr and Mrs Smith would be a lie.'

'Writing Mr and Mrs Locke is a lie.'

'But one day it won't be,' he said.

Elin followed him along the landing, thinking it over, smiling to herself, and then she remembered that Rose had told her men would tell you all sorts to get you into bed.

They passed the communal bathroom and WC, and then Al checked the number on the key and they were at the door of their room.

He held it open for Elin to go in before him. She looked around the room doubtfully, feeling awkward and not in the least bit romantic. The faint smell of furniture polish hung in the air. It seemed clean, at least. It was a large room with a worn patterned carpet laid over creaking boards. The bed was huge with a pale pink eiderdown, the colour of an anaemic tongue, and a mahogany headboard darkened with the patina of countless heads.

Against one wall loomed a giant double-doored mahogany wardrobe and, opposite it, the light from the window was half blocked out by a dressing table with a trifold mirror reflecting a pink lamp with a dusty shade.

Elin looked at Al, her arms dangling by her sides. She hardly knew him, she realised now. She was nervous that he would suddenly strip naked when she wasn't ready, and expect her to – she didn't know what he was expecting. She didn't suppose she was his first, and she started to feel resentful about it, and wanted to start a quarrel. It was true that before this, she had desperately wanted to have sex with him, but maybe that was only because they had nowhere to go.

Al was standing with his hands in his pockets. He went to sit on the chair by the dressing table, and he switched the lamp on.

Strangely, when the lamp was lit it made the room darker, and he switched it off again and stood up. 'Elin—'

'Yes?'

'I'm going to the bathroom.'

'Why?' she asked anxiously, grabbing at his sleeve.

He looked puzzled by the question. 'Well, you know,' he shrugged. He added, 'I won't be a minute.'

As the door closed behind Al, she thought seriously about leaving the hotel while he was gone. Just getting out of there, before it was too late. She hated the place. 'It's not you,' she would tell him if she ever saw him again, 'it was the room.'

She looked at herself in the mirror, her face multiplied into infinity. The furniture seemed to tower over her, and she turned quickly because the solid mahogany wardrobe gave her the creeps – you could hide all sorts of things in there. Daring herself to do it, she turned the dainty, ornate silver key in the lock and flung open the heavy doors. The interior tinkled with coat hangers. It smelled of wood, pleasantly dry. She looked at the rail curiously. She couldn't imagine who would stay in this room, in this hotel, long enough to need all this wardrobe space and all these hangers.

She thought again about getting out while she had the chance.

Then she wondered if maybe Al hadn't gone to the bathroom after all, but instead, he'd had the same feelings and left before her, got cold feet at the last minute and thought better of the whole thing.

Elin felt slightly indignant at the idea of being abandoned by him. She would find out sooner or later, she thought philosophically, one way or the other.

At the bottom of the wardrobe were two large drawers with blue glass knobs. She pulled the drawers open. They were empty, too. Suddenly she felt off-balance and realised to her alarm that the huge wardrobe was slowly tilting towards her. She pushed her hands out to stop it, but it was too heavy and the wardrobe toppled her backwards, and with a crash she was lying on the floor, enclosed, to her immense shock, with the coat hangers in the woody dark. 'Help!' she shouted, her voice muffled. 'Help me!'

The floor creaked and she heard Al's voice, also muffled.

'Elin! What the heck – hang on!'

Al began to lift the wardrobe off her and as he raised it off the ground high enough to let in a wedge of daylight, Elin managed to get into a crouch and she pushed it up too, as hard as she could, until they got it upright again, kicking the drawers shut with their feet. As it rocked back into place she shut and locked the heavy doors for good measure, and stood away from it warily, glancing at Al, wide-eyed.

'Are you okay?' He was very concerned. 'I heard a bang and suddenly you'd disappeared,' he said.

'I know! One minute I was standing here and the next thing – the next thing I was lying on my back in the dark—'

'You'd gone and the wardrobe was on the floor. I couldn't understand it,' he said incredulously. 'You might have been crushed.' His astonishment matched hers.

Elin stifled a giggle and nodded. 'I know,' she said soberly. 'I might have been.' She wiped her eyes. 'Oh, Al.'

He hugged her hard, and rocked her in his arms, and pressed up against his woollen sweater, Elin remembered why they were there.

After a few moments they kissed and his soft, gentle mouth fitted against hers perfectly, as if they were made for each other. It made wonderful sense now to take her dress off, and her slip. She stood in her pants and bra, and he looked at her for a moment without moving, and then he tried taking his clothes off all at once, struggling wildly out of his sweater and T-shirt and undershirt, getting all tangled up, until he stood there naked and she caught her breath.

He was not like the Welsh boys on the farms, all freckles and ribs.

Al had skin like honey and muscles that cast their own curved shade.

She put her arms around him, pressing her body against him, and his smooth throat was hot against her mouth. He was trembling and so was she.

They got into bed between the cold sheets. Al rolled over onto her and he put his warm lips on her closed eyes, and kissed her neck, her mouth. If they could just stay like this, she thought, being close and just kissing, it would be lovely. She only changed her mind when he stopped kissing her suddenly and jumped out of bed. She reached out for him with a whimper of frustration.

'I've got a condom,' he said, searching through his pockets. 'That okay with you?'

Elin nodded.

He put the condom on with his back to her and got back into bed and kissed her. They stared at each other, eyes wide open, and he slid into her. She had the sensation of a sudden happy shock. *This is it, this is it!* Plunging her hands into his thick dark hair, something amazing happened, feelings she had never expected, that wild tenderness, *again, again*, she thought. Afterwards, lying side-by-side under the sheets with the sweat cooling on their skin, hearts pounding, curiosity satisfied, Elin felt so close to Al.

In the silence, life seemed very simple and intense. She rested her arm behind her head and saw things with new eyes.

And the room looked beautiful.

*

Elin and Al were walking by the Mersey, and it was a sunny day in February, the first properly sunny day of spring, the kind that gives you hope that the winter has passed for another year.

Al was preoccupied, not talking much. He was leaning on the railings looking at the brown choppy water and she was staring at the gulls, the cruel yellow curve of their bills.

Without looking at her, he said, 'Elin, the ship is almost ready for departure.'

'Oh. Okay.' Now she understood. 'We knew it was going to happen,' she added miserably, looking out across the water. She shivered with resignation.

'Are you cold? Come here.' He moved her in front of him and wrapped his arms around her, warm as a cloak, resting his chin on the top of her head. 'Better?'

'Yes, much.' Elin wanted to ask him when he'd be back, just to give her a bit of hope to cling onto, to keep her going. But what was the point? It was better to face it. 'It's been so wonderful,' she said, trying to find the good in it. 'I've had the best time of my life, Al. I'll never forget it.'

He tightened his grip around her, squeezing the breath out of her.

'Marry me,' he said in her ear.

'What?' Elin struggled free and looked up at him.

He raised his dark eyebrows, inviting her answer. 'Well? How about it?'

'Shut up,' she said, half laughing, slapping him with the back of her hand.

'Is that a yes?'

'No.'

Al clutched his chest. 'You've broken my heart, Jenkins.'

'Now you know how I feel,' she said with a half-smile. She sighed. The wind lifted her fringe out of her eyes.

Al touched her face, stroking the tip of his finger gently down the lone dimple in her cheek. 'Give me one good reason why we shouldn't.'

'Just one? Where would we live?'

'Come to Pennsylvania. You know people there.'

She smiled.

'If I swap my liberty leave we can go and tell your parents right away. We'll do it properly.'

He was perfectly serious, she could see that now, and she thought of Rose warning her that he probably had a girl in every port. Rose was wrong.

'I've already told my folks,' he said. 'I've told them we're going to marry before I leave.'

'Have you? But you're leaving soon—'

'Yeah. Maybe in a couple of weeks.'

'What about banns and stuff?' she said vaguely. 'Don't the banns have to be read?' Elin wasn't exactly sure what banns were, but she heard herself ask the question like the voice of reason. Since when had she been so sensible?

She tried to imagine what her parents would say. Probably that she was too young to be rushing into marriage. They believed in things that could stand the test of time, and that included relationships. Her mother had a cousin who had been engaged for at least forty years. She wouldn't leave her mother and her fiancé couldn't leave his farm. Everyone except Elin thought that the situation was perfectly understandable.

But then the thought of living without Al was intolerable.

Pennsylvania.

Starting a new life in a new country with Al.

'What are you thinking?' he asked her.

All the things she and her friends thought they knew about men, that's what she was thinking about. No one ever talked about how hurtable they were, how kind, sexy, warm, hopeful, unsure, loving and good a man could be. And here was Al, happy to swap his leave to go with her to Wales to tell her father they wanted to be married. She put her arms around him and rested her forehead against his sweater.

'Elin.' He kissed the top of her head, thinking she needed to be persuaded. 'I don't want this to end.'

She knew how he felt. She would happily have carried on just like this, meeting up in their spare time, snatching moments together when they could, when their duties allowed, having drinks, sometimes spending an afternoon in the Sunrise Hotel. When she was with him, she was transported into a romantic life of glamour; she loved their lovemaking and his good looks and his gorgeous accent; she loved being away for a while from the messy, demanding, ugliness of sickness.

She imagined marrying Al in the chapel in Capel Celyn, with everyone there: her father in his suit, her mother wearing a hat, Eric as best man and Jane as a bridesmaid. Suddenly marriage seemed very easy and uncomplicated, and the obvious solution.

'I accept your proposal,' she said with a smile.

*

Elin's parents liked Al in their own quiet ways. Ideally, they would have welcomed a son-in-law who was local and could help on the farm, but it was in their nature to make the best of things.

'He'll be a good provider, at least,' her mother conceded, to console herself, as if that was the main reason to marry.

Al had gone out to the barn to ask Elin's father for her hand in marriage.

It was the moment her father had been expecting, and dreading. He told Al he would talk to Elin before giving his permission, and he went indoors in his work boots to find his daughter, trailing straw and mud through the kitchen.

Elin was sitting with her mother, waiting by the fire with her hands clasped on her knees. She looked up at her father anxiously, eagerly.

'I'd like to talk to you, Elin,' he said.

They walked by the clear river.

Against the sound of the water, she knew that she would miss the hum of bees, the sweetness of honeysuckle, the startling blue flowers creeping out of stone walls, the nettles adorned with butterflies, the gentle fragrant fields, the rugged hills, and the domineering mountains – it didn't seem so much that her father wanted to talk, but more that he wanted her to see all that she was thinking of leaving behind.

When they reached the stile, he leant against it and lit up a Woodbine.

Elin watched the smoke fray in the breeze.

'Tell me, how do you feel about marrying Al?'

'Dad, I can't imagine life without him,' she said passionately.

He gave her a weary, loving smile. 'Never mind a life without him,' he said. 'Can you imagine life *with* him?'

'Yes, I can. Him and only him. I'll miss you, Dad,' she said, almost in tears. 'But we'll come back to see you, and you and Mam can come and see us, can't you?'

Her father's expression didn't change.

He couldn't leave the farm, Elin knew that, but she desperately wanted him to say that he would.

'Aye,' he said gently. 'We'll work it out. There's always a way.' He stubbed the cigarette out in his tin box and put it away in his pocket. His eyes narrowed as he looked across at the hills. An eagle hung there focused, motionless, as if pinned against the sky. 'We'd better not keeping him waiting too long.'

At the house, Al was standing with his back to the fire, waiting for the verdict.

Elin's father went up to him and shook his hand without saying a word.

After the handshake he went back out into the yard where they could hear him talking to the dog.

CHAPTER TWELVE

In March 1956, having breakfast in Eric's dining room at Mountain Ash, was Robert Johnson, *Rob*, a new guest, come all the way from Liverpool wearing a smart trench coat and equipped with a briefcase and instruments.

For the last few months, the flooding of Welsh valleys to provide drinking water for Liverpool had been nothing more than a rumour. They didn't believe it would happen again, that Welsh land would be once more be flooded for English water. If it were true, they agreed, this time there would be a consultation and a great deal of opposition. It would be properly discussed with the people in the valley, the district council and the county council. People would be informed, and their voices heard. And yet, here was Robert Johnson, come to stay.

'Drinking water? What do they want more drinking water for? They haven't finished drinking Lake Vyrnwy yet,' Eric said bitterly.

Sunk under Lake Vyrnwy was the village of Llanwddyn. It had been flooded in the 1880s by Liverpool Corporation Waterworks to provide drinking water for Liverpool, with the loss of five shops, three pubs, two chapels, a church and thirty-seven homes.

They'd looked at his occupation in the guestbook. *Surveyor*, he said he was.

Rob Johnson was amiable, with light brown hair, an open face and a ready smile. He wore glasses which magnified his hazel eyes.

Jane wouldn't go so far as to call him good-looking – not by her standards. After all, she'd married Eric, who was striking and dark, like a sexy Dracula – but he was pleasant to look at.

Jane pinned her curly brown hair away from her forehead and applied Max Factor lipstick, coral, in order to interrogate Rob while Eric was making him breakfast.

She was full of questions as she pulled up a chair and watched Rob butter his toast, but she quickly established that he had no links to the area and he was just here to do a survey.

'What are you doing a survey of?' she asked him.

He was upfront about it. 'I've come to find out whether the valley is a suitable place to build a dam. It's only one of several possibilities,' he added, dabbing the crumbs from around his mouth. 'They're considering a few other places – Dolanog, Ceidiog, Hirnant, and the possibility of building a dam by Bodwenni to create one huge lake.'

'Bloody hell, man!' Eric said, coming through from the kitchen with the breakfast and catching the last bit of the sentence. 'You can't be serious! That would cover the whole of Bala! You're talking about drowning out a thousand people.'

Rob picked up his knife and fork. 'It's just a possibility,' he said.

Elin had given up her nursing job in Liverpool to spend a couple of weeks with her parents before she left for Pennsylvania to be with Al. They hadn't been able to get married before he left. The crew were given a day's notice, that was all, before the ship went back to the Naval Shipyard in Philadelphia with not even enough time to say a proper goodbye, beyond a last visit to the Sunrise Hotel before Elin waved Al off, tears in her eyes, a hot stickiness between her legs.

She was excited about joining them and his family seemed nice, welcoming – thoughtful, too. *My family can't wait to meet you*, he said.

Al's stepmother had sent her a card to say she was arranging a party so Elin could be introduced to family and friends all at once before the wedding on the 24th of March. And after the wedding Al was being posted to Japan; Elin would make a home for them while he was away.

Jane was sitting on Elin's bed in her room with rose-sprigged wallpaper at her parents' farm, and Elin was showing Jane her trousseau: silk lace-edged slips, salmon-pink corsets, and stockings.

'American Tan. Now that I've finished nursing, I'm never wearing black stockings again. They cost me a fortune. You can't see the ladders in these. And look!' Elin held up a pale, slippery nightgown.

'Easy to slip off,' Jane said with a knowing smile.

Elin was leaving the best till last. Her wedding dress was hanging on the door.

She took it out of the garment bag with a thrill of fresh excitement. It was the most beautiful thing she'd ever owned, made of white lace, with long sleeves and a high neck. Her mother had helped her choose it from Lewis's in Liverpool.

Elin held it against her slim, boyish figure and raised her dark eyebrows, feeling suddenly, uncharacteristically shy. 'What do you think?'

'Beautiful, it is,' Jane said softly. She met Elin's eyes and smiled wistfully. 'Put it on for me, Elin.'

Elin undressed and stepped into the cool silk lining of the dress, smoothing her hands over the white lace.

Jane buttoned her into it and stood back to admire it. 'Oh! You look so lovely. It's perfect. I can imagine it now, you and Al, and it's making me teary. Are you nervous?'

'No, I'm not! I can't wait! Undo me, will you?'

Elin stepped out of the gown and put it back in its muslin bag, dressed, and folded up the silk lingerie carefully, imagining

Al's face when he saw her in it. She closed her suitcase and put it back under the bed.

'You're getting out at the right time, you know,' Jane said. 'Liverpool is looking for places in Wales to drown for reservoirs.'

'I know.' Elin combed her fingers through her short dark hair. 'I read it in the *Liverpool Daily Post*. Likely to be Dolanog, it said.'

'Maybe so, but this surveyor that's staying with us, he's testing the ground by Hafod Fadog. I'm worried about it, to be honest.'

The news was a stone in Elin's heart. 'Please don't say that,' she pleaded. 'I feel guilty enough anyway, going so far away. My parents have been lovely about it and my dad joked and said it would save him a lot of money, me being married out there, but… you know. Anyway, don't worry about the surveyor, it will all be fine, I'm sure of it.' She didn't want to be dragged down. She was convinced that her happiness was shining its light over them all and that it would keep them safe. 'I love Al. I can't help it!' It came over her again in a kind of wonder, and she shivered with pleasure at the thought of him.

'Of course you do,' Jane said quickly, 'he's a nice boy, solid, and I'll tell you something about him, Elin, he's *neat*. Cleaning his room, it was so tidy that I was in and out in ten minutes. Don't roll your eyes, it's a good quality in a husband.'

'I can think of better ones.'

'Elin Jenkins!'

Elin laughed and fell backwards onto the bed, arms outstretched. 'I'm so happy I could burst.'

Jane said, 'Think of the mess!'

Elin giggled and stared up fondly at the rose of the ceiling light, and the pink lampshade, and the rose-sprigged wallpaper. She felt a rush of yearning for them, as if they were already just a memory. Jip was barking at magpies in the yard, and in the field beyond, the Welsh Black cattle lowed and the distant sheep chuckled softly. Everything that she'd got used to over the years she was hearing and seeing again.

'Just think, when I come home next, Al will be with me in this bed, right next to me, his head on this pillow, nose-to-nose and close-up tight.'

'Never mind that, before you leave, you should come and meet the surveyor,' Jane said, 'because a lot might happen before then. You're good with words; tell him to leave our village alone.'

'Tell him yourself!' Elin propped herself up on her elbow. 'Take him to chapel on Sunday and let him meet everyone. He'll get the feel of the place in his soul.'

'I'm not sure he's got a soul,' Jane said dryly. 'Hold still. You've got a feather in your hair.' She pulled it out along with a short strand of dark hair. 'Give me your hand. There.'

Elin looked at the white feather curled in her palm. It seemed a potent symbol of good fortune. 'When I was on the wards,' she said, 'we told patients that this was a sign that the angels were watching over them.'

'Better than blaming the pillows, I suppose.'

Elin put the feather by the side of her bed, linked her arm in Jane's and kissed her on the cheek. For a moment, they rested against each other in a warm and friendly silence.

'I suppose I'd better be going,' Jane said. 'It's getting dark and Eric will be wondering where I am.'

Elin straightened up and said on impulse, 'I'll walk back with you to Mountain Ash.'

There were a few small reasons Elin decided to walk back with Jane. She'd enjoy her friend's company a little bit longer, she had nothing else to do, and she felt like a walk.

Small reasons.

But they had consequences.

*

They found Eric and the surveyor sitting on railway sleepers around the bonfire, drinking cherry brandy.

Eric introduced Elin, shooting a glance at his wife which Elin didn't really understand.

'I was just saying to Eric, you're nice and high up here,' Rob said to Jane. 'If work goes ahead, it won't affect you.'

'How do you make that out?' Jane asked indignantly. 'Our parents live in the village. It will affect everybody.'

'My parents' farm's in the village, too,' Elin said.

Rob hadn't seemed to notice Elin at first, but he looked at her now with interest, his eyes large and gentle behind the lenses of his glasses. 'Is that so?' He turned his face towards the wide, glorious expanse of silver-streaked sky and black hills.

Eric followed his gaze. 'It makes me think of the temptation of Jesus, when the devil whispered, "All this could be yours." You can see why he had to stop and think about it, can't you, Rob?'

'I'm not a churchgoer,' Rob said. 'Granite is my thing.'

'Granite? Rob, forget granite, just let us know if you find gold,' Jane said, fanning the woodsmoke away. 'There's plenty in Dolgellau, and it's only twenty miles away.'

'We'd benefit from a gold rush,' Eric said. The cherry brandy was so sweet that he rubbed his tongue over his teeth to unstick them. 'People would come to stay from miles around.'

'We wouldn't need this place if we had gold,' Jane said dreamily. 'You wouldn't see me for dust. I'd go and live in The Ritz.'

'And then what? What would you do all day?' Eric asked, alarmed at this new side to his wife. He had a strong Methodist work ethic, and he wasn't sure he approved of this glimpse into Jane's fantasies. *I'd go and live in The Ritz, not 'we'.*

Eric knew Jane envied Elin and it made him insecure. She was a bad influence. Since she'd come back from Liverpool, he'd heard them talking outside at night, looking up at the stars sprinkled like talc on black velvet, and it seemed as if Elin had everything that Jane didn't. At eighteen, Elin still had the future laid out, unknown, in front of her, but Jane was only five years older and her future was just more of the present: keeping the guest house going, trying to survive. Even though Jane and Elin had been brought up in the same village, had gone to the same school, and attended the same chapel, their life paths were veering wildly.

'I promise I'll keep my eyes open for gold,' Rob said to Jane, 'and I'll tell you first if I find it.'

'Tell me, too,' Elin said, hugging her knees.

'But Eric told me you were going to America, so you won't be here.' Rob said it as mildly as he said everything else. But it seemed as if they all heard it differently.

Eric thought it was a challenge, and he laughed.

Elin took it as an accusation and was offended.

Jane was reproachful. 'Yes! It's all right for you, Elin, you won't be here! I don't know how you can leave, especially not now. I couldn't. I want to live here and work here, die here and be buried here. I'm glad I've married Eric, because he understands this place and he wants to live with me here. When we have children, I want them to grow up here so that they learn the language and the land and all the things that belong to this village. I would be heartbroken at the thought of leaving.'

'Well, we're different, you and I,' Elin said, still defensive, biting the edge of her thumbnail.

Reassured, Eric reached out and squeezed his wife's hand. 'We'll never leave,' he said.

'If they drown the valley,' Rob said, 'everyone will have to clear out whether they want to or not.'

They brought their attention back to him, their eyes gleaming dark in the firelight, red shadows dancing on their skin. The drowning was the subject they'd been avoiding, and now here it was again, laid out before them in its ugliness.

'Don't say that!' Elin's face was tight and her voice was high. 'That's an awful thing to say. You don't know it's going to happen yet. You might find that it's not a suitable place for a reservoir. That's true, isn't it?'

Rob scratched his head and turned away from the heat as a log crackled and shifted, disturbing the ash, resurrecting the flames. He didn't answer.

'You're supposed to agree with me,' Elin said to him fiercely. 'You're supposed to say you're right, it's not suitable.' She was on the brink of tears.

'Don't cry,' Rob said quickly, turning back to her. 'It's my job, you see. It's what I'm paid for. It doesn't mean I agree with the decision.'

'You should find another job, then,' Elin said.

'What difference would that make? They'd just send someone else.'

'Aye,' Eric said, mindful of his paying guest's feelings. 'I'm not blaming you, Rob.'

'Aren't you?' Elin's voice trembled. 'Well, you should be. I am.'

'Don't.' Rob was pleading, regretful, gentle. 'Don't be upset.' He took his glasses off and his eyes were naked.

Elin looked away quickly – she felt she'd stared straight into the man's heart. 'Sorry,' she whispered.

Rob squeezed his eyes shut. He put his spectacles back on and when he raised his head it was as if he'd retreated indoors to safety. The flames reflected off them. He folded his arms on his knees and hunched forward, looking into the embers.

Watching him, they were filled with foreboding. It was like noticing a crystal glass balanced carelessly on the edge of the table. It was like seeing a fledgling preparing to leave the nest. Something was going to happen, and for a moment they were sick with dread, but it was impossible not to watch him, and wait.

Rob only shook his head slowly, frowning.

Eric couldn't stand the tension any longer and he got to his feet. Elin was only eighteen and cherry brandy was strong stuff, no matter how innocuously it went down. He took her glass out of her hand, which was hot, and he threw the remains of the drink on the fire where it flared up in a blue flame. 'Righty-ho,' he said. 'Time to walk you home. Put the kettle on, Jane, I won't be long.'

Rob stood up, too. 'I'll walk with her,' he said to Eric.

'No you won't,' Elin said, 'neither of you, I'm going by myself.'

'Leave her be,' Jane warned, holding Eric back. 'She's in a mood.'

In the glow of the fire, Elin's face glittered with tears. She hurried across the yard and when she reached the track she blended in with the shadows and disappeared.

'She's younger than us, man,' Eric said, apologising to Rob. 'And for all she's been working in Liverpool, that nurses' home was riddled with rules. And she misses the Captain. She's just letting off steam.'

Rob stared across at the track with his hands on his hips as if he was expecting Elin to reappear at any moment. 'I know,' he said. 'I'm going to see if she's okay. Don't wait up, I've got my keys.' He patted his pocket.

'Aye,' Eric said, 'all right. Keep an eye on her.'

Rob rubbed his hands together and grinned. 'I will, don't you worry about that.'

Rob caught up with Elin halfway down the track.

She turned, startled, as he loomed out of the darkness behind her. When she saw who it was, she said indignantly, 'Rob? What are you doing here?'

'I've come to apologise. I didn't mean to upset you, Elin. Forgive me.'

'Leave me alone.' She wrapped her arms around herself and turned to walk away.

In one quick movement he was in front of her, arms out-stretched, blocking her path.

The moonless night made everything strange. She could hardly recognise his face in the shadows, and she felt a shiver of fear. 'Fine,' she said, backing down. 'I forgive you. Happy? Now let me pass.'

He remained standing in front of her, ominously silent and very still.

Elin was trembling. The cold wind was rustling the branches, whispering through the grass, plucking at her clothes. Only Rob, or the black shape of him, was solid and motionless.

'Prove it,' he said quietly in the darkness.

'What?'

'Prove you forgive me.' He added softly, 'Kiss me.'

There was something in his voice that scared her. It wasn't violence, or anger. It was worse than that; it was enjoyment.

'Cat got your tongue?' he asked, and she could hear the smile in his words. 'Come on. You kiss the Captain, don't you?' He chuckled to himself. 'And more besides, I bet.'

Standing in the blackness with Rob blocking her path, it felt serious, but Elin had no way of knowing how serious it really was. She couldn't tell how far he'd go, or how drunk he was. She'd dealt with drunks before, but never in a secluded place like this, not totally alone.

She tucked her hands in her pockets to stop them shaking. 'I'm warning you, Rob,' she said defiantly, 'Eric's got a short fuse. When I tell him you followed me—'

'Don't bother, he knows.' Rob sounded amused. 'In fact, he told me to keep an eye on you. I'm the only person who can stop the drowning, aren't I? It's all down to what I say in my report. Eric has to keep me sweet.'

Adrenaline rushed through her when he said that, as if Eric had sacrificed her for the sake of the land, but once the fight or flight surge passed, she suddenly felt stone-cold sober. Fear sharpened her mind as if her life depended on it.

In that moment, she came to a decision.

She wasn't going to scream, and she wasn't going to run – the thought of Rob chasing her, catching her, muffling her cries with his large, pale hands, brought panic flooding back again.

No. She was going to be sensible and talk her way out of it. She could do that. As Jane had pointed out, she was a good talker.

She swallowed hard. 'Okay,' she said steadily. 'I'll give you one kiss. To prove I've forgiven you.'

She moved towards him, close enough so that she could smell the sweetness of the cherry brandy on his hot breath. She raised her arms seductively and clasped her hands behind his neck, and as she pressed her mouth on his, teeth clashing against teeth, she brought her knee up sharply into his groin.

He jack-knifed sharply and doubled up in pain, cracking his head against hers. He let out a long squeal of pain.

Dazed, Elin pushed past him, her heart pounding in fear. She ran down the track as fast as she could, and his shrill wail chased behind her in the dark. She fled in panic, and it wasn't until she reached the bridge and saw the lights of the farm – like small, illuminated squares in the night – that she broke down and sobbed with sorrow and relief.

The following morning Elin's mother came briskly into the bedroom in a floral apron and opened the curtains.

'Up you get, sleepyhead. You've still got to finish your packing – don't leave it till the last minute or you'll forget things. Where's your list?'

Elin sat up in bed. She looked at the wedding dress hanging on the hook on the door.

Images of the previous night came flooding back – Rob's face, pale and featureless in the dark.

'My list? It's around here somewhere,' she said vaguely, frowning.

Her mother's face softened. 'Cheer up, girl,' she said. 'You've only got a few days to go and then before you know it you will be Mrs Captain Locke, starting your new life. It's all ahead of you, Elin.' Her bright smile turned wistful. 'Come on, I'll help you finish your packing.'

Elin got out of bed. 'I've got to go and see Eric first.'

Her mother looked surprised. 'Whatever for?'

'Because Rob Johnson the surveyor can halt the drowning if he wants to.'

Her mother plunged her hands in her apron pocket and looked sceptical. 'Now why on earth would he do that?' she asked. 'What's in it for him?'

Kiss me.

When Elin didn't reply, her mother looked at her closely. 'You look pale.' She felt Elin's forehead with the back of her hand.

Her mother's hand was cool and soothing. 'I feel as if I'm running out of time,' Elin said. *Like sand trickling through an hourglass*, she thought.

'I expect you're hungry, that's what it is. I'll put some eggs on for you.'

Once she'd gone out of the room, Elin washed and dressed quickly, then hurried downstairs.

'I'll have the eggs in a sandwich when I come back. I won't be long.'

When Elin got to Mountain Ash, Eric was sitting at the table cleaning the horse brasses. The smell of ammonia in the Brasso was strong, and as he diligently buffed the first one, the gleam lit up his face. 'Jane's out, getting groceries,' he said without looking up.

Elin curled her hair around her ear. 'That's okay. It's you I've come to see, Eric. Rob Johnson followed me into the woods and tried to kiss me last night.'

Eric's expression remained impassive.

'Aren't you going to say anything? I've always thought of you as my big brother,' she said, distraught.

The age gap between them had never seemed bigger. Eric still didn't meet her eyes, and she suddenly saw him not as a familiar friend but as a troubled man struggling with his conscience.

He wiped his dirty hands on a cloth. 'Do you think it's easy for Jane and me?' he asked Elin, his dark eyes shining with anger. 'Making him feel welcome, one of the family, giving him extra portions, letting him feel at home when like that,' he snapped his fingers, 'he's trying to destroy the land we love? And you come here complaining because he asked you for a kiss?'

Elin bit the inside of her cheek, close to tears.

Eric sighed. 'I'm sorry.' He rubbed his hands over his tired face. 'Like it or not, he's our last hope, our only hope. We can show him the human face of Celyn. The talk of demonstrations, petitions, the letter to the Queen in fancy writing – what difference are any of those going to make? Who cares if a village of twelve houses and farms and a few shops is submerged for drinking water? It's nothing to them. But we've got a good chance of convincing Rob. Do you think I don't know that people are talking about Jane and me behind their hands? But if that's the only sacrifice I have to make, a bit of gossip and my good name, I can live with that, Elin, and so should you. Stop being so selfish.'

'Oh,' she said, deflated. She understood, now.

He picked up his polishing cloth and put it down again as if his heart had gone out of the job. 'Put the kettle on, will you, please?'

'Sure.' Elin went to the kitchen to make the tea and sat opposite him to drink it.

They were silent for a few moments, thinking their own thoughts. 'About Rob…' she began, and hesitated, thinking of her mother's scepticism.

'Yes?'

'Do you trust him?'

Eric ran his hand through his black hair. He seemed to be giving the question some serious consideration.

'He's a weak man,' he said at last, 'but he's not a bad man. At least, I don't think he is. Do you understand what I'm saying?'

'You're saying that because he's weak, you can, *we* can—'

'Persuade him,' Eric finished for her. 'Yes, Elin. That's my belief.'

Later that same day, Elin went to the post office with a heavy heart. She knew what she had to do.

'Heart alive, Elin, you're soaked,' Bethan Parry said in alarm from behind the post office counter, watching her dripping on the wooden floor. She was a kind woman who saw herself as a go-between for the outside world and the village.

The post office smelled of paper and ink. 'I've got to send a telegram to Al.' Elin had written it down, feeling all the time that she was drowning in sadness. She'd come out in the rain, delaying her errand for as long as she could until the road was empty, the rain was keeping people indoors, which was good, because she didn't want to talk to anyone.

She couldn't leave, not now. She was *Doing the Right Thing*, she reminded herself miserably, hoping that someone would stop her from actually doing it.

She hoped her parents would talk her into going to join Al, but they were worried about the farm and they had gone to the defence committee where the atmosphere veered from indignation to fear.

Al would be disappointed and maybe even annoyed that Elin was changing the wedding plans at the last minute, but he loved her and he would understand, she was certain of that. A few months was nothing out of a lifetime together.

'You'll be off to America soon, won't you?'

'I was supposed to be going on Friday,' Elin said miserably. She took her notepad out of her handbag and tore off the sheet with her message to Al written on it, raindrops from her sleeve smudging the ink. 'I'm staying on now for a bit, just until they've found somewhere else for the dam.'

'Ah! Bless you, *cariad*. You will be a comfort to your parents.'

'I'm only staying until it's all sorted,' Elin said quickly. 'Rob says they could still choose Dolanog or even the Lake District instead.'

Bethan Parry snorted. 'Rob, is it now?' she said, folding her arms. 'Scumbag.'

Elin caught her breath, shocked. She hadn't expected that from Bethan Parry, who was very polite and proper. But there it was; the villagers' hostility towards Rob was out in the open. Even worse, it sounded as if it was something Bethan Parry had said before.

'I think there's a chance he's on our side, or he will be.'

'Don't kid yourself, he's on the side of Liverpool,' Bethan Parry said scornfully. 'To be honest with you, I don't know how Eric can let him stay at Mountain Ash, this whole business is breaking his mother's heart and I've told him that to his face. He didn't like it, but he knows it's true. And I'm warning you, Elin, mind you don't get tarred with the same brush. Now what can I do for you?'

Elin passed her the sheet of paper.

Bethan Parry read it out loud:

DEAREST AL, CRISIS, VALLEY MAY BE DROWNED, NEED TO BE HERE FOR NOW, SO SORRY, MUST CANCEL WEDDING, HEARTBROKEN, WILL WRITE TO EXPLAIN, UNTIL WE MEET AGAIN, ALL MY LOVE ALWAYS, ELIN.

'Dew!' she said. 'It's going to cost you a fortune to send this! There's a charge per word, you know.'

Elin flushed; she'd never sent a telegram before.

Bethan reached for a pencil. 'Brevity is the soul of the telegram. You want to keep it brief. You don't have to put *WILL WRITE TO EXPLAIN*', she said, crossing it out. 'Just write. You don't need to tell him the valley might be drowned.' She crossed that out, too. 'You want to keep *CANCEL WEDDING*, because that's the crux of it, but you don't need *ALWAYS YOUR ELIN*. Save the endearments for your letter, see? Now then, that's got it down to a decent price for you now.' She handed the edited note back to Elin.

Elin looked at the shortened version. 'It doesn't say how sorry I am.'

Bethan Parry took it back from her and amended it.

CANCEL WEDDING, REGRETS, ELIN.

Elin chewed her lip. She still felt fragile from her encounter in the dark with Rob and was having a hard time thinking straight. She looked at the message doubtfully. 'Um… it doesn't say much, does it?'

'It says what needs to be said, doesn't it? The telegram is for emergencies. You can put all the details and the "all my love always" and that kind of thing in a letter.'

'I suppose so. I hadn't thought of it like that.'

'That will be £2.10 shillings,' the postmistress said, filling in the form.

Elin was shocked. It was still a lot of money, even just for those few words.

Bethan Parry stamped it with vigour, and Elin cringed. It felt as if she was stamping on her heart. 'I'll have an airmail letter, too, please.'

She trudged home in the drizzle. Walking along the wet road was like wading in quicksand; her legs didn't seem to move properly, they felt heavy and stiff. She had the feeling that she'd done something terrible but necessary, that she'd offered a great sacrifice in order that the village would be saved. She stopped to nuzzle the horse and his damp whiskers feathered her face.

When she got home, she sat on her bed and poured her love, her feelings, her hopes and her longings into a letter to Al, her tears smudging the page.

Dearest Al,

Please understand how hard postponing our wedding has been for me, but I know that above all you are a kind, good man, and that you will understand why I have to stay here a while longer for my parents' sake.

This is so hard for me to write. The valley may be flooded to create a reservoir, but I am confident that a better, less destructive location can be found soon. I long for you with all my heart and I can't wait to be in your arms again. When you come back from your voyage, I will be waiting for you, and we will start our happy lives together with no guilt to tarnish it, knowing our joy in each other is enduring, abundant and well-deserved.

Ever yours, my darling,
Elin

She went back out in the rain to the postbox. She listened to the letter drop. *There.* It was done.

CHAPTER THIRTEEN

Al's stepmother, Betsy, was talking to him about camellias. Camellias were little waxy pale pink flowers that she was particularly fond of. She wanted to wear a camellia corsage for the wedding, but more than that, she was eager for Al to want it too.

'Pretty, aren't they?'

'Really, they are,' he said obligingly. They looked too perfect to be real. Until that morning, he hadn't even known what a camellia was. Thought she was talking about chameleons.

'Now, Al, do you think your bride will like them in her bouquet?'

He nodded. 'She's sure to, she'll love them,' he said, handing her the blossoms back. Elin would be delighted with any flowers that Betsy chose, she was good-natured that way. For both of them, it was marriage that they wanted more than a wedding, and if they could somehow have done it without any fuss, they would have.

Betsy had lists of things to do for the wedding, pages of them. She checked flowers off in her book.

Hearing the doorbell, she patted Al's shoulder and hurried to welcome the Episcopalian minister who had come to check that Al fully understood the sanctity of marriage, and after pouring him a bourbon she enthusiastically ticked him off her list too and encouraged him to join Al in the sitting room.

Without the bourbon, the minister wouldn't have been able to bring up the subject of carnal temptation, because he was a sensitive man, slight, with fair, thinning hair and the apologetic air of someone who had been bullied over many years. The alcohol allowed him to at least skirt around the subject, once Betsy left them to it.

After she'd closed the door, the minister sat on the edge of the plum-coloured sofa, swilling ice cubes around his glass. He cleared his throat. 'If I may speak frankly, Japan has a reputation for unsavoury activities,' he confided to Al. 'Women, and the like. I'm afraid it is my spiritual duty to warn you of that. You will have to be on your guard. It's very easy to fall into bad company when you're far from home.'

Al hid a grin.

As if he didn't already know.

But he took the advice as seriously as it had been given. 'I understand,' he said. 'But don't worry, Elin's the only girl for me.' It sounded lame and unconvincing. He wasn't good at expressing his feelings, but he gave it another go in an attempt to explain how it was with them. 'She's not just any woman, you see. What I mean to say is, I want to survive the odds and Elin's the girl I want to live for.'

This is why he wanted to marry her before he went to Japan – he was going to be away a while. Most of the crew had remained at the naval barracks, but Al had come home to help Betsy with the wedding arrangements. He couldn't wait to see Elin again. It was all he thought about.

In the days before departure, they all went crazy, each man in his own way: leaving behind pregnancies, reunions, break-ups; going out gambling and drinking; everything they could fit in on a last wild spree. They were always apprehensive before the ship sailed; they never knew what was ahead of them, and when or if they'd be back. The ship was like a small city ruled by the dictatorship of discipline, so the sailors let off steam while they could.

He saw himself through the minister's doubtful gaze. This was his madness, he thought, being separated from the girl he loved.

The minister frowned and fortified himself with another sip of bourbon. 'I understand from your mother that Miss Jenkins will be staying here before the wedding?'

'That's right. But don't worry, I'll be sleeping at the Delmans'.'

'Ah!' The minister's face brightened. The Delmans were old friends and generous supporters of the church. 'Their eldest, Virginia, is going to be the maid of honour, I understand?'

Al grinned. 'That was the trade-off,' he said.

'And are your bride's parents happy with the arrangements?'

Al rubbed his jaw thoughtfully. 'Yeah, they seem okay with it, apart from it being a bit rushed, I guess. They want Elin to be happy. We'd have been married in her village chapel, but there wasn't time.'

'I'm sure she'll become a valued member of our congregation and find a spiritual home from home here,' the minister said. 'Let me assure you, you won't have to worry about her while you're away.' That was it, he'd said all that he came to say, the lecture was over. As he finished his drink the ice cubes clashed against his teeth.

Elin would laugh about it when Al told her.

He called Betsy to let her know they were done and went to the door. As the minister said goodbye, he saw the mailman coming up the yard, slapping a telegram against his thigh with every step.

'Telegram for Mr Locke.'

'That's me.' Al's heart sank. He wondered if it was from the ship, alerting him to a change of plan. He opened it.

Al saw it was from Elin and he read:

CANCEL WEDDING, REGRETS, ELIN

He went cold and he felt his skin shrink and prickle. His vision narrowed with adrenaline. He watched the mailman saunter back along the path as if he was watching him through a telescope, and then he turned quickly to look at Betsy.

She was smiling up happily at the minister, talking about her lists and plans and her camellias, and he felt a painful rush of pity for her, but an overwhelming hollowed-out abandonment made him want to vomit. As Betsy said goodbye to the minister and closed the door behind him, Al felt saliva rush into his mouth.

Just then, his stepmother turned and looked at him. Her smile faded to concern. 'What's wrong, Al?'

He handed her the telegram.

She held it at arm's length and took an age to read it. 'Well, I do call that rude! The minx!' Betsy burst out furiously. 'And to leave it until now to tell you – I don't know what your father is going to say. He always thought it was a hole-in-the-corner affair.'

'That's enough!' Al shouted. 'I love her.'

He walked out of the house to get away, to burn off energy, leave the nausea behind. He would drive back to the barracks and get drunk senseless with his buddies.

Virginia Delman tooted her horn as she drove past him and parked up outside her gate. He watched her getting out of her father's car, or rather, he first saw her pale legs from the knees down, and her black patent shoes setting down on the kerb. More of her emerged – a black-and-white checked dress, and then her head, her blonde hair pinned back in a French pleat.

When Virginia noticed Al looking at her she raised her hand and waggled her fingers at him. She walked towards him, swinging her patent handbag, reflecting flashes of sunlight.

'I was just going to call at yours, because Betsy asked me...' Virginia stopped suddenly. 'Are you okay, Al? You look positively awful.'

'The wedding's off.'

There it was, he'd said it. He'd dropped the bomb. It sounded louder than it had in his head.

Virginia covered her mouth with her hand and her eyes became rosy with tears. 'Al,' she said briskly, 'I'm glad you've seen sense before it's too late. After all, you hardly knew her. You've been every kind of fool, you know.'

He'd never been the sort of man who went from woman to woman. He'd only had three relationships; and that was including Virginia. They'd known each other for years, but the spark wasn't there, not on his part anyway.

He hadn't been serious about anyone until he met Elin. Elin made his life light up. He felt a deep ache in his chest, and he looked into the distance and thought, *she's broken my heart.*

'Come home with me,' Virginia said, putting her hand on his forearm. 'Come and have a drink. You look as if you need it.' She added, 'My folks are out.'

'Good old Virginia,' he said. He couldn't imagine Virginia breaking a man's heart, she was too nice, too sweet.

In that particular moment she was a port in a storm, a safe harbour. And not that sweet, as it turned out. Bryn Mawr was proving a learning experience in more ways than one, and she took him upstairs to her bedroom, undressed and got into bed, looking up at him, folding her arms patiently as she waited for him to join her.

Al was standing in the shade of the curtains, going through his options. *Apologise and leave… or get into bed with her.* Veering from one to another.

He stripped and joined her under the covers, staring at her suddenly unfamiliar face. He closed his eyes. Everything about her was strange, the feel of her, the smell of her, the softness. Afterwards she pushed him off her in a panic and reached for her alarm clock.

'Al, my folks are due back!'

He dressed quickly and hurried downstairs. Mitzi, the cat, slinked around his ankles. He scratched behind her ears, feeling that he was going to burn in hell for what he'd done. He felt worse than he had before. He was ashamed of himself.

*

The next day Al went back to the ship. He wanted to get away from his father's philosophising and Betsy's spin on Elin cancelling the wedding. Following Virginia's inadvertent misunderstanding, Betsy eagerly followed her lead and let it be known to the guests that he'd seen the error of his ways and changed his mind about marrying a British girl. She managed to get a world of contempt into the word 'British'. 'Better now than after the wedding,' she kept saying.

Al threw himself into the physical work of preparing the vessel for its journey to Japan. He pinned a picture of Virginia above his rack.

They were married before he sailed, keeping the original plans in place. As a result, everything was exactly as Betsy had planned it, including the camellias, and the only difference was the bride.

The day he sailed, Virginia gave him some letters, to keep him company, and included little drawings of her cat, Mitzi, and of a new frock that her mother had made for her. Al read them over in his bunk, and this was how he got to know her and her world, a gentle world where a disaster meant only that her mother burnt an apple pie.

CHAPTER FOURTEEN

By Easter, the atmosphere was tense.

'Bloody hell, Elin, you're frightening the postman,' Eric said. 'Don't you know by now he only brings bloody bills?'

'Leave her alone, she's waiting for a letter from Al,' Jane said, defending her. 'She hasn't heard from him for weeks.'

'It won't come here, will it? It'll go to the farm.'

Elin was helping out at Mountain Ash – it suited them all. She needed the money for her trip, and they had four permanent weekly residents to look after: three managers from the Arenig granite quarry and Rob.

Jane and Eric had taken Rob to chapel on Sunday, so that he could see how warm and friendly the people of the village were. They were seeing it purely from their own perspective. It would be a lovely experience for him to get to know and understand the warmth and culture of the place.

But they hadn't considered it from Rob's point of view. Like when they tried to go sit in Eric's parents' pew, and Eric's mother had refused to move up.

It had caused quite a stir.

They hadn't thought it through. The service was in Welsh and incomprehensible to Rob, and this was a man who confessed he knew more about granite than God. He'd stretched his feet out of the side of the pew and gone to sleep with his head flung back and his mouth open – only for a few seconds, mind, till Jane had nudged him awake. But those who saw it made sure the ones who hadn't seen it knew about it.

It was Mr Griffith preaching, and he liked to do a bit of shouting and threatening and fist-waving in the pulpit. It was the kind of sermon that would keep you awake no matter how tired you felt, so it came across as rudeness, all that yawning, as if the preacher was doing a lukewarm job, but truthfully Rob was just bored. He didn't see the community's warmth, because there wasn't any, not towards him, anyway. This was the man who was poking around in their land with a view to flooding them out of it. He only saw their hostility. And it was a lot easier to hate people when they didn't speak your language.

'He's on our side,' Elin protested to her mother, miserably. She hated upsetting her.

'Even if he is, how do you think Al would feel if he knew you were accompanying another man to chapel? You're not to see him any more, Elin, not while you're living under our roof. He's giving you a bad name, and us, too.'

In the face of her mother's righteous disapproval, Elin moved to Mountain Ash where she could concentrate on influencing Rob into sparing the village.

Elin's job at Mountain Ash was to make the residents a tray of tea at 6 a.m., and take it up with the daily newspaper, knocking on their bedroom doors and letting herself in to put their trays on their bedside tables.

Jane was happy with the arrangement because she didn't like the intimacy of going into strange men's rooms, into the warm, stale air they'd been breathing all night. 'I'm married,' she protested. 'It's not right. It's different for you, Elin, you're a nurse. You've seen all sorts. I've only seen Eric.'

'There's nothing *to* see,' Elin said, feeling it was something she should be indignant about. Nurses had a terrible reputation as it was. 'You could always make them come to the dining room for their morning tea and papers.'

'We have to look after them properly, it's a regular income for us,' Jane said, 'and twelve months a year, too, guaranteed. I don't know what we'd do without them, to be honest. With tourists we have to depend on the weather. Nobody wants to come here in the winter.'

Strangest of all was going into Rob's room in the morning. Even though the curtains were shut, and he was lying in the dark wrapped in his bedclothes, drowsy at being disturbed by her knock on the door, she could smell soap and toothpaste in the room, as if he'd got up too early by mistake and then gone back to bed.

One morning Elin had the feeling he was watching her, and as she was putting his tray down on the bedside cabinet, she reminded herself of what Eric had said: *He's a weak man, but he's not a bad man. I don't think so, anyway.*

The bedclothes rustled. Rob sat up and patted the bed. He said in a low voice, 'Why don't you come and sit by me for a moment, Elin?' In the shocked silence that followed, he chuckled softly. 'You should see your face! Anyone would think you were scared of me.'

'Behave,' she said sternly, tossing her head, 'or Eric will be bringing you your tray from now on and he might take you up on it.' As she opened the curtains, letting in a square of cold morning light, Rob jumped out of bed with a twang of bedsprings and stood between Elin and the door with a smile on his face.

His smile scared her more than anything – it was the awful inappropriateness of it. Far from smiling back, her heart was hammering against her ribs. She stood with her back to the window, afraid to move.

His face tightened. 'What's wrong with you?' he asked querulously. 'I'm just opening the door for you, see?' He held it open for her.

'Oh, sorry. Thanks.' She hurried past him, wondering if she was going crazy, and took a gulp of air as she hurried back to the safety of the kitchen where Jane was cooking sausages.

The fat was spitting, turning the air a hazy blue.

Elin told her what happened. 'And him in his striped pyjamas,' she said, and shuddered.

Jane laughed. 'He can't help it. He's sweet on you, and he's a shy man. You should feel sorry for him; the poor thing is hopelessly in love.' She turned the sausages and puffed her cheeks in exasperation. 'Look! They've burst out of their skins! They're cheap, see; I might have known. Anyway, it's all for the best that Rob wants to impress you. He'd be happy to let the place drown if it weren't for you. He's sending in his report any day now.' Jane fanned the air. 'Just be nice to him for a bit longer. It doesn't hurt to be *nice*, Elin.'

Just then, the quarry managers came down for breakfast. They were in their late fifties, quiet types.

Eric said they liked being away from their wives for the whole week because it made the weekends bearable, but he had absolutely no evidence to back this theory up. Elin only ever heard them talk about the quarry and the railway which carried the gravel for track ballast. They sat at their own tables, but they met up in the common room in the evening to listen to *The Archers* on the radio or play dominoes. Eric and Jane went to their private quarters.

Elin sat and talked to Rob. He continued to reassure her about the steps he was taking behind the scenes to save Capel Celyn, and she believed him.

Elin had been to the rally at Bala and the public meeting at Corwen, and the demonstration in Liverpool where to her shock she saw Rose in the jeering crowd, and she'd supported the deputation that went to Liverpool City Council to give their side of the argument and were refused. She couldn't help but think that it was all a waste of time because she was fully confident in Rob's assurance that he could find somewhere more suitable for a reservoir. She just wanted him to get a move on so that she could put all of this behind her and join Al.

By July, the bad feeling against Rob and against Eric, Jane and Elin, by association, had intensified. Despite the loss of income, Eric told Rob to leave and find somewhere else to live. He had tried to be fair and Christian about it, but he was resentful that he'd been made a fool of.

Elin felt the same, to a degree, but she didn't blame Rob in the same way that Eric and Jane did because she had other things on her mind.

She was desperate to hear from Al. She missed him terribly. And she had news for him; she was pregnant, no doubt about it, and she wanted to marry him before it showed. She was determined to keep it a secret from their families. That way, after the birth, she and Al could tell everyone it was a honeymoon baby.

They wouldn't be the first. During her stint on the maternity ward, she'd known a few full-term mothers who'd convinced their families that their eight-pound baby was three months premature and conceived on their wedding night, a story families were usually happy to buy into.

Now it was almost four months since Al had left, and three months since Elin had sent the telegram, and she still hadn't had a reply to her letter. She couldn't understand why.

She hadn't thought of him writing to her at her parents' house. In her letter she'd asked him to write to her at Mountain Ash, in case her parents opened her mail, which for some reason they still felt they had a right to do.

Her mother was baking when Elin arrived. She stared at her as if she hardly knew her and she wiped her hands on her floral apron. 'Hello, Elin.'

'I was wondering if anything had come from Al,' she said awkwardly, getting straight to the point.

'When did you last hear from him?' her mother asked.

'Not since he left.' Her mother's expression alarmed her. 'Why? What's happened? Has something happened?'

'Thomas, come in here!' her mother said sharply, calling him through the kitchen door.

Elin's first guilty thought was – *they've read Al's love letters to me.* She felt a sudden wave of panic as her father came in, tapping a cigarette out of the packet.

'What is it?' he asked. 'Oh, hello, Elin.'

'Hello.'

'What have you done with that letter?' her mother asked him.

He didn't ask which one, which made it seem as if only one had come. He put his cigarette in his mouth and took out his matches, avoiding her eyes. 'It's still in the letter rack.'

Her mother took a cream envelope out of the letter rack and handed it to her. She was brisk, but also sad. 'It grieves me to give you this,' she said.

'What?' Elin recognised Al's writing. 'You've opened it,' she said accusingly, cringing as she imagined what they must have read to make them this serious.

She nervously took the card out of the envelope, and saw that it wasn't a card, it was a wedding invitation, cream, with embossed roses.

Mr and Mrs John Delman
invite you to celebrate the marriage of their daughter
Miss Virginia Margaret Delman
to Coxswain Albert Locke

on
Saturday, 24th March, 1956

Scribbled across it in Al's unmistakable handwriting, defacing the invitation, was the message: *No Hard Feelings*

Elin stared at it, horrified, and felt as if life stopped for her.

She sat down by the table and felt herself burning up with humiliation, as if she'd been caught out doing something shabby.

Al had stopped loving her, he had abandoned her, deserted her, made a fool of her, cheated on her, gone back to Virginia Delman.

As she faced the truth, she had the sensation that she was dwindling and becoming very small. She was alone now, with the baby coming, worthless, the lowest of the low. Her mouth was dry and full of ashes. The past was gone, and her future had gone, too, erased from the page. She'd been following a path that led nowhere. She was destroyed.

Mortified, she slid the invitation back in the envelope.

'Oh, my girl,' her father said gently, putting his hand on her shoulder. 'Better you know what he's like now than after you're married. I wouldn't have had this happen to you for the world.' He sat down next to her, his cigarette still unlit.

Elin looked at him. 'I can't believe it,' she whispered. She scratched at the green chenille cloth on the table and raised her face to her mother, looking for comfort.

'He didn't wait long, did he?' her mother said, tight-lipped.

'I should have gone when I said I would. I broke my promise.' The room seemed to have got dark and her father got up from the table and switched on the light in the frosted glass shade. 'When did it come?'

'Not long ago,' her mother said vaguely. 'Your father was going to bring it up to Mountain Ash, but it wasn't as if it was urgent, was it? It was the kind of bad news that could wait,' she said and shook her head. 'It's cruel, what Al's done.' She added quickly, 'Stop picking at that cloth, Elin. You're making a bald spot.'

Elin clasped her hands together and pressed her knuckles against her eyes. 'No hard feelings,' she said suddenly. 'What does he mean by that?'

Her parents looked at her blankly.

'Seriously. Does he mean he doesn't bear hard feelings towards me for not coming, because he's fine? Or is he asking me not to have hard feelings about him getting married to Virginia Margaret Delman?' It seemed vitally important to know what he meant.

'Does it matter?' her mother asked.

'Yes, of course it does!' Elin said. She was fixated on it, the importance of the answer. *Why send an invitation at all?* 'I could go to the wedding,' she said.

Her father scraped his chair away from the table and stood up. 'Don't be soft, Elin. Have another look at the date on it! It's already been.'

She took the invitation out of the envelope and studied it again, the embossed invitation with Al's neat black handwriting: *No Hard Feelings.* It was indescribably cruel of him and she kept her tears back by force of will. 'That's the day he was going to marry me.'

Her father felt her pain as if it were his own. He put his cap on and went to the door. 'I'm going to see Bill,' he said gruffly. Jip followed him out.

Her mother sighed. 'Well, that's that. There's nothing to be done.' After a moment she said, 'You can help me with tea, Elin, if you're staying.'

Elin peeled the potatoes and her mother chopped the carrots, and Elin imagined telling her about the baby while they were busy with something else and didn't have to look at each other. Her mother might say: *I thought you were different, Elin.*

How would they cope with the shame?

'What will you do now? Go back to nursing?'

'Maybe,' Elin lied. The Welsh weren't welcome in Liverpool any more.

After a long silence, her mother said, 'What you want to do with your wedding dress? Meirion's daughter's getting married in the summer. I haven't said anything to her, mind. I was going to talk to you first.'

Elin's spirits plunged lower. 'Yes, she can have it. Of course she can.' It was a lovely dress, a lovely, pointless dress. 'What will you tell people?'

Her mother dropped – no, flung – the carrots in the pan. It was the first time she had showed any emotion. 'I'm going to tell them Al fell overboard and got eaten by sharks,' she said furiously. 'Came to a tragic end and serves him right.'

Tears threatened to rip out of Elin's throat, become a howling agony that she couldn't control, because there was no turning back and no way to put it right now. Pain tore through her body, a physical pain, and she felt light-headed at keeping her feelings in. She had to get away. 'I've just remembered, I've got to go back to the guest house. I'm working tonight,' she lied.

Elin walked back up the track to Mountain Ash with her heart breaking.

Jane and Eric were sitting at the table going through the bills.

Elin took the invitation out of the envelope and slid it across to them.

They looked at it in astonishment.

Eric picked it up, read it carefully and held it up to the light as if he wasn't sure what he was seeing. Finally, he handed it to Jane. 'The Captain didn't wait,' he said to her incredulously. 'He didn't even give her a chance. I can't believe it of him. "No Hard Feelings", indeed.'

Jane took Elin's cold hands in hers, tears silvering her eyes in sympathy. 'How could he do this to you? Come and sit down before you fall down.' She pressed her into the chair. 'Get her a cup of tea with a splash of rum in it, Eric. Look at her! She's in shock.'

As she said it, Elin felt a low sharp cramp, deep in her abdomen, like a bad period pain. She took her hands from Jane's and put them protectively on her stomach.

Eric saw the gesture and knew instinctively what it meant. He stared at Elin, the blood rushing to his normally pallid face. 'No... Elin? Don't tell me you're...' He couldn't bring himself to say the word and he stared at her, hot with shame. 'But how?' He was a fastidious, self-righteous man.

The look on his face made Elin recoil. 'How?' She gave a harsh laugh, like the shriek of a gull. 'Don't you know yet, Eric? It's easy, the easiest thing in the world!'

'It's Al's, is it?' he asked.

'Of course it's Al's! Why would you even wonder?'

He pressed his hands to his temples. 'But I don't understand you, Elin! You must have known you might be expecting! What on earth made you stay here in the circumstances?'

'You did!' Elin stared at him, astounded at the sheer injustice of the accusation. 'We were making sacrifices to save the village, remember?'

'Aye, but Elin, you should have stuck to your plans for the baby's sake.'

'I didn't know I was pregnant, then.'

Eric dragged his eyes from hers and took another look at the wedding invitation on the table. 'Does he know?'

'No.' Her voice tightened, as if the word was choking her. 'There's no point in telling him now, is there?'

A new thought troubled Eric. 'What are people going to say?'

Her chin trembled. 'I don't care what they say.'

'No, I suppose *you* don't,' he said bitterly. 'But it's our reputations, too.'

She gave a strident, humourless laugh. 'It's a bit late for that now, isn't it, after all the time you've spent living with the enemy under your own roof, making a fool of you!'

Elin had hit a nerve. Eric jumped to his feet, energised by anger. For a moment he towered over her and then he controlled himself and said, 'I'm going to The Lamb.'

'Aye, you do that,' Jane said to him soothingly, patting his shoulder. 'A drink will do you good.'

Eric made sure he slammed the door behind him, leaving behind a gust of cold wind.

Elin shivered.

'Don't mind him.' Jane put her arms around her friend and gave her a fierce hug. She smelled of lavender. 'I'll make us hot tea with a splash of rum in it,' she said.

Coming back with the drinks, she added, 'You know what Eric's like, Elin. It's not personal. I don't know why he didn't join the clergy and be done with it; he's more pious than they are.'

Elin gave a tremulous smile.

'That's better! Cheer up!' Jane sipped from her cup and smiled through the steam. 'This is what we're going to do. We're going to get knitting. I've got a lovely pattern for a matinee jacket and matching bootees and bonnet. Let's go to Bala tomorrow, for wool. White? Or yellow's nice.'

Elin began to cry with relief at her friend's kindness.

'Hey, stop now, your tea's getting salty,' Jane said.

Elin caught a teardrop with the tip of her tongue. 'What am I going to tell my mother? She's got enough to worry about.'

'Listen to me,' Jane said, 'a baby will take her mind off her worries. I remember her rearing newborn lambs, her face lit up with happiness. How much nicer is it to welcome a baby into the house than a lamb? A baby is a joy, a blessing.'

Elin nodded, her eyes gleaming with tears.

'That's better. From now on, you've got to look forward, Elin, for the baby's sake. The past – it's no use thinking about that any more,' she added firmly. 'It's done with.'

Elin knew that by the past, Jane meant Al. The pain came back as strongly as ever, as if it had been lying in wait to surprise her afresh. 'I know,' she said sadly.

'I'll come with you tomorrow when you tell your mother. She loves you. She'll tell your father when the time is right. They both know it's not your fault that the Captain broke his promise.' She turned the invitation face down and got up and bent to kiss the top of Elin's head. 'Now, let me find those knitting patterns.'

Eric came back from the pub two hours later in a philosophical mood, soothed by brandy. 'We'll make the best of it,' he declared, folding his arms.

'That's the spirit,' Jane replied.

A calmness had descended on Mountain Ash. But it wasn't to last.

'Thanks, both of you, for being so – you know,' Elin said, gathering up the patterns with their pictures of bonny babies.

As she got up from the table and turned to the door she felt the cramping sensation again, an intense wave of pain that seemed to roll through her whole body, making her light-headed. She wanted to close her eyes, lose herself in it.

'What's wrong?' Jane asked her.

'I think the baby's coming.' Her eyes burned with tears.

'Oh, dew,' Eric said in panic as if the roof was falling in, 'you can't have it here! Go back to your mother's! She'll know what to do with you!'

Elin held onto the door, bracing against the pain. When it passed, she said calmly, 'Put the kettle on.' In the momentary quiet she felt pure and cleansed, clear-headed. 'Get some towels, Jane.'

'How far gone are you?'

'Four months.'

'Oh, dear.' Jane hugged herself. 'Will it be okay?'

Elin thought of the premature babies in Alder Hey, translucent and as veined as baby pigeons. Her stomach hardened, and it was like being gripped in a vice, front and back. Her body was labouring to squeeze the life out of her.

'Can I do anything?' Jane asked anxiously.

In the kitchen, the kettle whined.

Holding her breath, Elin felt a strange hot dampness in her pants. Tears were running down her cheeks. 'Help me to the toilet, will you?'

They were almost there when Eric came up clattering behind them, holding a tea tray with china cups dancing in their saucers. 'Where do you want me to put these?'

'Anywhere you like!' Jane said. 'Where's that hot water?'

'I've just made the tea with it, haven't I?'

'She wants hot water, not tea! You can't clean a baby with tea, man!'

Elin just wanted them to be quiet so she could concentrate. She hobbled towards the bathroom, holding herself in by force of will. It was like a severe case of gastroenteritis, as if her body was violently trying to get rid of what was upsetting it, the part of Al he'd left her with.

She shut the bathroom door and sat on the toilet and looked in her pants at the blood and mucus. 'Oh,' she sighed. She pushed them down to her ankles and kicked them off; her body convulsed in one huge pain-filled heave and to her anguish the baby slid out into her hands, a miniature baby, white as a mushroom, limp and still, with none of the furious writhing anger of a newborn. Elin cleared the baby's mouth with her fingers, and blew her breath into her, but the baby had gone. She heard Jane's footsteps on the tiles.

'Elin, you okay in there? I've got the towels. Eric's boiling another kettle. *Twp*, he is.'

Elin couldn't think of any words to say. The baby's body fitted neatly in her cupped hands, she was still warm from her womb, the cord was still joining them, and she opened her blouse and held the baby hopefully against her breast. With her finger she stroked her thin, thin arms and thin, thin legs, her new-formed fingers; it was the softest skin she'd ever touched.

'Elin? Can I come in?' Jane opened the door with her foot, towels in her arms, and saw her sitting on the toilet. 'Oh, sorry!'

'It's okay, she's come,' Elin said, her voice tight with misery, feeling the slow, deep pull of the placenta. 'Let's wrap her up. We'll need to cut the cord.'

'Oh, *cariad*,' Jane said tearfully, looking at the still little form. She covered her mouth and the tears dripped off her knuckles. 'Oh, the little thing.' She wrapped the towel gently around the baby as if she was keeping her warm. 'Stay there. I'll fetch the scissors.' For a moment they stared at each other, distressed by the magnitude of what had happened.

Jane went away and came back with the scissors and she knelt next to Elin.

Elin felt the afterbirth coming. She felt as if her soul was separating from her body, as if it had gone rogue, making its own mind up about things.

Eric tapped on the door, his voice muffled. 'I've got a bowl of hot water here,' he said. 'I won't come in.'

'No, don't. Do you want to get cleaned up, Elin?' Jane asked.

Elin nodded. She looked down at the tiny form of her baby and tried to imagine what it would be like if she was fine, and just sleeping, but her mind refused to conspire to play those kinds of games. Numb, Elin gave it to Jane and stood up and washed and dried between her legs.

Jane laid it down on the nest of towels and fetched Elin a sanitary towel and a belt. 'I've told Eric what's happened. He's going to drive you to hospital,' she said.

Elin folded up the damp bloodied towels. 'Why would I go to hospital? It's too late now.'

'To give them the baby.'

Elin thought about it. The products of early miscarriages were clinical waste, no different from amputated hands and cancerous growths. She'd heard a rumour of one nurse in a situation much like her own, who had paid the undertaker to put her baby in a casket with a dead woman so that it would have a proper funeral. 'No, I can't do that.'

Jane shivered. 'What are you going to do, then?'

'I don't know. I can't think.' Elin rested her head in her hands.

'Shall I get your mother here?' Jane asked, frightened of the responsibility.

'No. It will break her heart.' Elin leaned on the windowsill and looked out. The sky was dense with fog, and she couldn't see the mountains.

'Do you want me to fetch the minister, then?'

Elin shook her head. 'No.' This was a matter between her and God; she didn't need the minister to speak for her. *The baby was known to Him and now she'd returned to Him, as we all do*, she thought. She had changed her mind about being born and who could blame her? Elin thought of the way things might have been and she said, 'I'm going to take her to Hafod Fadog, to the Quaker cemetery.' It was her happy place, even now.

Jane looked startled. 'Why? You're not a Quaker,' she objected, as if that was the biggest of their problems.

Elin gave a faint smile and rested her forehead against the cool glass. She turned back to Jane. 'Don't worry, you don't have to come.'

Jane put her hand to her throat, flushing with obvious relief. 'All right then, I won't, if you're sure.'

Don't bloody come then, Elin wanted to say even though she'd only just given her permission not to.

'Elin—'

'Yes?' she replied hopefully.

Jane tucked her brown hair behind her ear and nodded at Elin's chest. 'You're all undone, girl. Button yourself up before you go.'

Later that evening, Elin went down the lane with the bundle in towels and a spade. A blurred sun was screened by fog as thick as smoke, the world on fire, birds muted.

She left the road by the side of Hafod Fadog and saw lights on in the kitchen. The dog barked once inside its kennel, and she climbed the sloping field, and put the bundle on the stone that marked the grave of Margaret Evans.

She cut into the top layer of grass and moss with the spade and peeled it back, exposing the matted pale roots, and viciously dug out the soil beneath it, the jolt and ring of metal on stone, bursts of furious energy, digging it deep, mind, her face washed with tears, dirt and the sweat of exertion. She picked up the neat bundle and wondered about one last look but she didn't unwrap it. It was entitled to its own privacy now, daughter of the soil.

She covered her over, rolled the lid of turf back, pressed it down. She went to the crumbling stone wall and picked up a stone that was white and regular and heavy, and carried it over and laid it on top. She wiped her face with her sleeve and the pain felt like the heavy white stone on her chest, a straining bulkhead, holding back her feelings.

Elin walked down to the road, bent with sorrow and pain, using the spade as a walking stick, and passed Dafydd putting the milk bottles down outside his house. He stopped and turned.

'Who's that?' he asked curiously.

'Elin,' she replied.

'Good evening to you, *cariad*,' he said warmly.

'Good evening, Mr Jones.' She longed for her mother. She was only half a mile from the farm. But she couldn't go home. She looked down at herself. *Look at me. Filthy. Dafydd must be especially short-sighted not to notice.*

Back at Mountain Ash, she was met by the astringent smell of mint sauce. The quarry managers were having roast lamb for dinner.

She startled Jane, who scooted her off to her room, 'Look at you, Elin! You're getting mud on the carpet!'

'Sorry.'

'Go and get cleaned up and I'll bring you a sandwich,' she said.

Elin ran a bath, four inches of water, and thought about her locked-away grief and emotion, and all the things they'd seen and done, nursing, that they'd packed away and didn't look at. Well, she would pack this away too. *It's not your job to cry*, Sister had said.

The weight of the bundle in the towels had been heavier than she expected.

CHAPTER FIFTEEN

'Let's get this clear, Elin, I don't want to know anything more,' Eric said firmly later that evening, his hands clasped over his knees. They were in the sitting room, and the wind was wailing down the chimney. The glass of the picture frames shone squares of light on them.

Elin shrugged.

'We're going to say we know nothing about it, if anyone asks,' Jane added.

It was obviously something that they'd been talking about. 'Who's going to ask? Nobody knows,' Elin said.

'Not for sure, they don't. I mean, there have been rumours, haven't there?'

'Rumours? Who said?'

'Doesn't matter who it was. Bethan Parry is just filthy-minded and we're happy to leave it at that.' Jane shook her head and her face crumpled. 'Oh, Elin, I can't believe it.'

'Don't, don't, don't,' Elin said quickly. She felt emotion well up in her and it was an effort to hold it back. 'I'm not going to tell anyone about it. I'll keep it to myself, and you must, too. I just want to forget it. I understand how you feel, Eric, you don't want to be tarred with the same brush, but you've got to keep quiet as well, Jane.'

'I know she's got a mouth on her,' Eric said, 'but trust me, she won't say anything.'

Elin looked doubtfully at Jane, who had secrets bursting out of her. 'Promise me, Jane, on Eric's life.'

'Hey, steady on,' Eric said.

Jane sat up straight. She closed her eyes and tears leaked from under her eyelids. She shook her head and finally she said the words slowly and clearly, 'I promise you on Eric's life I will never tell anyone. We'll just forget it ever happened.'

'If you ask me,' Eric said, 'the miscarriage is the best thing that could have happened. There's no harm done. It's all worked out for the best.'

That night, Elin lay scared in bed and against the curtains the shadows of the black trees lashed furiously at the wind, pattering leaves against the window. She had raised this storm from hell and against the roaring of the wind she could hear the dead, still silence that her baby had been born into. How could she forget it had ever happened?

I want my mother. I want to go home, now, this minute. She tried to imagine telling her, sharing her pain with her, crying in her mother's thin, strong arms and being comforted. *Is that how she would take it?* No. It would break her. Her parents had enough on their plate as it was.

'Elin, I thought you were different,' her mother had said bitterly once when a neighbour reported she had seen her and Al kissing.

'Why?' she'd asked, surprised.

'Wishful thinking, I suppose,' her mother had said tiredly, pushing her work-reddened hands into her apron pocket.

But from the relative safety of her bed, Elin was too scared to step outside into the wild dark. She could hear a distant clang and the metallic beat of a dustbin lid bouncing on its edge, and it seemed to get louder until it came right up to her window where it dropped with a crash that made her jump. Her tears flowed silently on and off through the long night, not brought on by her thoughts but by her body which was mourning its own loss, holding the ache where the baby had been.

Eventually, through half-closed eyes, Elin saw a cut appearing in the sky, bleeding red, the birth of a new day. The trees shook their red-tinted branches.

She got out of bed and crept down the hall to the bathroom. She washed quickly and went back to her room and got dressed. At seven thirty, she went downstairs and heard noises from the kitchen. Jane was wearing a pink bed jacket and pyjama trousers, her hair net keeping her curls in place, swearing at the hob, trying to get it to light but the matches kept breaking. This morning the guest house had taken on a kind of autumnal dampness, the vague smell of fungi and rotting wood. She turned sharply and saw Elin in the doorway.

'Oh, it's you,' she said irritably.

The mood had changed overnight. It wasn't that easy to forget a nightmare.

She'd shared her burden with them, and already it was proving too heavy a weight for them to carry.

Eric came in from outside, breathing hard and struggling to close the door and keep the wind out. 'Damned gales,' he said, 'we've lost some tiles off the roof.' He saw Elin standing in the doorway to the kitchen, didn't say a word to her, walked past her as if she wasn't there, and lifted the kettle and shook it to see how full it was, he and Jane were standing by the cooker with their backs like a wall against her.

'I'm sorry,' Elin said to them, waiting to be forgiven.

Eric turned to face her. 'Dragging us down with you, you are,' he said fiercely. 'We couldn't sleep all night. You think that covering things up means they don't exist, but they're here,' he said tapping his temple so hard that his fingers knocked loud against the bone. 'And you left that muddy spade by the door, too.' There was sorrow in his eyes, knowing the sad purpose it had been used for. 'You're too much of a responsibility, Elin. We can't take on your troubles as well as our own. We've done our best for you, but you need to go home now. Let your mother take care of you.'

'I'm sorry.' She'd forgotten about the spade. 'I'm sorry about everything,' she said. 'I want to stay. Please can you forgive me?'

The zip of Jane striking the matches, the momentary smell of sulphur, the howl of the wind.

'No.' He said it calmly, but it was as harsh as a blow. 'We've made our decision.'

'Fine! Die in hell, Eric,' she said in a rush of furious energy, and she went back to her room to pack her case. She'd become repellent, rejected, abandoned; ashamed and alone. He was right though, about everything. She was the most disgusting, contemptible creature and they couldn't be expected to take on her troubles. Nobody could. It was one burden too many.

There was just one person in the world she could think of who, no matter what she'd done, would greet her with a smile. She only had one place left to go.

*

By asking around, Elin found Rob's small caravan at the caravan site in Fron Goch where the construction workers were staying. He was sitting outside pumping a Primus stove on a red Formica-topped table, giving it his full concentration and cursing softly to himself. His brown hair was messed from sleep. There was an oily smell of paraffin shimmering in the air.

He was too engrossed in his task to notice her at first.

'Hello, Rob,' she said after a moment, feeling awkward and out of place.

He looked up at her, surprised, and gave her a sudden welcoming smile that lit up his face. 'Good morning, Elin! What are you doing here?' Then he noticed her bag and his smile faded. 'Ah,' he said knowingly. 'Kicked you out too, have they?'

She nodded.

'Ingrates.' He got to his feet, moving his chair towards her. 'Here. Sit down. I'll put the kettle on just as soon as I've got this thing started.' He took his glasses off, polished them on the tail of his shirt and put them back on. He pumped the Primus again and with a combustible pop it lit, burning a clean blue flame. 'Perseverance,' he declared, pleased. 'That's all it takes.'

He went into the caravan and came out with a blue tin kettle with a whistle on the spout. He put it on the stove. 'There. It won't take long to heat up.' He sat on the steps of the caravan and folded his arms. The sun had brought out his freckles.

Elin sat clutching her bag on her lap, wondering what to say to him. She was tired of thinking, planning, scheming for herself.

'Listen.' He leant forward. 'Whatever Eric said about me, I tried my best for the village.'

Elin nodded. 'Okay.' *Maybe he had.*

'When do you leave?'

'I've already left,' she said, confused.

'I mean for Philadelphia.'

Tears filled her eyes. 'I'm not going. It's off,' she said. 'Al's married someone else.'

A flash of exultation flickered across Rob's face which he didn't try to hide. 'The man's an idiot.'

Despite everything, she wanted to defend Al.

Rob jumped to his feet, went to hold her, but she recoiled so strongly he pulled back again. 'What can I do for you, Elin? Tell me what I can do!'

A shrill scream startled them both.

'It's okay, it's only the kettle. Look, I've taken it off.' The whistle quivered to a feeble gasp. 'Hot sweet tea, that's what you need,' he said. 'Wait here.'

Tears of misery were welling up in her sore eyes, running down her face from a bottomless source of grief, clogging up her nose, her throat, corrupting her like seawater, exhausting her. Her stomach ached. She closed her eyes. If she could just sleep for a few days or weeks, and wake up on the other side, she could get through it.

A thin, blonde woman with her hair in a spotted scarf came out of the next caravan with a basket of washing to hang on the line between the caravans, avid with curiosity. She looked at Elin for a moment. 'Is she all right?' she asked Rob.

'She's had her heart broken. Not by me,' he added quickly, putting the cups down. 'By an American sailor.'

The neighbour pegged out her husband's work shirts, which were enormous and flapped like sails in the breeze. Once she'd finished, she picked her empty basket up and looked at Elin again until Elin returned her gaze.

Her expression softened. 'Do you want me to read your cards for you, love?'

Elin shook her head.

'Are you sure? I can tell you if your sailor's going to come back to you or not,' she said. 'You'd be surprised by how many do.'

Elin was superstitious about that sort of thing, about having her fortune told. It might give her hope, or it might take away hope. And even though she didn't believe in it, she was scared of what it would reveal. She pinched her lower lip. 'There's no point. It's too late now.'

'I've seen it often enough in couples,' the woman said. 'There's nothing new under the sun. People getting restless, and then regretting it. Sometimes it's nice to find that things aren't always what they appear.'

She had a wise, reassuring way of speaking, as if she could see far into the distance into the whole wide spread of life and knew about the rightness of things that were still hidden from Elin.

Elin took her handkerchief out of her sleeve, rubbed the tears from under her eyes and blew her nose.

'She's right. There's no point. Al's made his choice,' Rob said with his slow, lazy smile, 'but I'm still yours for the asking, Elin.' He turned to the woman. 'You can read my cards instead if you like? I'm a sucker for a happy ending.'

The woman shifted her empty basket onto her hip. She slid her eyes towards Elin and then looked back at Rob again with a faint knowing smile. 'All right, then. Give me ten minutes to prepare. We'll have to do it indoors. It's too windy out here.' The large shirts bounced and waved on the line.

Rob made the tea and Elin sipped it slowly, feeling the steam bathing her tight face.

She couldn't imagine why Rob wanted his fortune told. 'Do you believe in readings and that sort of thing?' she asked him.

'Not really. Do you?'

'No, not really.'

He glanced at his neighbour's caravan, as if he was wondering if she could hear – the walls were very thin. 'I like to keep an open mind, though. She might tell me which horse is going to win the Derby.'

'Then what?'

He laughed. 'Then I'd back it.'

Elin smiled weakly, still holding the mug. 'No, I mean and then what if you won?'

'If I won, I'd go travelling, see the world. I'd go to South Africa and Australia, and I'd stop where the mood took me. I'd stay in the sun all year round and never live through another winter again.'

Elin rubbed her palm against her temple, unsure whether he was serious or not. It was a nice dream, even so.

For a moment, she thought about the adventure she had been expecting to have. She tensed, thinking she was going to cry again. Her tears didn't seem to come from her eyes, they came from her chest, from her heart, and she stopped them right there, put a barrier in the way. 'What else?'

'I'd paddle down the Amazon to look at piranhas. I'd ride a horse on the pampas. I'd get a leather hat with a brim. What's that expression?' he said. 'You don't like the hat?'

'I do like it.' She sipped her tea and looked at him over the rim of the tin mug.

The door of Rob's neighbour's caravan opened. 'Come on in, Rob,' the woman said. 'I'm ready for you.'

Rob crossed his fingers and waved them at Elin with a grin. He followed the woman inside and closed the door.

Elin could hear the mesmeric murmuring of the woman's voice. The walls of the caravan were thin, but they weren't thin enough to make out the conversation. For a few minutes the woman talked softly, her voice lifting and falling, and then there was silence.

Elin kicked the grass under her feet and wondered what it would be like to live in a caravan for any length of time. *Worse than living in a village*, she thought. The caravans were all bunched together, no space inside to wander around, no space outside to call your own, no privacy. There were so many building workers living on the site, attracted by the good wages and decent employers, that they had a permanent police presence to keep order.

They doubled the population of Fron Goch, which was just a village, really, with a few shops.

She was distracted by the sound of Rob saying sharply, 'What do you mean?'

It sounded as if they were having an argument.

'I'm just warning you,' the woman was saying. 'It's up to you to take notice.'

'I don't get it. What's in it for you, saying that?'

'That's enough!' The woman sounded angry, but not just angry, nervous, too. 'We're done here,' she said firmly. 'I'm not saying any more, so don't ask me to.'

Elin could hear Rob protesting. Moments later, the door opened and he came out and stared at Elin as if he'd forgotten all about her. Frowning, he sat down on the steps and rubbed his eyes under his glasses.

'What happened?' she asked him, alarmed. 'What were you arguing about? What did she say?'

He shook his head. 'Nothing much.' Behind the glasses, his hazel eyes looked scared. 'It's a lot of nonsense, anyway. A waste of time.' He seemed annoyed, not just with his neighbour but with Elin too.

Elin whispered, 'Did you have to pay her, Rob?'

'No,' he said. 'She didn't want my money. She said it was unlucky.'

Elin raised her eyebrows. 'How can money be unlucky? I wish my money was unlucky. I'd never have to pay for anything again.' She only said it to make him forget what had happened, but he shrugged and shook his head. Turning away from her, he lit a cigarette.

She had never seen him in this mood before and she grew indignant. 'This is exactly why I didn't want my cards done,' she told him. 'It only upsets things and puts ideas into your head that you could perfectly well live without. No one can really read the future, it's just a creative guess. She's got no right to upset people like that.'

'I'm not upset.'

'Oh. Good.'

'I'm *not* upset,' he said again.

Elin put her hand on her brow – she felt as if her emotions were burning up inside her head and she stood up and picked up her case. 'Well, thanks for the tea,' she said politely.

'Where are you going?'

'Home, where else?'

Rob rubbed his hand round the back of his neck. He stubbed his cigarette out on the sole of his boot. 'You don't have to go. You can stay here.'

'No, I can't. I'm not over Al, yet.' Elin raised her sharp eyebrows. 'And living here would be asking for trouble, wouldn't it?'

'You can't blame a man for trying it on with a beautiful girl, can you now? And you certainly gave as good as you got,' he added ruefully. 'Stay,' he pleaded. 'I won't lay a finger on you. I promise. Not until you want me to.'

Elin stared at him for a moment, undecided. The lenses of his glasses were so smeared with fingerprints that she couldn't see his eyes. She shook her head hopelessly and turned to walk away, ducking under a clothes line.

'Hey, wait,' he called to her, 'I've got something to tell you.'

'What?' she asked, without looking back.

'I'm crazy about you!' He shouted it desperately, as if the admission was painful to him.

She stopped walking and held her dark, windblown hair away from her face and considered what he'd said. Even though he knew that Al had abandoned her for another woman, and that Eric and Jane had thrown her out, Rob was still crazy about her.

His words felt gentle and sweet, like a kiss on a wound.

He's weak, but not a bad man, Eric had said.

She was weak, too.

Elin tried to process this new state of events. She'd always known he fancied her. And it was nice to be loved. Could she give him a chance?

She had nothing more to lose.

CHAPTER SIXTEEN

A month went by, and Elin still didn't love Rob, but she didn't mind being loved by him.

She was grateful to him for keeping his promise and accepting there couldn't be anything physical between them until she was over Al. At night they slept opposite each other on the caravan benches, an arm's length away. Sometimes he would reach out to her, and she would look at his outstretched, upturned palm, white in the darkness, and wait until it gave up its need for her touch and retreat back under the bedclothes.

Her body was healing, but her mind was troubled. Some nights she lay awake looking at the flowers on the curtains. Through the light from the caravan next door, she could see faces in the blooms and the buds. They were ugly, jeering, and even though she knew it was a trick of her imagination, when she shut her eyes and opened them again, the devils' faces were still there, easy to find.

One evening in December, Rob was unexpectedly late coming home from work. The lamb chops she'd cooked him had curled up, cold and dry, and he took off his coat and looked at the plate with that inappropriate smile that made her shiver.

Then he looked up at her, still holding the smile in place. 'Aren't you going to ask me where I've been, Elin?'

'I suppose that's your business,' she said cautiously.

'That's where you're wrong,' he said mildly. 'I've been to see your parents.'

'Why did you do that?' Her heart gave a double thud against her ribs and she looked at him in alarm.

'I went to tell them you're safe, and that I'm looking after you.' He added reproachfully, 'They've got a right to know that, Elin.'

She bit the edge of her thumbnail anxiously. 'What did they say?'

'To be honest, they didn't seem that grateful. I sometimes wonder why I bother. Anyway, they've washed their hands of you. Parents, eh?' Rob sighed. 'They bring you up and they put you down. Isn't that always the way?' He raised his eyebrows, waiting for a reply.

'I suppose—' she said.

'You *suppose*?' He looked at her with interest, as if waiting for her to elaborate. 'It's a fact! You should have seen them! Your name was a filthy word!' He paused and added petulantly, 'You're lucky you've got me. I don't think you appreciate all I do for you. Can you guess what I did after that?'

Elin shook her head.

'No? You could at least give it a try. Go on! Don't spoil it. Guess!'

Elin didn't want to guess. She shrugged uneasily.

'You give up? Okay, I'll tell you. I called in on Eric and Jane.'

Elin chewed her lower lip. 'Did they ask about me at all?'

'You think a lot of yourself, don't you? I don't think you were uppermost in their minds, Elin. You burned your bridges when you left. No, I filled them in on developments; it was the least I could do. Now that Liverpool can present the Bill in Parliament, the planning phase is done and dusted. The clearance dates have been scheduled. People are going to have to leave the village whether they want to or not.'

She looked at him in dismay. 'So soon?'

'It might seem soon to you, but it's been dragging on long enough,' Rob said. He took out his packet of cigarettes and tapped one out. 'Eric's parents' house is the first one to be scheduled for demolition. Believe me, it gave me no pleasure to tell him that.' He lit the cigarette, exhaled a plume of smoke and watched it roll across the caravan ceiling like a cloud. He giggled. 'Well, maybe a little pleasure; I'm only human.' Behind his glasses his hazel eyes were clear and guileless as his gaze roamed over Elin's face and body.

Elin closed her eyes and faced the reasons things had gone wrong. She took responsibility for it. She hadn't only postponed her wedding to please Jane and Eric, or to support her parents.

She'd postponed it because she wanted to be the person to convince Rob that Capel Celyn deserved to be saved. She'd seen that look in his eye, his interest, and it gave her power over him. She wanted Capel Celyn to be the legacy she left behind, she wanted to be waved off in triumph, she wanted people to say that if it hadn't been for Elin Jenkins they wouldn't be here now. *Let me tell you about her. Went to Philadelphia, she did, like the Quakers.*

If she'd gone when she planned, her parents might be grandparents, looking forward to her letters arriving in the post, propping up the latest photographs on the mantelpiece, proud that she'd done well.

Instead, she was sleeping in a caravan with the enemy, unmarried, an outcast – alienated from her friends, and cut off from her family who had washed their hands of her.

As the nights went by, she still didn't love Rob. Sometimes she hated him.

*

Elin took a job as a cleaner for a local woman, Mrs Owens. The advert had gone up on the caravan site noticeboard and there were a lot of applicants, but she got the job because she spoke Welsh.

Mrs Owens was the wife of the local butcher. She was a talker, not a listener, which suited Elin as she herself had nothing to say. Mrs Owens was a fair woman to work for. As the months passed, she stopped checking on Elin's work and took it for granted she was doing a thorough job. She was a gentle woman who had her hair set once a week and refused to advance money to their workers as a matter of principle, even though they had plenty.

'Neither a borrower nor a lender be. That way, we all know where we stand,' she said firmly to Elin.

Rob looked after Elin's wages for her. He'd kept her at his own expense for long enough, and for what?

At first, she thought paying her way would ease the tension between them.

But it didn't work that way.

He had a litany of resentments over the way she was treating him: 'It's time you got over Al, don't you think?' 'Give me a chance to prove my love.' 'I've been a patient man, haven't I?' 'You're taking advantage of me because I've got a gentle nature.'

All of which were true; Elin knew that.

As she cleaned Mrs Owens' house, she thought her only chance of freedom was if Rob lost patience with her and fell in love with someone else. It was what she prayed for.

*

In October 1958, it was through Mrs Owens that Elin heard about the auction in Capel Celyn as she was drying the dishes.

Mr and Mrs Owens were getting ready to go out. Ivor Evans was auctioning some livestock from one of the farms affected by the clearance and Mr Owens wanted to add to his small herd. In addition, there was a tractor he was interested in, if the price wasn't too steep. Mrs Owens said she was interested in a china tea service, as long as it wasn't chipped.

Normally Elin pretended that she was working too hard to listen to their conversations, but this was different. She folded up the tea cloth and gave an embarrassed cough. 'Excuse me please, whose farm is it?' she asked, interrupting them.

'Pen y Bryn. Once that's empty there'll only be the school and the chapel left standing. They're leaving them until last.'

'That's my parents' place,' she said with a jolt. 'Please can you give me a lift there? I'll come in tomorrow, to make up for it.'

They looked at her curiously, as if it hadn't occurred to them that she might have a life outside cleaning, and gave the request some consideration, examining it from all angles, for catches.

'Aye, all right then,' Mr Owens concluded in the end, putting on his overcoat. 'You might be able to tip us a wink.'

They went in the cattle truck and as they crossed Tryweryn Bridge they were met by the strange sight of cars parked bumper to bumper in the street.

To Elin's shock, most of the houses in the village were already empty and being reclaimed by nature. Tendrils of ivy were creeping through window frames, the grass was waist high, moss was greening the roof slates.

Elin jumped out of the truck and ran to the farm. The crowded yard was like a marketplace, the roar of voices raised against the lowing of cattle, grim men wearing caps and overcoats; sympathetic but looking for a bargain, too. The auctioneer was standing on a box in his trilby, holding up his walking stick. Some boys were playing chicken with the cows and dodging the horns.

On the doorstep of the farm, looking on, was her dead-eyed mother in her blue-and-white headscarf with her navy coat buttoned up.

Elin was pushing through the men to get to her mother. 'Mam!' she called, desperate to comfort her. She could never have come here because of her own needs, but she was here for them, to stand by them.

For a moment she braced herself for rejection after all this time apart. But she needn't have worried. Her mother's resigned face softened as she saw her. She pressed Elin's hand to her mouth.

'Don't say anything, Elin,' she said quickly, 'I'm not going to let them see me cry.'

Elin couldn't believe the worst was actually happening. She stood on the doorstep next to her mother, shoulder to shoulder. She searched the jostling crowd, looking for her father and saw him encircled by the crowd of men. He was standing by his best cow, his face like flint.

'Everything's got to go!' the auctioneer shouted. 'Where shall we start?'

Willing him to see her, Elin stared at her father until he felt the pull of her gaze; his eyes met hers and for a moment they flashed alive with hope. So now it was the three of them together again, taking part in the proceedings. Elin thought she couldn't bear it, but it was amazing what a person could bear.

It was hard to die of unhappiness, that was the hardest thing about it, that you kept going, miserably, indefinitely, through the drag of time. It was just a matter of standing tall, ignoring the noise, waiting for it to pass and be done with, she thought.

She'd known that this day was coming, but for a long time that's all it was, a day that was coming. And now it had come.

She'd never expected it to be here, this day, now.

The new owners led the cows to the cattle truck. Jip rounded up the sheep for the last time and the spoils of the farm were divided amongst farmers from Bala and Corwen, and then the men went back to their cars and the boys got into the back of the trucks and left them behind in a blue haze of exhaust smoke.

The farm was silent.

'So that's that,' her father said as they stood in the empty yard. He looked confused, because despite seeing everything sold, he wasn't prepared for it having gone.

Elin couldn't stand the silence of the farm any longer; she said she had something to do and she would be back shortly. She left her parents and headed for the quarry, her anger newly refreshed, blotting out her thoughts.

After asking around, she found Rob at the top of Arenig quarry with a clipboard in his hand.

'You're not supposed to be here,' he said mildly.

She looked down across the west of the valley, trucks rumbling over it, the noise, the dirt. The clearance had started, and every tree, every bush, every hedge, every shrub was being cut down, destroying all evidence of nature and beauty. 'My parents have just sold their livestock,' she said furiously, energised by grief and anger. 'Are you proud of yourself?'

He looked at her uncertainly. 'You can't blame me for that.'

'You said you'd find somewhere else! You promised us.'

Rob took off his glasses and polished the dust off them carefully. A truck was approaching, piled with gravel, and he pulled her aside to let it pass in a hot rumbling gust of fumes. He raised his hand to the driver in acknowledgement and turned to Elin. 'You'd better go,' he said, 'you'll get me into trouble. Let's talk about it at home.'

'Home? I haven't got a home. I'd rather sleep under a hedge than go back with you now. I hate you,' she said furiously, 'for all this destruction.'

'Destruction? Construction, you mean.' Rob corrected her automatically, without thinking. He gazed across the valley, frowning. From up here, the brown dust settled over the land like a cloud layer.

He rubbed his hands over his face and when he looked down again he seemed to see it suddenly for the first time as it really was.

In the same way that Elin had found clarity, Rob found it too.

All his certainty left him. Then he said, as if the truth had dawned on him like a shocking revelation for the first time, 'You're right. We're wiping it from the face of the earth.'

'I will never, ever forgive you.' It gave Elin some satisfaction to know she still had the power to hurt him.

'Don't say that. You don't mean it.'

'Yes,' she said viciously. 'I do.'

'You came to live with me because you know we belong together,' he said shrilly.

'I had nowhere else to go!'

Rob rubbed his mouth with his sleeve. 'But you love me. I know you love me, Elin.'

'I don't love you!' she spat at him. 'You're weak and pathetic! I hate you! I've hated you since that night you followed me down the lane!'

As her words sank in, he suddenly looked pitiful, stooped, defeated, as if all his certainties had left him. He walked to the sheer edge of the track and looked down at the brown scars that they'd torn into the green countryside.

He turned back to her, his coat flapping, his mouth curved in that strange, familiar smile. 'I love you, Elin,' he said helplessly.

She gave a harsh laugh. 'Liar! You don't know the meaning of the word!'

'I do,' he protested. 'You're my whole life. I can't live without you.' He was crying now. He turned away from her and raised his arms and spread them wide as though he was embracing the damage that had been inflicted on the valley.

She watched him with her hands on her hips. 'Bloody drama queen,' she said in disgust. 'Go on! Jump! Do it! See if I care!'

'Elin,' he whimpered.

She turned from him, filled with anger and contempt. She couldn't bear to look at him any more. Walking away was like leaving a crucifixion scene. She'd gone a few yards when she felt a dark heaviness come over her. At the last minute, she turned back – Rob was a black cross leaning desolate against the evening sky, leaning and then toppling rigid off the steep side of the quarry, plummeting with the crash of thunder onto the rubble below.

CHAPTER SEVENTEEN
Present day

High-pitched, excitable voices floated on the breeze and three young women in shorts and T-shirts walked across the yard, flushed with exertion and heat.

Sophie greeted the new arrivals and they shrugged off their backpacks with relief.

One of the group, a tall, dark-haired girl, pushed her orange baseball cap to the back of her head and gave their details. 'Hi there! Regan Brooks. Three of us, for one night.'

'Come on inside.'

In the lobby one of the girls pulled off her boot and sock and examined her heel. 'Gross!' she exclaimed, pressing the spongy, white raised circle of flesh. 'Look, it's straight out of *Dr Pimple Popper*. I'm going to pop it.'

Regan turned and said sharply, 'Seriously, Belle, do you have to do that here? Do *not* pop it, you'll just make it worse.' She pulled at the peak of her orange cap, looked cheerfully at Sophie and jerked her head towards her friend. 'Tell her, will you!'

'Don't pop it,' Sophie said obligingly.

'Oh, but it's all squidgy,' fair-haired Belle said longingly. 'I *love* popping things.'

The third girl, pink-haired, wearing camo, was kneeling on the floor, looking through one of the pouches of her backpack. 'She does,' she confirmed. 'It's disgusting. She'll pop anyone's.' She produced a small green container and threw it to Belle. 'Belle. Catch.'

'What's this?'

'Plasters. Read the label,' the girl said impatiently.

'Compeed' Blister Plasters.' She took one of the flesh-coloured plasters out of the container. 'Yuk, Molls! It feels weird. Like chicken fillets.'

Sophie gave them their registration forms to fill in and Al came into the lobby from outside to find his route blocked by the backpackers and their luggage.

'Where have you guys come from?' he asked.

'We've just climbed Arenig Fawr mountain. We've walked absolutely miles and it's only taken us six hours even though it's all up and down. Six hours,' Regan repeated, hooking her thumbs into her shorts and looking at Al with interest. She seemed fascinated by his shiny brogues. 'Are you on a walking holiday too?'

'No, not a walking holiday. I'm looking for Abraham Lincoln's ancestors.'

'Cool,' she said. She drank from her water bottle and wiped her mouth with the back of her hand. 'He was on *Doctor Who*.'

'Who was?'

'Abraham Lincoln.'

'He was born in 1809,' Al pointed out.

'Yeah but... there's only one Abraham Lincoln, right? And like, Doctor Who is a time traveller, you know, on the show? When Peter Davison was Doctor Who he saved Lincoln from an assassination attempt. And then Paul McGann was a different Doctor Who and he tried to stop him from going to the theatre where he was shot, but he went anyway.' She lowered her voice. 'Spoiler alert – he got killed.'

Al was tugging thoughtfully at the loose skin on his neck. 'You don't say.'

Sophie was leaning on the counter enjoying this riveting, although surreal, conversation.

'And that's on *Doctor Who*?' Al asked.

'Yeah. It's very educational. That's why my dad makes me watch it. Haven't you ever seen *Doctor Who*?'

'Can't say I have.'

'You should watch it,' she said kindly. 'You'll find out all sorts of things.'

Al raised his eyebrows. 'No doubt.'

'You can put it on your list of things to do, Al,' Sophie said with a grin as she unhooked three locker keys. 'Come on, I'll show you where everything is.'

Belle tucked her sock in her boot and hobbled behind them to the locker room.

When Sophie came back, Al was sitting in front of the birch screen in reception in a beam of sunshine, his eyes closed, his face relaxed into folds.

He sensed her standing there and opened his blue eyes. 'I wonder how much persuasion it took for their families to let them come on a walking holiday, alone. They're so young.'

'I know. They're over eighteen, though.'

Al frowned and shut his eyes again, retreating into the past. 'Elin was eighteen when we met. I've never considered how young she was before now.'

'Yeah, it's young.' Sophie gathered her hair and tied it up in a high ponytail with the band from around her wrist. 'But don't forget, you were young then, too.'

'True,' he conceded. 'It's strange, lifespan doesn't seem to come into the equation, does it, where memory is concerned? One's ego seems like a constant that remains unchanged. Part of the illusion of self, I suppose.' Al rolled his thumb back and forth across his index finger. Then his tone changed. 'I got a telegram from Elin, you know, three days before she was due to come to America.'

'Ah.' Sophie lowered herself into the swivel chair. She was curious, but at the same time she didn't really want to hear Al's story. He seemed so full of pain still, all these years later, it was a depressing thought. Time heals, that was the prevailing message, that's what you got told, and she'd adopted it as her mantra. *Time heals*. With everything that had happened to her, she didn't really want to take on Al's heartbreak. *Bad luck*, she wanted to say to him. *We've all been hurt. Get a grip, Al. We've all been there.*

They sat in silence for a few moments.

A bird flew past the window, casting a momentary shadow over Al's sunlit face. '"The Green Banana" we called it,' he said. 'The letter that said you're dumped. I read that telegram from Elin and it was like my world blew apart, and the shell fragments were the wedding, our children, our joy, our safety, our future, our lives. I felt myself break into pieces. Pow!' He spread his arms wide, banging them against the birch screen, startling Sophie. 'The pain took up all my senses, all my energy. It destroyed me.'

You're still here, aren't you, she wanted to argue. She held back and asked, 'What did the telegram say? Did Elin mention the flooding?'

'She didn't give a reason. She just wrote "Cancel wedding",' he said, miming speech marks.

He pursed his lips in thought. 'We had a small window of opportunity before I was deployed to Japan. We knew what the Japanese were like during the war, their kamikaze attacks on our ships. Dying in glory. The rumour went that killing you was doing you a favour because it was a brave death, it was like they were giving you a gift.'

'You were scared.'

'Yes. I'm not ashamed to admit it. That's why I wanted to marry Elin. I didn't want a girlfriend, I wanted a wife.'

'So, Elin cancelled it and you went to Japan. And that was that, was it? Neither of you got in touch again?'

Al rubbed his hands roughly over his face as if he were washing it clean. 'I got a letter from her after that. The mail was slow, it took a while to get to the ship, so it arrived some months later. When I opened it, I read "My Darling Al", as if time had gone backwards. I couldn't look at it. I set it alight and let it fall into the sea. But before it hit the waves, it floated back up again in flames. If I'd wanted, I could have reached out and caught it.'

They heard the girls coming back from the bunk room.

'Beer?' Sophie asked him.

He gave a rueful grin. 'You read my mind.'

The five of them sat together at the wooden table in the cool of the afternoon, and Al was right, it was easy to forget what being young was like, and just as easy to remember. The girls were friendly, open, warm.

'You're American, aren't you?' Regan asked him.

'That's right.'

'Did you know there's a memorial up Arenig Fawr to eight US airmen? They crashed their plane into the mountain on a training mission in nineteen-forty-something.'

'Nineteen forty-three,' Al said. 'I've seen it.'

'Oh.' Her young eyes searched his sympathetically. 'Did you know them?'

'No. I was eight years old at the time. I'm a navy guy, myself.' He smiled at his own pride. *Old was old, to the young*, he thought; *and how old was irrelevant.*

He remembered it wasn't an easy walk up Arenig Fawr when Elin had taken him there. It was misty at the top, no view, the mountain blended with cloud, and debris from the bomber lay embedded below the summit. They'd stood looking at the names of the dead for some time, it seemed to him, Elin resting her head on his shoulder. The mist beaded her hair and clothing like tiny lights in the cloud-drained sun.

Sophie was stamping damp circles on the table with her bottle. *Thud thud thud.* 'They've put a new memorial up there now because the names had faded off the original. Dilwyn Morgan from Bala fundraised for it.'

'Cool,' Molly said.

'I think it's cool, too,' Al agreed. 'Wales remembers everything through its memorials. Maybe it's true of every country, and it's only in Wales that I truly noticed them.'

'You have to keep tradition going.' Sophie was frowning slightly, as if he'd been critical. 'Otherwise, things get lost in time.'

She was thinking, *how could you not have read Elin's letter? How could you be so angry that you would destroy it without reading it? And why have you come back to look for her, what do you want to happen, what do you want from her?*

She knew what it was like to be the victim of a break-up. Her friends had sided with her afterwards, of course. She got all the sympathy and all the unpicking of the relationship during drunken nights out that ended in vomiting and tears.

But she knew what it was like to be the perpetrator, too. She and Max changed roles a few weeks in. He had accused her of stalking him.

It wasn't actually like that. Stalking wasn't the right word. Stalking is what you do when you hunt a person down. She just casually passed him by near his office, looking wonderful. She wanted him to notice her and feel a pang of loss or longing, and call out to her; she just wanted to give him the opportunity to realise he'd made a mistake. She was making it easy for him.

When he ignored her, she started thinking, *well, maybe he didn't see me after all.* It seemed entirely possible, because after Max broke up with her she felt as if she'd faded from sight, become less solid and more of an illusion. Her sense of certainty deserted her.

As it turned out, Max had seen her. *Of course he had.* He just didn't want to. When he blocked her on social media, she told herself it wasn't because of her, it was because he was having mental health problems, or a midlife crisis. She sent him a link for a relationship counsellor and then a psychotherapist. She was looking for a reason, really. She wanted him to work out what was wrong with him.

It took Sophie a long time to realise that there was nothing wrong with him. He'd just stopped loving her. She didn't know how that happened, or what she could have done to stop it. Been a nicer person, maybe.

Despite that, Max still lodged in her head; he inhabited part of her memory. On their first date she was wearing heels and a tight skirt, and as she jumped out of an Addison Lee cab Max opened his arms to catch her and she kind of fell into them. They hung on to each other and he said, 'I've been waiting for this.' *Me too.* Sophie would never forget that feeling, and she didn't want to. She *was* nice, in those days.

What would she do if a letter came from him today? She couldn't imagine him writing, but if he did, and she saw his handwriting on the envelope, then what? Would she get as far as, 'My dearest Sophie' and get angry and burn it? She picked up her beer.

Across the table, Al was laughing at something that one of the girls had said.

Sophie smiled. They hadn't made him feel old, they'd made him young again.

We're always trying to go back, she thought wistfully. *Always wanting to go back.*

CHAPTER EIGHTEEN

The following morning, Jane came to clean for Sophie. She liked to keep an eye on the place. She was dusting the pictures on the wall in the common room and Sophie was wiping down the skirting boards. They were chatting companionably about nothing in particular.

Jane ran her blue J-cloth over a photograph and then stopped, because it was of her and Eric when they first started the guest house, looking so young, standing arm in arm, full of optimism and doubt. She could see her reflection in the glass, laid on top of them, and it shocked her. 'Dew, I've got a face like a crumpled tissue,' she said. She dabbed at the picture gently, like a mother wiping a child's mouth.

'Jane, can I ask you something?'

'Go for it.'

'How come you lost touch with Elin?'

'Mind your own business.' Jane checked her cloth for dust and refolded it. Her lips were pressed together as if the truth would come blurting out without her permission. 'I don't pry into your past,' she said coldly. 'I don't expect you to pry into mine.'

'Sounds as if someone's got a guilty conscience about something,' Sophie said, nudging her with her elbow. It was meant as a light-hearted comment, so she wasn't prepared for Jane's extreme reaction.

Jane turned on her, flicking the J-cloth at her in sudden anger. 'How can you say that! You! Look at you, holier than thou, you know nothing about it,' she said, her face flushing with fury. Her voice hardened and she threw the cloth at her. 'I've had it with you. You can do your own cleaning.'

It was so unexpected, so out of character, that Sophie just watched Jane in astonishment and jumped as she slammed the door behind her.

Her heart was racing with adrenaline at the confrontation because it seemed to come from nowhere. *What the hell just happened?* She didn't feel she was in the wrong. Indignation rushed through her. *Fine. Let her go if that's what she wants.*

But Sophie could imagine her marching along the road in her red coat despite the summer heat, a small elderly woman energised by anger, and she went to fetch her car keys.

Jane was in her eighties, she'd worked all her life, and there was no question that she was capable of walking home, but still.

She jumped in the car and caught up with Jane just before she reached the dam. She slowed to a crawl and shouted through the window, 'Jane! Get in! I'll drive you home.'

Jane didn't even turn her head.

The car behind her sounded his horn impatiently and Sophie stuck her finger up at him and put her hazards on. 'Hey, Jane!' she called again, 'I'm sorry! Forgive me! Come on, get in! Please?'

'Leave me alone!'

If someone won't accept an apology, what are you supposed to do?

'Fine, if that's what you want,' Sophie yelled back.

She pulled away from the car behind and turned around in the lay-by to the dam. Too bad if Jane changed her mind now, she thought, glancing at her as she drove past. But Jane didn't look as if she was about to change her mind, didn't even look her way. Sophie swore loudly and headed along to Trawsfynydd to get herself a coffee and calm down.

*

Al was at a loose end. The three young women had left after breakfast, and Sophie had gone out somewhere, he wasn't sure where.

When planning his trip, he hadn't thought he would need a car. He'd only intended to walk down the track to the village and back, enjoying the familiarity of the place. The bunkhouse was so quiet without Sophie that he felt a sudden need for company and on an impulse he sat on his bunk and called Virginia.

'Darling,' she said, sounding husky from sleep. 'What time is it?'

He'd forgotten about the time difference. 'Did I wake you?'

'Yeah,' she replied vaguely, her voice fading as grief settled over her once more. 'Are you having fun?'

'It's no fun without you,' he pointed out. 'And,' he admitted, 'I haven't got very far at all.'

They lapsed into silence, and then spoke at the same time. 'Today I think—'

'Have you been to Bryn Mawr yet?'

'No.' He hadn't intended to go to Bryn Mawr at all – that was part of Virginia's ideal trip, not his. 'We've always said we'll go there together,' he said wistfully. They'd planned a tour to the original Bryn Mawr and a trip to Wrexham to see the grave of Elihu Yale, founder of Yale University, as well as the visit to the Quaker grave that he'd told her so much about.

'But we haven't been able to, have we? You do it for me, Al. Take plenty of pictures,' she said, 'won't you?'

'Well… okay, of course I will.' It would at least give him something constructive to do.

She yawned listlessly and said, 'Enjoy!'

Al listened to dead air with a certain disappointment and a renewed feeling of loneliness. *Bryn Mawr*. He tried to find it on his phone, and it had its own Wikipedia page, in Welsh. He would get a cab from Fron Goch. He took a soda out of the fridge and went outside to sit in the sun to drink it.

He watched a cloud of dust approaching, and Eric Oswald Hughes drove up and parked in front of him. For a few moments he sat grimly in the car with the sorrowful expression of a broken man. As usual, he was dressed in black. He reminded Al of an undertaker, a profession that in his old age he tried to keep his distance from.

Even when they were both a lot younger, Al wasn't at all sure what to make of Eric. The man kept himself to himself and let his wife do the talking. Al suspected that sometimes his thoughts were too dark to express.

Eric opened the car window. 'Is Sophie around?'

'No. She's out.'

Eric looked at Al with cold, dark eyes. 'Did she say when she'd be back?'

'No.'

'Did she mention Jane at all?'

'No. I haven't seen her since breakfast when I went for a walk by the lake.'

Eric rested back against the headrest. 'Women can be hard work sometimes.'

'Isn't that the truth.'

Eric seemed consoled by Al's agreement. He gave a brief smile and slid the window shut, and then had second thoughts and opened it again. 'What are you up to today, Captain?'

'I'm going to Bryn Mawr.'

'In Dolgellau?' Eric looked surprised.

'That's right.'

'How are you getting there?'

'By cab,' Al replied firmly.

'Dew, man,' Eric said, 'it's twenty miles to Dolgellau! It will cost you a fortune.' He turned off the engine, got out of the car and leant on the hood. Shielding his eyes from the glare of the sun, he looked out at the hills and he came to a decision. 'I'll take you there myself. It will be home from home for you.'

'How's that?'

'It was Rowland Ellis's place before he left to go to Pennsylvania. Your neck of the woods.' He looked at the gleam of Al's brogues. 'It's a bit of a walk, mind.'

'I've got walking boots in my locker.'

'Good, you'll need them. Bryn Mawr means big hill, and sure enough, big it is.'

It was a generous offer, and Al took him up on it, glad of the company and pleased to have a lift. 'Give me five minutes,' he said, and he hurried inside for his boots, wallet and phone. He filled his canteen with water and got in the car with Eric.

As Eric drove, he told Al about a book he'd read called *The Secret Room*, which had made an impression on him. It was set in 1672 and it was based on the life of Rowland Ellis, a landowner who had inherited Bryn Mawr from his grandfather and became a Quaker before moving to the wilderness and religious freedom of the New World. 'I find it very significant that he named his new home Bryn Mawr, don't you?' Eric looked over at Al.

'In what way?'

'Well, he obviously didn't want to shake off his roots, despite everything; and that sums up the Welsh character, to my mind. Firmly rooted. *The Secret Room* brought that whole period of history to life for me. I will lend it to you. The walk we're going on is based on the places in the book. It's a Quaker walk,' he said, changing gear. 'I've got a lot of time for Quakers.'

'I know very little about them, except for a general feeling that they're slightly oddball, like the Amish.' It suddenly seemed the wrong thing to say. 'I didn't know you were a religious man.'

Eric laughed, and it was such a good, hearty belly laugh that Al started laughing too, without really knowing why. 'Religious,' he repeated. 'Why wouldn't I be? Mind you, think of all the mockery and scorn the Quakers suffered for it.' His smile faded and he gave Al a brief intense look. 'Reading that book made me wonder – why would a person do that, Al? Why would they put themselves through so much suffering for their new beliefs?'

He was stuck for an answer. 'I can't really imagine.' His own experience of religion was attending weddings, baptisms and funerals. He'd met some good chaplains during his time in the navy and for a moment he visualised a folded US flag on a casket; his own casket. He'd always intended to talk it over with his son, Charles, when the time was right. 'Like most people, at my lowest ebb I've appealed to a greater power; even railed against it,' Al said grimly, 'but I can't say I've ever suffered because of it. Or that I would feel strongly enough about it to want to.'

'No,' Eric agreed.

'What exactly was it that got them into trouble? I've never understood that. It always seems a gentle religion.'

Eric sucked in his loose cheeks thoughtfully. 'The problem was, they discovered that the light of God is inside us all. Pure and unsullied.'

Unsullied. There is something in the way he said it, his emphasis, that seemed to light a flare of hope in Al, and he wanted to keep hold of the feeling. 'What's so wrong about believing that?'

'Well for a start, it meant they didn't need clergy to mediate between them and God, so they refused to pay the mandatory taxes to the Church of England.'

'Tax evasion? That sheds a different light on it altogether,' Al said. He was a traditionalist at heart; you couldn't make a career in the military without being a traditionalist.

Eric didn't make any effort to argue and in silence they entered a tunnel of trees bowing across the narrow road.

But Eric hadn't finished yet. 'Even worse, they believed we were all equal in the eyes of God.' He shot Al a swift, unguarded look. 'Imagine that as a concept, Al, in those class-driven times! What that could do for a man! It's all very well if you lived in poverty. You'd love to know you're the equal of other men, wouldn't you? No more saluting, doffing of hats. Dew! It would do wonders for your self-esteem if you could believe that. However, if you're gentry, the last thing you'd want is equality with your servants. It must have been terribly annoying that the Friends had no respect for class, or wealth, or slavery, or any of the outward manifestations of wealth. They stripped everything back to the love of God and their fellow man.'

'I can see how that would be a problem.'

'Yes! Nevertheless, Al, the *Bonheddig*, the noble class, the pure Welsh, they embraced it, despite the fact they had so much more to lose.' Eric's voice was fervent, a kind of awed whisper. 'Anyway. You'll see for yourself.'

Al watched the countryside go by and consoled himself with knowing that at least he could take a photograph of Bryn Mawr for Virginia and buy a souvenir postcard to send her.

Wish you were here.

They reached the town of Dolgellau and parked next to the River Wnion. Eric took a pair of Nordic walking poles out of the boot. 'Follow me.' By the river wall he pointed to an area of still black water, the surface undulation betraying the current beneath it. 'That spot there was where they drowned those who they declared to be witches,' he said. 'The purity of the Society of Friends and the drowning of witches ran along side by side; it's difficult to credit, isn't it? It was the duty of every Christian to denounce dissenters as quickly as possible. Like Twitter,' he added, glancing at Al.

'At least we don't kill people for thinking differently any more.'

Eric looked sceptical. 'Don't we, though?'

Al followed him through the grey buildings of the town at a brisk pace. At the end of a street stood a grand house, with a sign saying: Y MEIRIONYDD.

'Now this restaurant is where Dolgellau jail stood,' Eric said, shielding his eyes against the sun's reflection. 'For hygiene reasons the floor of the cells consisted of a metal grid so that the prisoners could piss and shit onto the earth beneath it. But Quakers were deemed the lowest of the low, so that's where they put them, underneath the grid, to get pissed and shat on until they died or changed their ways. Imagine,' he continued, turning his fierce dark eyes on Al, 'having everything taken away from you, your possessions, your livestock, your land, your freedom, your health, because of the miraculous wonderment of your faith, the discovery of this new relationship with God. Captain! I envy their belief! What a time that was.'

He was like some fervent old preacher, lit up with fire and passion.

Al looked at him warily, wondering if Eric was trying to convert him.

There was a menu in the window of the restaurant. The stone building had shaken off its dark history and now appeared warm and welcoming. Al looked at it hopefully.

'When they left for Pennsylvania the Quakers could worship freely, lit by that inner light. Of course,' Eric said over his shoulder as he started walking again, 'when they did relocate, it was a bit tough on the cautious remnant who were left behind. They fell into a state of apathy and married non-Quakers and the like, and that was the end of that, more or less.'

They crossed a bridge and followed a lane past stone houses and into a dark, wooded area. Through the black trees Al could see a window of light in the distance. He was breathing heavily, and the woods smelled of ferns and moss. It was steep and hard going on uneven ground.

Eric was way ahead of him, a distant figure, his black jacket flapping wildly, a man with a mission.

In the dim seclusion of the trees, twigs cracking under their feet, Al looked out for a good stout stick of his own, just to be on the safe side, and found one with a decent balance to it. He swung it at the brambles like a baseball bat.

Eric waited for him to catch up and he pointed to a buzzard swooping and rising, holding a limp, small creature in its mouth. They walked on, and soon all Al could see was his bald head above the green ferns and flowers.

A cloud of midges lifted up from a black swamp with silver-rimmed puddles, and Al's boots squelched in the mud. The woods muffled most sounds except for their harsh breathing. The tall trees leaked patches of gold light and now the ground was soft and cushioned with brown pine needles.

Stones from the path fell into the nearby stream as they walked by, and presently Al followed Eric up a bank and they emerged into the sunlight again.

The green meadow was like paradise; the world was spread out before them, and the bright, sheep-shorn grass was dense and velvety. In the distance the grey town shimmered with its grey slate roofs, and beyond that were endless dreamy blue-grey mountains.

Al sat on the stile, opened his water bottle and drank gratefully, his shirt clammy with sweat, his heart thumping with an irregular beat that made his eyes throb.

Eric was waiting for him by a tree growing up the side of a rough track, and he pointed to a sign. 'This is it! Bryn Mawr!'

Al looked at a derelict single-storey stone building which had lost the tiles from its roof; the rafters showed like bones, bleached grey in the sun.

Eric had painted Al a picture of the past, and Al expected at the end of it he would see something magnificent that had been left behind, forfeited to the eager search for the freedom of the New World. 'It's smaller than I expected,' he said.

Eric gave him a strange look. 'Hold on, man, this is just part of the estate, we're not there yet.'

They descended into a ditch with a wooden plank at the bottom of it, climbed out, and there it was, the original Bryn Mawr: a modest two-storey house with a slate roof and stone lintels.

'There's not much of the original building left,' Eric said. 'Rowland Ellis emigrated in 1686 and this part was rebuilt around 1750. But it retains the atmosphere, doesn't it?'

Al walked around the building. To his surprise, he came across an overgrown burial ground, with upright gravestones, which seemed to belong to the house. Coming back round to the front of the house he tried the door, but it was locked, so he looked in through the window. The place was modern inside and comfortably furnished and he was just about to comment on this to Eric when a man's face materialised in front of him and started shouting.

'Get off my land, you bloody vandals!'

A dog barked, too close for comfort.

'Run!' Eric yelled, and he headed back the way they came.

Al had propped up his stick against a wall, and he was about to get it when the front door opened and with a snarl, a flash of black dog bounded towards them.

Al ran as far as the boundary, when Eric, some way ahead of him, turned, looked alarmed, and threw his Nordic pole at the dog like a javelin. Al caught up with Eric and they half ran, half slid down the dry scree. Al stumbled over Eric's remaining pole and landed in the ditch at the bottom, the breath knocked out of him.

Eric, further up the bank, rolled up his trouser leg, examining his grazed knee and said accusingly, 'What did you want to look in the windows for, Al? Dew, man, we almost got savaged.'

'I didn't know there was anyone living there! I thought it was a museum! You should have warned me!' He checked his racing pulse and it was off the scale. 'Did you see the size of that dog?'

'He was a mean bugger, all right.' Eric pursed his lips. 'We've survived, though,' he said in a tone of amazement. 'You have survived, haven't you, Al?' He straightened his trouser leg, got to his feet cautiously, lost his footing and slid down in a flurry of limbs until he came to rest alongside Al. For a thin man, he was surprisingly solid.

Al started to laugh and after a moment Eric laughed too; they lay helplessly against the bank until it was all out of their systems.

'Do me a favour, Captain,' Eric said when he recovered.

'What's that?'

'Go back and fetch my walking pole, will you,' he said. 'I feel awkward with just the one.'

They started laughing again. Eric looked at him, suddenly concerned. 'Oh dear. You look as if you've been in a fight, man; you've got twigs in your hair. I don't know what Sophie is going to say.'

The laughter built up again inside Al – a side effect of adrenaline. He felt kind of proud of his war wound. 'Let's get a photograph, Eric.' He put his arm around him and took a selfie; two old boys who should know better.

'I haven't got into a scrape for years,' Eric said as they hobbled back along the path. 'I normally keep away from bad influences.'

'Me too. I need a brandy. Let's get one from the jail.' As they walked back to the restaurant through the shady woods, Al could feel his elbows smarting but despite everything he felt triumphant.

Thanks to Virginia's vigilance, Al hadn't experienced the wonderful medicinal properties of brandy for a long time. 'Hair of the dog,' he told Eric.

'I've had enough of dogs for today. Just the one then,' Eric said.

He chatted to the bearded barman and described the size of the dog. 'Huge, all teeth and temper, it was.'

'You mean Keith,' the barman said, deadpan. He winked at Al.

'Get away with you!' Eric looked offended. 'Who calls a dog Keith?'

'Keith's wife. Every time she called for her husband, the dog came running, so they decided to change its name, for simplicity.'

Eric mulled this over for a moment. 'So the owner's a regular, is he? Ask him to bring my walking pole in and keep it for me, will you?'

Back in the car, Al started whistling 'Bridge over the River Kwai'.

'It's a lost art, whistling,' Eric said wistfully.

'I agree. I suppose people don't need to make their own music now, with a pair of earbuds they can enjoy bands, orchestras, or anything they want.'

'True. Me, I'm old style. I prefer self-sufficiency,' Eric said.

'I'm much obliged to you for taking me. We had a personal interest, as my wife went to Bryn Mawr College in Pennsylvania.'

'Did she now. Didn't she want to come and see the place for herself?'

There was something in the way Eric said it, as if it was something he honestly wanted to know, that made Al open up.

'We'd always planned to come together,' he explained. 'My son, Charles, generously gave us the airline tickets for my eighty-fifth birthday. It was a trip my wife and I had talked about for years. "Just do it, Dad," Charles said. So here I am. It was to be our grand tour.' Al smiled faintly. 'We'd booked a luxury coach and four-poster beds.'

'Ah.' Eric shot him a quick, curious glance. 'Your wife changed her mind, did she?'

'Yes, that's it,' Al said. He nodded, and for a moment his vision blurred with tears. 'She changed her mind.'

*

Back at the bunkhouse, Sophie's car was parked in its usual spot by the fire pit.

Eric parked up next to it, sighed, and turned to Al. 'Did Sophie tell you that she and Jane had an argument?'

Al was surprised. 'No.'

Just at that moment, Sophie appeared in the doorway, raising her hand in greeting; the cuff of her white shirt flapped around her wrist.

The men got out of the car into the sun, cool from the air con.

'Hello,' Sophie said. 'What have you two been up to?'

'We walked to Bryn Mawr from Dolgellau,' Al said. 'It was quite a trek.'

'Why didn't you drive up?'

'We could have *driven*?' He turned to Eric, but Eric was no longer the wry, easy-going storyteller. He was staring at Sophie, his black, lowered eyebrows casting a shadow that hid his eyes.

'You've upset Jane something awful, you know.'

'Yeah, I'm sorry about that. I didn't mean to.' Sophie's gaze drifted from Eric to Al and back again. 'This is something that we should talk about in private.'

'I'll get out of your way,' Al said, quick to take the hint, heading towards the door.

Sophie was moving aside to let him pass when Eric called him back.

'Hold on there, Al. It's time we cleared this up once and for all. Sophie has been getting some wild ideas in her head and upsetting Jane over it.'

'No, I haven't!' Sophie protested. 'I just asked her why she'd lost touch with Elin.'

'You blamed her for them breaking up.'

'Eric, where did you get that from? I did no such thing. I know why they broke up, Al's already told me. It was because of Elin's telegram, cancelling the wedding.'

Al tucked his hands into his trouser pockets and nodded. 'It's true.'

Eric flexed his jaw and gave a harsh laugh. 'And then what did you do in retaliation?'

Al squinted in the sunlight as if he was trying to peer back into the past. He shook his head.

'I'll tell you what he did. He married someone else. He sent Elin a wedding invitation, just to rub it in. She showed it to me, I read it with my own eyes,' Eric said. 'Despite what Al says, what broke them up wasn't the telegram, it was his marriage to someone else on the same day he was due to marry Elin. If you're accusing people of having guilty consciences, you should point the finger at the Captain first.' He turned to Al and his face was cold. 'Day after day, Elin waited for your letter. She was sure you'd wait for her. But you didn't, did you? You married a girl who went to Bryn Mawr! She couldn't compete with that.'

'That's not... what are you talking about?' Al asked, perplexed. 'My wife's education had nothing to do with it. I've known Virginia all my life, our parents were good friends, she was...' He stumbled to a halt.

'You wrote: "No hard feelings". You wanted Elin to know how little she meant to you.'

In the silence, a blackbird trilled a refrain that filled the warm air.

Al gripped his temples. 'Yeah,' he admitted. 'You're right. I did. She broke my heart. I thought for a long time about what to write. I wanted her to know that I'd moved on, that I was happy, that I had someone else to love me. I wanted to reassure her on that matter and, at the same time, to rub it in her face. I did have hard feelings. I still have them now,' he said.

In the burning glare of the sun, Sophie shielded her eyes and looked at Al. She said bitterly, 'I can't believe you did that.' She was furious with herself for being taken in by Al's romanticism. All her illusions about his love for Elin, her belief that love could endure despite everything, her hope for a happy ending, he had destroyed all of that. Relationships, so-called love, always came down to the same thing in the end: disillusionment, dislike, betrayal.

She left them to it and went through to her own room, slammed the door shut and drew the curtains, shutting out the light. Her head was hot and she pressed it against the cool marble mantelpiece, feeling sick, as if she was having a migraine.

She heard Eric drive away.

People don't change, Sophie thought, *and how depressing is that?* They just carried on as they were, getting older and older, muscles diminishing, collagen diminishing, brain cells diminishing. It was only people's emotions that stayed bright and true and diamond-hard, reflecting the same old facets of themselves, jealousy, resentment, self-justification, things they couldn't control, talking only about the choice bits of their stories, the good bits, the bits that that suited them best, protagonists and antagonists alike.

Back when she was pretending to accidentally bump into Max, to show him what he was missing, she actually enjoyed seeing his expression change to irritation. She wanted him to feel *something* for her, and if it wasn't love then she'd settle for an emotion equally powerful. It was satisfying, that she could have that effect on him, the sly snicker of knowing she was behaving badly. Still thought of herself as the good guy, though, even as she was doing it.

She'd lost her mind for a while, back then, it was as simple as that. That's how she chose to see it now. She'd discovered a part of herself that she didn't like.

If Al had lied to them out in the yard, it would have been different. When he admitted he wanted to hurt Elin, she got it, but she still held it against him because she understood him perfectly.

What she didn't understand was why the subject of Elin bothered Eric and Jane so much after all these years. Whatever happened back then, Al's visit had stirred it all up again. She'd never thought of them as having hidden depths. She had always been happy to accept what she saw on the surface.

Maybe it was safer that way, best not to look too hard.

Everyone's got a dark side, she thought.

CHAPTER NINETEEN

Al headed down the leafy track to the lake. He clambered down to the water's edge, inhospitably studded with mossy boulders and shrouded by trees. He imagined he was the only person to go down there, but he was wrong because he came across a cider can, a screwed-up tissue and a used condom that hadn't been there before; these remnants that people had left behind. It was profoundly distressing.

He headed to the smooth, flat rock he already liked to think of as his own, and he sat on it and looked out across the restless, sparkling water. From where he was sitting, he could see people walking across the dam, with their dogs or alone, taking a stroll, standing with their backs to him and looking down the grassy dam wall and the sluice gates. As they returned to their cars, if they cared to look up they would see the words '*Cofio Dryweryn*' painted in white across the wall of the substation: *I remember Tryweryn*, the valley in which the village once thrived.

He thought of the hikers talking well into the early hours as he lay in his bunk last night. Their voices were light, almost musical. They weren't talking about anything deep, but what they talked about they were taking seriously, and their words were like a holiday in his head.

He had lived eighty-five long years, with a life behind him that seemed to amount to very little at all except for regrets.

For a moment it seemed like he felt the vibrations of trucks on the road, and then he realised it was his phone vibrating in his pocket. He saw it was his wife, Virginia. 'Hello, honey,' he said, surprised and pleased that she was calling him.

'I've been down in the basement,' she said. Her voice was cold and slightly slurred. 'That wall needs a lick of paint, Al.'

Her words filled him with alarm. 'Don't even think of it,' he warned her, and it came out a lot harsher than he meant it to. 'And don't touch my desk.' He watched the white gulls circle and land on the chopping water, bobbing gently together like little craft. His voice carried and he softened his tone. 'I've got important stuff down there that I need to keep. Just leave it be. I'll sort it all out I when I get home.'

Virginia's voice was distinctly hostile. 'Does that include her telegram, Al?'

For a moment he did a double take. 'Huh? You've been through my files?' It was his turn to be outraged. He groped for a pebble to throw in the lake.

'You know I'm not a jealous woman, Al,' she said, 'but there are limits.'

The pebble splashed and the gulls flew away, screaming.

She *was* a jealous woman, actually.

He could remember the scenes she'd made at dinner parties, the sulks, the rows. And the excuses afterwards: *PMS, pregnancy, the menopause.* But he also knew that he was to blame. She was jealous because, while he was posted in Liverpool, he'd given her reason to be.

'I chose you, didn't I?' As soon as Al said the words, he knew it had been the wrong thing to say. His phone was hot in his hand, hot against his ear, as if she was breathing fire.

'Oh, you chose me, did you? Only because she ditched you.'

Now, sitting by the lake where the village had once been, he knew what he'd done to her. He said, 'I love *you.* I've been a good husband, haven't I? I've looked after you.'

Virginia ignored the question. She hadn't finished yet. 'Have you seen her?' she asked in a high, tight voice.

'No.'

She made a little sound that was halfway between a sob and a sigh. He wanted her to drop the subject.

'Do you intend to meet up with her?'

Al was silent.

Again she gave that little mewl of pain. 'I don't understand why you've lied to me for all these years. Do you know how that makes me feel? What's wrong with you, that you'd rather lose yourself in the past than live with me in the present?'

God forgive him, but it was true. 'I'm so sorry, Ginny.'

He couldn't tell her that when he retreated into his imagination, leaving his sorrow behind, Elin only knew the best of him, the young, carefree man he'd once been. He liked the man he had been when he was with her. She had made him feel better about himself, like a bigger person, as if she alone had seen Al's true self. Thinking of her gave him a way out of his misery, like a good bourbon.

'I should have come with you,' Virginia said, 'but I couldn't leave.' Her voice broke. 'Do you understand? I was afraid that when we got back, Charles's spirit wouldn't be here any more.'

'I know,' he said gently. He nodded, even though she couldn't see him. He did understand. 'It will be okay, Ginny. We'll talk about it when I get home. I love you, you know.'

He stared at the dazzling lake, waiting for her response until his eyes hurt. Purple discs of light swirled inside his eyelids. She didn't say it back and he hated himself for minding. *What the hell am I doing?* he wondered, not for the first time. He tucked his phone away.

In the rustling silence, with the pale blue sky reflected in the shimmering water, he looked across at Arenig Fawr, and from that visual bearing he tried to work out the layout of the village as he remembered it.

Across the valley, about a mile away from where he was sitting, he could make out the straight, flat track where the old railroad was. Hafod Fadog farm and the Quaker burial ground must be a good few yards to the right of where he was sitting. He felt the pull of the past, compelling and physical.

He climbed back up to the road and headed west along the path above the lake. A few minutes later he came to a lay-by. At the far end, set back from the road on a base of grass-embedded cobblestones, was a huge boulder.

He stepped over the low wooden fence onto the grass. Embedded in the boulder was a metal memorial plaque. He ran his hand over it, and the words were hot under his palm.

Under these waters and near this stone stood HAFOD FADOG, a farmstead where in the seventeenth and eighteenth centuries Quakers met for worship. On the hillside above the house was a space encircled by a low stone wall where larger meetings were held, and beyond the house was a small burial ground.

From this valley came many of the early Quakers who emigrated to Pennsylvania, driven from their homes by persecution to seek freedom of worship in the New World.

Al rested his weight against the warm stone, moved to tears.

Under these waters was the grave that Elin had showed him. He was so close, he thought, so very nearly there.

CHAPTER TWENTY

When Eric got home, there was a letter for him in a white envelope with the address written in block capitals.

'You've been a long time,' Jane said.

'Sophie wasn't there so I took the Captain to Bryn Mawr. And when he came back, I made him face what he'd done. Never mind blaming you.'

'I deserve it. I should have persuaded her to go to join him in Pennsylvania, as she planned.'

'Hindsight.' Eric glanced at his wife. 'The wedding invitation, I'm talking about. The one he sent her.'

'Never mind the Captain! When are we going to face up to what we did, Eric? We treated Elin without an ounce of love or compassion or understanding. We were her friends! How could we have told her to go home when she was in that state? What does it say about us that we were so priggish and pompous that we could wash our hands of her suffering? I've carried this guilt for too long. I hope Al does find her so that we can make amends.'

Eric stared at his wife. He didn't have an answer to that. In stubborn silence, he turned away from her, slit the envelope carefully with his brass letter opener and sat down to read the letter. He took his time, and when he reached the end, he read it over again, his face creased in a frown.

Jane looked at him curiously. 'Who's that from? It's not bad news, is it?'

Eric sighed. Beneath his dark eyebrows, his face was troubled. 'It is. And not only bad news but sad news, that's the way I would put it.' He took a deep breath. 'A relative – John Oswald Hughes – has died.'

'No!' Jane sighed and shook her head sorrowfully. 'That's dreadful news! And on such a sunny day, too. Who was he, Eric?'

He read the letter again. 'To be honest,' he admitted, 'the name doesn't ring a bell. I don't know why not, as we've got something of a dearth of Johns in our family.'

'It's one of those names,' Jane said, 'that you either have lots of them, or none.'

'None, in my case. You'll never guess where he died.'

'Then I'm not going to bother. Where?'

'Jiangxi. Where's our world atlas, Jane?'

The atlas was propping up one leg of the coffee table.

Eric lowered his glasses to look at it. 'Oh yes, I'll mend that in a minute, I'm glad you reminded me, it's on my list of jobs, only three or four from the top,' he said, retrieving the atlas and putting his glasses back on to look through the index. 'Jiangxi… here it is! I thought so.' He slammed the atlas shut. 'China.'

'What was he doing in China?'

Eric went back to reading the letter. 'Well now. It doesn't say, specifically. One thing I can tell you, he was in investments.'

Jane leant over to the coffee table and slid the envelope towards herself with her fingertips. She picked it up and looked at the address in block capitals, and said, 'It's got a Welsh second-class stamp on it.'

'Well, why not? That's just good sense, because they get delivered at the same time as first class, give or take a day or two.'

'But you'd expect it to have a Chinese stamp on it,' Jane pointed out.

'Ah. Yes, it would have normally, I'm sure, but listen.' Eric went back to the first paragraph of the letter. 'It's been posted on the sender's behalf by a friend who is travelling to the United Kingdom.'

'Fair play, I expect it's quicker than sending it from China.'

Eric grunted. 'Slightly quicker.' He didn't have a very high opinion of Royal Mail.

'And does it mention a funeral?'

'No, no funeral. Come on, Jane,' he said briskly, 'even if it had, let's face it, we wouldn't have gone to China for the funeral of a man I can't place.'

'I know that, but we could have sent flowers. Out of respect.'

Eric sat back in his chair, deep in thought. 'I don't think it's customary to send flowers to Chinese funerals. I've a feeling you give money, for the afterlife, like Druids. Anyway, it's irrelevant, because they haven't given the contact details of the funeral directors and for all we know, it's already been and gone. In any case, that was not the purpose of the letter. John Oswald Hughes was a bit of a financial whizz-kid by the sound of it. He put aside $11 million for an investment, but, this is the thing, he died before he could go through with it.'

'Was it a heart attack?'

'Probably. Something quick.'

'You never know what's around the corner even when you've got money. Who is the letter from? John's wife?'

'No. He was either a widower or a bachelor, because he died all alone. I hate to think of him dying all alone in China. He was friendless too, because this letter has been sent to me by his bank manager, Mr Ai Wong.'

'Very thoughtful of him, isn't it? The personal touch.'

'There's a touch of self-serving about it, to be honest,' Eric admitted. 'That unused $11 million investment money is still lying in John's bank account, unspent. The bank manager is willing to give us fifty per cent of it, as beneficiaries, and keep the other fifty per cent for himself. Fixer's fees, I suppose.'

'And expenses. He's got the cost of that second-class stamp to take into account,' Jane said dryly. 'Ignore it, Eric. That's my advice.'

But Eric had a gleam in his eye. They had nothing very interesting to look forward to in the foreseeable future. And now here was something he could get his teeth into to take his mind off Elin Jenkins. 'I don't know if I want to do that,' he said.

'You don't even know a Mr John Oswald Hughes. The whole thing sounds shady to me,' Jane said.

'Yes; and to be fair, even Ai acknowledges the shadiness of it. He makes no bones about it. But if we don't share the investment money, it will go to the Chinese government, which is why he wants us to "act quick on this as soon as possible", as he puts it.'

'Who?'

'Ai Wong, the bank manager. He's given me his email address which is handy because I haven't a clue about the time difference in Jiangxi and I wouldn't want to get him out of bed.' He skimmed the letter again. 'His English is very good, I must say, except for a bit of tautology, which could happen to anyone.'

'I wonder how Mr Wong found you?'

'Technology,' Eric said. 'You can find anything with technology these days.'

'Except for Elin.' They had avoided talking about her for all these years and now she couldn't think of anything else. 'Would we still behave like that now?'

'They were different times,' Eric said impatiently. 'No worse, no better. That's how we were, then. We had our reputations to consider. Now this letter…'

*

Later that same afternoon, Greg turned up unannounced at Mountain Ash. He was wearing a black T-shirt and baggy shorts and his skin was tanned – he looked totally edible, Sophie thought, looking up at him as he leant on the counter.

'You got any room tonight?'

'Yes. For you, I'd kick someone out.'

He laughed.

Sophie rolled her shirtsleeves up, something to do to save staring at him. 'What would you like to drink?'

'I would love an iced coffee,' he said.

She took their drinks outside. Greg had pulled the deckchairs into the dappled shade of the mountain ash tree and they lounged back, side-by-side, tilting their faces under the leaves hiding the clear blue sky.

'I've got some news,' he said, stirring his coffee, the bamboo straw ringing against the side of the glass. 'I'm going to Everest.'

'Seriously? How come?'

'I'm going with a film crew. They're doing this documentary on the clearing up of the trash on the mountain – paying Sherpas based on what they bring down, by weight, and so forth. So, you know, I can feel I'm doing something and not just spending a shedload of money on fulfilling my own dreams.'

'Good for you,' Sophie said, pleased for him. He would be away for months; it would be strange without him. She watched a yellow butterfly meander across her vision like a leaf fluttering in the wind.

'Have you ever climbed Snowdon's Great Gully?' he asked her.

She sat up and turned to face him. 'I have, actually. I was twenty-five, and I was with a guide. It was the toughest experience of my life. Ferocious. It took six hours, way longer than I thought, but I ticked it off my list.' Studying Greg's expression, she had the strong feeling he'd read her online climbing log and already knew all that.

'Do you want to come and climb it with me?' he asked her.

Sophie felt a rush of nervous excitement, and she wasn't sure if it was the idea of the climb or climbing with Greg. She ran her nails back and forth along her lower lip. 'I'll think about it. Maybe. I don't know.'

'That's decisive.'

She laughed. 'Yeah. I'd sort of… put that part of my life behind me.'

Greg narrowed his eyes. 'And you don't miss it?'

She shrugged. 'I don't have time to miss it.'

'I can see that,' Greg said, looking at her in her shorts with her tanned legs outstretched. 'Look at you, rushed off your feet.'

'I know!'

He laughed and rested back again. 'How's Al's search for Lincoln coming along?'

Sophie took in a deep breath and let it out in a puff of exasperation. 'Urgh. He thinks the key is that girl he knew, Elin Jenkins. I decided he was still wildly in love with her, which let's face it, is romantic, right, after all these years? But he went and married someone else and sent Elin their wedding invitation as a way to end it. Can you believe it? And he's still married to his wife, and he still wears a wedding ring.'

'And that's got you pissed off with him.'

'Who says I'm pissed off with him?'

'Aren't you?'

'Yeah,' she conceded, 'I am, actually. I don't get it. The whole Al and Elin thing. I'm not getting involved any more, that's it; Al will have to work it all out by himself.' She finished her iced coffee, put the glass under her chair and asked plaintively, 'What's life all about, Greg?'

He took a deep breath and made a thoughtful humming noise. 'I have absolutely no idea,' he concluded.

For some reason, his response made her smile. People usually acted as if they had all the answers and she hated that.

CHAPTER TWENTY-ONE

That evening, after supper, the three of them, Sophie, Greg and Al, went to The Lamb.

The meal had been a subdued affair, and Al was glad to be somewhere lively and crowded. There was no sign of Eric and Jane. Owen, the grocery delivery man, was there, leaning on the bar in a boisterous good mood, and when Sophie said he could stay over in the bunkhouse he was in an even better mood.

Dai, the landlord, had stocked up on tomato juice especially for Al.

Al drank the Bloody Marys without really tasting them. He felt tired and old. He knew that he was, in some profound way, making a mash-up of things.

He found himself listening to some story he couldn't follow about some people he didn't know, and he excused himself and went outside to clear his head.

The air was fresh, and the horizon was a strip of deep orange, the dark sky pricked with starlight, the cool of the night invigorating.

His ears were ringing, and he took a few moments before turning to head back into the brightness, warmth and noise of The Lamb.

But by the door, listening to the roar of voices, he stopped and considered his circumstances.

He was a married man in a strange land without his wife. He was free, with a full belly and plenty of wine inside him. He was Al, 'the Captain', a man with a mission. Right now, he didn't have to think about his wife, or the state of his marriage, or Charles. And he had no one to worry about him, either. He was filled with the heady freedom of youth. He changed his mind about going back inside and decided to walk to the lake.

After passing the bunkhouse, the last bright stain of sunset faded to black and he was swallowed whole by the claustrophobic throat of the track.

He began to whistle 'Bridge over the River Kwai'. He'd taught his son to whistle as soon as he had his retainers out. He taught him to blow into the neck of a bottle so that it sounded like the deep hoot of a ship. He taught him how to make a camp in the woods. All these years, and he'd never actually had a conversation with Charles. He'd showed him how to do stuff instead.

As he descended down the bank to the lake's edge, a bat flitted and wheeled above his head.

As soon as it had gone, Al saw that the lake was a black hole.

He sat on his rock and let the black water lap at his shoes. He could sense the remains of old walls and foundations baptised by the water, cleansed.

He knew what he would find under the surface – he could swim along the road past the farmhouses, the cottages, the school, the post office. He could swim along the shore to the fields above Hafod Fadog.

Impulsively, he took off his shoes, removed his socks and folded them carefully. He rolled up his trouser cuffs, got to his feet with some effort, feeling slightly stiff, and hobbled tentatively into the shallows. The cold gripped his ankles, numbing them instantly, sending shockwaves all the way up to his head in a rush of excitement.

He retreated to dry land and took his jacket off. Now, flexing his shoulders, the night air seemed warm and cosy on his skin. He took off his shirt and pants, and his underpants too, and stowed them safely behind a rock.

He stood on the shore, naked in the night.

When he entered the water again the cold pinched his feet, ankles, knees. Sharp stones jabbed at his soles, and to avoid them he cautiously moved deeper, diving out of the night's silence into the dumb roar of the lake, into nothingness. He opened his eyes to find he could see nothing at all, and then emerged exhilarated and gasping, liberated, his heart pounding.

Swimming out in an easy front crawl through the cold black water, Al kept close to the line of the shore and looked out through the tangle of trees for the large boulder with the memorial plaque so that he would know when he'd reached the burial ground. When he was sure he could see the bulk of it, he trod water and looked around.

He was feeling lucky; the water was shallower here. Weeds entwined around his ankles and tickled his skin; and he ran his hands over the bedrock, feeling for the gravestone which would unlock the secret. Under his hands he disturbed gravel, rocks, debris, and he surfaced, breathing hard, turning and floating on his back, letting the water take his weight.

He gulped in air and stared up at the starry spinning sky and started laughing uncontrollably at the thin-lipped moon.

No doubt about it, I'm drunk, he told himself. *What would Virginia say?*

She'd say, *Al! Take a pill. Dull the pain!*

There was nothing that couldn't be cured by a pill, in Virginia's view. She had pills that rubbed the edges off that embarrassing inconvenience, human emotion.

And yet, who lived into old age without suffering?

The secret was not to think about things too hard.

He dived again, away from thoughts of his wife. He could feel something under his fingertips, but he had no way of knowing whether he was touching a gravestone or concrete.

This time when he surfaced, the chill gripped him and his teeth started chattering. The cold tightened like a band around his head. His arms were tired and he swam along the shoreline until he could feel the ground beneath his feet, the submerged path from the village. He waded out of the water, once more heavy, cumbersome, and saw his clothes next to the rock, piled up in the darkness. He trod carefully towards them, reaching out for his shirt with shaking hands to dry himself quickly, but once he'd reached for them, they dematerialised and there was nothing there but shadows.

He stumbled, sending sparks of pain to his shins. Crawling on his hands and knees he groped around the rock. *Get a grip, buddy. Think!*

The closeting, private darkness had become a wilderness.

Think! He tried to rub warmth into his hands.

Somewhere along the shoreline was the familiar path to the water: fact. He looked for the gap in the thick line of trees, and felt he was looking into a forest. In the dark everything was shades of black and grey.

Although the word 'think' had come easily, Al was unsure how to do it. He stood up and brushed the gravel off his hands, baffled, confused by illusion. Folding his arms over his chest for warmth, he thought about his options deeply for some minutes. He had sobered up, or at least he was sober enough to realise that he was wasting time looking for his lost things in the dark.

One day I'm going to look back on this and laugh.

That was a moot point, wasn't it?

His heart had stopped pounding now and he checked his pulse. A solitary beat. And after a pause, another. Slow and steady. His head was clear. He sat down and picked up a rock. He held the cold rock in his hand. It was flat enough on one side to use as a pillow. *Like Jacob.* His mind slipped to Jacob's ladder, the rope ladder they had used on the ship. If he climbed it, he would find himself in his bunk.

Reason returned.

There was no ladder, and no bed.

If he rested by the shore until daybreak, he would find his clothes easily. He was very tired and the stone was very comfortable.

He shut his eyes and heard ducks echoing across the water. He fell into a contented dream in which the sky turned pink and gold in the cleft of the hills and he was high up, coloured by the sunrise, looking down on himself, as pale as a grub on the grey rocks.

By force of will, eager to get going, he opened his eyes again and found it was still dark. He braced himself against a boulder and looked around.

Naked or not, he knew he had to get back.

He'd tell them he took a midnight dip. That's what holidaymakers did, no one could argue with that.

Al climbed up the bank, heading towards the trees that separated the road from the reservoir and hurried along the pavement, keeping close to the shadows. In a sudden flare of headlights he saw the lane.

The effort of moving purposefully helped him feel better and he kept to the grass in the centre of the track, trying to distribute his weight evenly, and when he smelled the dead badger he knew he was close to home.

The porch light was on but the bunkhouse was in darkness. He briefly patted his naked body down for the keys, without thinking. *Oh yeah*. The door was locked and he hobbled round the back of the bunkhouse and stood outside the darkened window. He knocked on the glass.

'Keep the noise down!' came a muffled voice from inside.

He waited for someone to investigate but the place fell quiet again. He hammered on the glass and the curtains moved. Greg was staring through the window, cupping his hands around his eyes, looking straight at Al without seeing him.

'Greg,' he called hoarsely.

'Al?' Greg opened the window, baffled. 'What's up, mate?'

'The door's locked. Can you let me in?'

'Shit, man. Er… yeah, okay. Hang on.'

Al went back round the bunkhouse to the front door where Greg was waiting with a robe for him to put on. He handed it to Al without a word.

'Thanks.' Al put it on quickly, wiped his feet on the doormat and followed him inside. 'I went for a swim and lost my clothes.'

Greg grunted, scratched his stubble and turned to go back to the bunk room. Something stopped him. 'Where did you swim? The reservoir?'

'Correct.'

'Crazy,' he said, shaking his head. 'And then you walked back? Why didn't you call someone?'

'My cell phone's in my shoe. I hid my stuff behind a rock, but rocks all look pretty similar in the dark.'

'Oh, right, yeah.' Greg scratched his jaw. 'You hid your stuff behind a rock. Why? So no one would find it?' He gave a brief grin. 'Come into the kitchen and warm up. I'll make you a hot drink.' He pulled out a chair, put the kettle on to boil and went off to the drying room. He came back with a pair of wool socks, still warm from the heating rail. 'Give me your feet.'

The socks were indescribably blissful. Al had never been so appreciative of warmth in his life.

They sat in silence, listening to the kettle coming to the boil.

The sound of a teaspoon ringing in a mug woke Al, music that he briefly incorporated into a dream…

'Al, don't fall asleep yet, mate,' Greg said. 'Here's your tea. You want to warm up a bit first.'

'Yes.'

'Can you hold the mug? Got it?'

'Yes.' The tea was hot, sweet and strong. When Al finished drinking it, Greg took the mug from him, rinsed it and put it upside down on the draining board.

Al waited for him to demand an account of his adventure, but Greg just looked at him, saying nothing, so in the end he volunteered the information.

'That memorial stone is down under the lake,' he said. 'You know. The gravestone that I'm looking for.'

'Oh,' Greg said with sudden understanding, 'so that's what you were doing down there in the dark.' He was silent for a moment, then he looked at Al again, eyebrows raised. 'Luminous gravestone, is it?'

Al ignored the sarcasm. 'I thought I could work out what the letters were by touch, you know?'

'Yes,' Greg said, 'fair enough, you probably could. How far out is it?'

'Not far at all. It's quite near the shore.' He glanced at the clock. It was very late. He got to his feet. 'Thanks.'

The bunk room rumbled with snores and smelled of alcohol fumes. Al got inside his cool sleeping bag and shut his eyes. Instantly he was back in the vast starry darkness.

I need to do it again, but properly this time, in daylight, with a snorkel at least.

He opened his eyes as the bunk above him dipped and creaked. 'Night, mate,' Greg said.

CHAPTER TWENTY-TWO

Al woke up early with a sense of urgency, thinking about the midnight swim and his clothes neatly stowed behind the rocks. He rolled out of his bunk, determined to return and recover them before some curious dog walker came across them and jumped to the wrong conclusion. He could imagine the fuss it would cause. He dressed without showering, grabbed his kitbag and headed down the lane.

In the morning light, mist lay over the water and the rocks were a uniform shade of grey, but as Al looked around he could see that his possessions had been scattered, splashes of colour flung far and wide. He picked up his jacket, clammy to the touch, and to his great relief he found that his keys and his glasses and his carved wooden spoon were still in his pocket. He gathered up the rest of his damp clothes, rolling them up carefully and packing them into his bag.

Mission accomplished, he sat down on a rock with a feeling of great relief, knowing he'd got off lightly after his impulsive behaviour of the night before. At the same time, he was deeply, agonisingly frustrated. His time here was running out and he had nothing to show for it. No Elin. No Quaker connections. No insight into Nancy Hank's origins. He tried to imagine what comment his son would have made about this precious, wasted trip. Knowing Charles, he would have been understanding.

You gave it your best shot.

Had he, though?

The lake was as sleek as foil under the clouds, and it was so beautiful that a wistful feeling of longing came over him. Despite a cool, fresh wind, the valley was warm and benevolent, as if it had had a personality change overnight.

If I can't find Elin, I can at least give the search for the grave marker another go, he thought as he headed back to the hostel.

Greg and Owen were up and in the dining room eating toast. They greeted him with grunts.

'Where would I get a snorkel from around here?' Al asked, dumping his bag by his feet and pouring himself a coffee.

'I've got a snorkel you can use,' Owen said. 'Are you going to the coast?'

'No. I'm going to see if I can find that grave marker in the reservoir. It's near a wall, and the water isn't too deep. I think with the right equipment I could find it.'

Owen stroked his beard and looked at him steadily. 'Makes sense,' he said. 'I'll come with you. I'm free until twelve. I'll bring my underwater sports cam, as a kind of extra pair of eyes.'

Although Al was intending to do it alone, the idea of having Owen's company was very appealing. 'I really appreciate that.'

'Yeah, well,' Owen said, 'I don't want you losing my snorkel. Hiding it behind a rock, or something.'

Al looked accusingly at Greg, and he grinned.

Sophie came through with sausages, bacon and eggs in serving dishes. She was wearing a white halterneck cotton dress, and she looked fresh and lovely.

'Help yourselves,' she said, putting the dishes down with a clatter.

Al looked tired, she noticed. His lips had a blue tinge to them and he was flushed, clasping his hands together on the table so that the veins on his knuckles showed blue.

Hangover. 'You were up early.' It was none of her business and she knew that.

'I've always been an early riser,' he replied.

'Me too,' she said cheerfully, 'I'm always ready to get started on a new day.'

Owen said to Sophie, 'Guess who came home naked after a swim last night?'

'Hey!' Al said.

Sophie looked at him in disbelief.

The colour was coming back into Al's lips and he put a couple of rashers on his plate.

'I wondered where you'd got to,' she said, keeping it light, but inside, she was genuinely panic-stricken. *Are you crazy? What the hell were you thinking? What if you'd drowned or died of hypothermia, and I'd have you on my conscience for the rest of my life because I was mean to you?*

'We're going back today, see if we can find that grave,' Owen said.

'You're not supposed to swim in the reservoir,' Sophie pointed out, folding her arms. She hated the self-righteous way she sounded, as if she hadn't broken rules in her time.

'How else am I going to find it?' Al asked.

'Good for you.' Greg sounded impressed. 'You're married, aren't you, Al?'

The question seemed to take him by surprise. 'Yes, I am.'

'And your wife didn't mind you coming all this way?'

'She suggested it.'

For some reason, this made them laugh.

Sophie shook her head in despair. She refilled the coffee jug and came to sit by the table.

Owen brushed the crumbs from his beard and got to his feet. 'I'm going to pick up the car from The Lamb, get the snorkels, and I'll be back in about thirty minutes.'

Greg got up, too. He was going to meet someone at the Pen y Gwryd Hotel, at the foot of Mount Snowdon. 'I'll see you at Arenig Fawr after two, Owen. We'll be back around six.'

'Greg is going to climb Everest next year,' Sophie said, wanting to keep him there a little longer.

'You are?' Al asked, sounding impressed.

'I feel it's my duty,' Greg said. 'Everest was named after a Welshman.'

Al was drinking his coffee and he choked violently. Greg patted his back until he recovered.

'Is there nothing that the Welsh haven't put their name to?' Al croaked, his eyes watering.

'No, mate, nothing,' Greg said seriously, clasping his shoulder. 'Good luck with your search.' He looked at Sophie and tilted his head.

He had a warm and direct way of looking at her with his brown eyes, amber with the light in them, that made Sophie's breath catch in her throat. She liked his face, the contours of it, and his nose: it didn't seem to be too big any more. She wanted to run her hand over his short hair. She imagined what it would feel like. 'Climb safely,' she said.

He looked surprised, and then he smiled. 'I will,' he said with a lilt to his voice, as if it were a given.

When he'd gone, she sat opposite Al.

They looked at each other and raised their eyebrows at the same time in a kind of 'so here we are' gesture.

'Are you sure about going back to the reservoir?' she asked him.

'Perfectly.'

He sounded brusque.

'Are we good, Al?'

'Sure.'

'Sorry about yesterday,' she said. 'I don't know why I got worked up.' She wasn't responsible for him, or his past. He'd been in the military, he was a fighting man, a naval man, and she wasn't his daughter, she wasn't his wife. She owed him nothing except the bed and board which he was paying for. She stirred her coffee, watching the light break up on the surface. She felt Greg was partly the reason she suddenly felt so rational and unburdened, even light-hearted. 'What would you do if you found her?'

No need to ask who 'her' was.

'First of all, I'd tell her how much she meant to me.'

Sophie laughed and rested her bare heels against the legs of her chair. 'And then what?'

'I don't know. That's as far as I've got.'

'You could take up where you left off and move in with her around here,' Sophie waved her hand, 'some cottage with a plot of land towards Bala and live happily ever after, gardening and walking the dog.'

'In the evenings, we'd go to The Lamb and tell our life stories to anyone who'd listen, in return for a Bloody Mary.'

'And we'd buy you one to keep you quiet, it would become a tradition,' she said with a smile, feeling for her lost shoes with her dusty feet. When she looked up she saw that he was pinching the bridge of his nose. 'I'm so sorry,' she said, aghast that she'd upset him. 'I didn't mean—'

Al waved his hand impatiently. 'I know. It's just that I'd give anything to talk to her one last time.'

He looked at the bacon on his plate and put his cutlery to one side. 'I'd better have a doggy bag. I never like to swim on a full stomach.'

He was as nervous as she was, Sophie thought.

Al carried the wetsuits down to the water, full of trepidation. The alcohol he'd drunk last night had given him a hefty dose of Dutch courage.

This morning it had all worn off.

People thought if a guy had been in the navy he must be used to water, but the one thing that the crew aimed to do was to keep themselves out of it. Yachtsmen who can swim are more likely to drown than non-swimmers, because they have a go at saving themselves, whereas the non-swimmers stay close to the boat and wait to be rescued out of necessity. If you have the misfortune to end up in the ocean, it's still, quite often, a choice between dying fast or dying slow. It's not something he had ever had to put to the test, and he was grateful for that, even now.

A ship felt safe, until it didn't, because there was nowhere to hide, nowhere to escape. When he retired, Virginia had arranged a Caribbean cruise as a surprise, thinking he would enjoy going to sea for pleasure rather than business, and he had a bad feeling about it. Made her cancel. The truth was, he didn't even like taking a bath – give him a shower any day.

He struggled into the wetsuit while Owen checked his video camera. He wondered how the hell he'd got into this situation at eighty-five years of age. He should be taking it easy, lying back in a La-Z-Boy with his feet up. He wondered if he should ring Virginia to explain everything, in case it was the last call he ever made. Give her a chance to talk him out of it.

Owen zipped him up and handed him the mask; he spat in it, not easy with a dry mouth, and swirled it around in the water. He put it on and Owen handed him the swim fins and then the snorkel.

There was no going back now.

'Ready? Are you okay to follow me?' he asked Owen.

'Yes.'

Despite the sun, and despite the goggles, they were kicking up mud and the water was murky. For fifteen minutes or so, it was like being very short-sighted. Mostly what he could see was a lot of rubble and very little that was recognisable.

Owen surfaced, and they trod water. 'The visibility's not good.'

'This area feels right to me,' Al said. He didn't know why. A feeling is all it was, an instinct, some deep-rooted recognition.

They were in shallower water now, swimming in water as thick as turkey gravy. He swam over something that caught his eye in the glow of the sun. Beneath the rippling, dappled water he noticed the silt outlining the objects on which it rested. An oval white stone caught his attention and the green weed growing on its smooth surface gave it a phosphorescent glow in the mud.

Al floated over it, fascinated, because it was the kind of flat sun-bleached pebble you would find on a beach, pure, perfect, worn smooth by the tide.

On his next approach he widened the search for the memorial stone he'd been looking for, but it was impossible to make it out through the silt.

He heard Owen call him and he lifted his head and took the snorkel out of his mouth.

'What's up?'

'We'd better pack up, mate. We've given it a fair go, and I'm going rock climbing with Greg this afternoon up Arenig Fawr.'

'Ten more minutes,' Al said.

'What difference is ten minutes going to make? We can't see a thing. It's like swimming blind.'

'I'm going to find it.' But even as Al said it, he knew he was only going to come across it by chance, by sheer good luck. He knew that the feeling he had was not to be trusted, it was the same as the way he'd felt certain he was going to come across Elin in the village. Look where that had got him.

Owen was already standing on the shore, wiping down his camera, his wetsuit peeled down to his waist, his red dragon tattoo bright on his freckled arm.

Reluctantly, Al dragged himself out of the water. They didn't say much to each other, just packed away in silence. The mission had been a total failure. It was not their fault. Owen was right, they'd given it a fair go.

He didn't know what more he could do.

CHAPTER TWENTY-THREE

After Al and Owen left for the reservoir, Sophie cleared up and phoned her mother to see if she was free to meet for lunch.

'Why?' Mary asked suspiciously. 'Are you in some sort of financial trouble?'

'No.'

'Pregnant?'

'Mum! Steady on! I just thought we could have a chat.' That sounded unlikely, so she gave up the pretence. 'If you must know, I want to talk to you about Jane and Eric. I've sort of fallen out with them.'

'Hah! Have you really?' Mary asked eagerly, sounding delighted. She'd never forgiven them for luring Sophie back to Wales, fifty miles away. 'Where shall we meet?'

'The Grosvenor Hotel, Pulford?' Sophie loved its glamour: the velvet chairs, the fairy lights in the trees, the winding staircase. It held plenty of happy memories for her, it was a beautiful setting for a serious talk, and the food was good if everything else went wrong. 'I'll see you at one o'clock.'

Mary and Eric didn't have a particularly close sibling relationship. There was a big age gap between them, so by the time Mary got to an interesting age, Eric had already started working.

They had absolutely no values in common, not in outlook, politics or attitude. But they did, unfortunately, look very alike. Mary was vivid, striking, but there was something about her features that despite carefully applied make-up and lipstick made her look, in a cruel light, like Eric in drag.

Sophie changed out of the white halterneck, worn for Greg, into a teal-blue silk Nicole Farhi shirt dress belonging to her previous life, the life her mother approved of.

The drive to Chester took a little over an hour.

Her mother was waiting for her on a striped, velvet chaise longue in the foyer, below a curving staircase.

'Sophie!' Mary greeted her daughter energetically, looking her up and down, taking in her dress. 'Nice.'

'Nicole Farhi. You look great!' *Kiss, kiss.*

Mary was wearing a red shift dress, and she was carrying a pale grey wrap over her arm – the air conditioning at the Grosvenor Pulford was extremely efficient.

She looked as vivid and striking as Snow White's wicked stepmother. Her hair was black and freshly blow-dried. She was attractive, literally – people were drawn to her – and it was a family joke that even on their holidays abroad she was bound to bump into someone from Wales who knew her from somewhere. She would talk to anyone, would Mary.

Mary had left Capel Celyn in her teens. If it hadn't been for the drowning, she might not have got away from her parents so easily, but as everyone was in a state of depressed trauma anyway, her leaving home for London hardly made a ripple.

She became a nanny to the three children of the Loveridge family in Hampstead. She replaced her Welsh accent with an English one, met playwrights and poets, and eventually met and fell in love with Howard at an auction in Christie's and moved with him to Chester, in the north. She was still in touch with the Loveridges to this day. That, in Mary's view, was the definition of progress.

However, even though she had shaken off the accent, she hadn't managed to shake off the fervent Welsh curiosity about the human condition.

They went into the dining room and the waiter showed them to a table. They sat. Sophie didn't even put her handbag down because she knew what was coming next. Mary made a point of never sitting at the first table she was shown. She always moved twice before she was happy. So she waited for her mother to get up and they sat at a different table, nearer the window, for all of two minutes.

'The table's a bit small, don't you think? What about that one over there?'

'Fine with me,' Sophie said. Generally, in restaurants, she was just happy to get a table at all.

'Perfect,' Mary said at table number three, looking around, fully satisfied beneath a bower of twinkling lights. She snuggled into her wrap which was a fluffy, creamy grey and draped it around her shoulders – 'the air conditioning, you know'. The waiter was back. 'Let's order first and then you can tell me all about it.'

'I'm going to have a glass of wine, a small one.'

'Me too. And steak and salad. Medium rare.'

'Same.'

'So, what's Jane up to?'

Sophie couldn't take her eyes off her mother's wrap. 'She's got very proficient at spinning,' she said. 'She can spin and watch television at the same time.'

'To be fair, she could do with getting some of that weight off. Where's the class? Bala?'

'Not cycling spinning – spinning thread with a spinning wheel.'

'No!' Mary's eyes widened. 'She's got a spinning wheel?'

'Antique mahogany,' Sophie said.

'She's got a spinning wheel,' Mary repeated, blinking. 'I've heard it all, now.'

'She's using it to make yarn out of dog hair. It's got all sorts of medicinal properties. It cures rheumatism.'

'Whose dogs?'

'Anyone's. She does it on commission. She's knitting a hat for Hywel for the winter from Shep.'

'Shep's never still alive!'

'No, this is young Shep. His fur is just right, not too short or too coarse. She can judge a good dog coat from metres away. Their guest room is full of bags of dog hair.'

Mary shuddered. 'Jane's always been unconventional,' she said. 'Obviously, I'm glad she's got a hobby,' she added generously after a pause. She stroked her wrap as if it was a comfort blanket.

'I love your wrap,' Sophie said.

'Jane gave it to me for my birthday.' Mary looked at it and made a face, as if she was seeing it for the first time. She whisked it off her shoulders and sniffed it. 'It doesn't smell of dog, does it?' she asked, handing it to Sophie.

Sophie buried her face in it and handed it back. 'No. Alpaca,' she said confidently. *Why ruin something lovely?*

'I was thinking alpaca, too.' Mary stroked it. 'Cosy,' she said.

When the wine came, along with warm bread rolls, Mary dispensed with the small talk, folded her arms on the table and said, 'Now, what's all this about, you falling out with Eric and Jane?'

'This guy has come to stay. He's American. Ex-US Navy.'

Mary brightened. 'Is he your boyfriend?'

'Steady! He's in his eighties.'

'Why on earth is he staying in a youth hostel?'

'Bunkhouse. Nostalgia, mostly. He stayed with Jane and Eric before the dam was built, when Mountain Ash was a guest house.'

'Did he?' Mary's sharp eyes took on a new focus.

'His name's Al Locke.'

Mary twirled the stem of her glass. 'You know, I do remember an American coming to Capel Celyn when I was young. Caused quite a stir, he did, in his uniform, and for the week he was around we were all in love with him, he was a good-looking lad. He was dating Elin Jenkins from the farm.'

'That's the guy!'

Mary's eyes widened. 'What's he come back for? Has he been looking for her?'

Sophie thought about the way he'd arrived, showered, got changed and gone straight out again. There was something about the memory that moved her to pity every time. 'Yes, but he's also looking for Abraham Lincoln's great-great-great grandmother.'

'Really? Is she still alive?'

'Ha ha, hilarious.'

'Who was she?'

Sophie shrugged. 'No idea. He's forgotten her name.'

Mary took a deep, happy breath and said, 'I wonder if he'll remember me?'

'He's sure to. You haven't changed a bit.'

Mary looked at Sophie sternly from under her black eyebrows. 'Now you're just being silly,' she said. 'So, what was the row about?'

Sophie broke off another piece of bread. 'They were annoyed because I was asking about Elin. Jane says they lost touch years ago and that's that. She won't talk about it. They weren't even in The Lamb last night.'

'Hmm. They could do with a night off for the sake of their livers.' Mary leant forward and tapped her daughter's hand consolingly. 'To be honest, Sophie, it doesn't surprise me – they've always had a self-righteous side to them. I'm amazed you haven't seen it before.'

'Anyway, I thought you might know what happened to Elin in the end. Any ideas? Al's only here for a few more days.'

Mary played with the stem of her glass. 'Why does he want to find her now?'

'He's worried he might not have long left.'

'Has his wife died?'

'No.'

'Oh. That's usually the reason, isn't it?' Mary looked at Sophie from under her dark eyebrows. 'I'd left home by the time of the flooding, to live in London, so I had my own life to lead, but I'll tell you what my mother told me – with some astonishment, mind, as she was a lively little thing – she said that Elin Jenkins saw the light.'

'What do you mean? Which light?'

'Sophie, you're a heathen! She found God.' There was no trace of Mary's English accent now – she was thoroughly Welsh again.

Sophie sat back in her chair, took a deep breath and let it out slowly. 'Are you saying she joined a convent? Became a nun?'

'Where did you get that from? She didn't become a nun, but she did become deeply religious and retreated from the world, which was a surprising turnaround, because she used to be a handful when she was young.'

'Yeah. That's what Eric said.'

Just then, the waiter came with the steaks and salads; they made appreciative noises and admired their plates.

Mary started to eat at once, but Sophie was still thinking things over. 'Do you think she just wanted to put love behind her?'

'What, darling? Oh! I've no idea. Mustard?'

'No thanks.'

'You have to remember that it was a terrible time for Celyn. I think that had a bearing on it.' Mary chewed rhythmically, her eyes distant. She shrugged.

Sophie persevered. 'Elin must have gone back home, back to the farm, I suppose, when it didn't work out with Al.'

'Well no, I don't think she could go home. She had no home to go to, did she? Once the bill was passed to flood the valley, the clearances started quite soon after that. The whole thing was heartbreaking for our families. Even though it was clear Celyn had lost the struggle, demonstrations continued and then there was the bombing, and jail sentences, the whole thing got nasty. There was a lot of anger over it. Three lads blew up the power source at the dam.' She gazed around the room, at the twinkling lights, the beauty. 'Great depths of emotion have a tendency to turn people into extremists. How is your steak?'

'Wonderful.'

'I hope that's answered your question,' Mary said sweetly. 'What was it again?'

'I wanted to know why Eric and Jane lost touch with Elin.'

'Oh, yes. I think the last straw was when Eric heard Elin had become a Quaker. It touched a nerve with him; for some reason, he seemed to think it was a slight against him personally, you know what he's like. It's always about him.'

CHAPTER TWENTY-FOUR

When Sophie got back from Chester, she found Al in the dining room hunched over his laptop with his glasses perched on the tip of his nose and a notebook open on the table, studious as a schoolboy.

'Hi, Al. How did it go?'

He looked up at her gravely. 'Couldn't see a thing. It was a waste of time.'

'I'm sorry. It was worth a try though, wasn't it?' Sophie hooked her bag on the back of the chair, with her own good news to tell him. 'Guess what, I've just had lunch with my mother and she…' suddenly, it didn't seem like such a good idea to get his hopes up about the Quaker connection just yet, when it might not come to anything and he would be disappointed again, '…she remembers you.'

He laughed. 'I remember her, too – she was a moody adolescent last time I saw her, with those strong family characteristics, the widow's peak, the stubbornness. Dominant genes.' He added quickly, 'I'm sure she's charming now.'

'Yeah. She can be.'

'Sophie, have you ever heard of a place called Llanfor?'

'What? Oh – Llanfor, yeah, that's not far from here. Why, what's there?'

'A very old parish church. I thought it might be worth looking at some graves to see if I recognise any of the family names.'

'Let's do it.'

*

That afternoon they headed to St Deiniol's Church at Llanfor, an ancient building constructed of rubble and sandstone. Raised up from the road and visible from a distance, it carried a dignified air of history and age. A row of stone houses abutted the churchyard wall, and stone cottages clustered in the lanes around it. A couple of gleaming cars were parked up in front of it, but the place was silent; no barking dogs, no birdsong, no living thing to be seen. They climbed the steps to the lychgate and surveyed the solitude of the churchyard. In the sunlight, the neat grass was luminous green.

'Where do we start?' Sophie asked.

'As with everything else in this life, there seems to be a fashion in headstone construction,' Al said, kicking his way through the soft grass.

Some of the tombs were boxlike, enclosed on all sides. Worryingly, to Sophie's mind, one of these boxes had split open as if it was about to topple apart and reveal its contents. She gave it a wide berth. But behind the church, two of these tombs had been placed side-by-side, with a discreet gap of a few inches between them, like twin beds pushed together. A bush was rudely growing in the gap between them like a determined chaperone, filtering sunlight and flickering shadows over the worn Welsh inscriptions.

They walked around, hands in their pockets, taking their time to stop and read the names blurred by the mould of seasons and speckled with bird droppings.

Sophie was obsessively drawn to the ages of the people interred: seventeen, three, fifty-four. There were clusters of deaths around the late nineteenth century, too late for the plague and too early for Spanish flu.

Al straightened up from reading an inscription and rubbed his back with his fists. He'd obviously been doing the same thing. He looked up at the relentless blue of the sky. 'Thirty-five,' he said. 'My mother died at the age of thirty-five.'

'Yeah? That's young.'

Al's face was tight with the memory. 'Let me show you something.' He reached into his pocket and handed her a carved, wooden object. 'Do you know what it is?'

'Of course I do,' Sophie said, studying it carefully. 'It's a Welsh love spoon.' The carving in the wood was smooth and worn, polished to a mellow patina by hands through the generations, a symbol of love and commitment. 'Is it yours?'

'Yes. It belonged to my mother. She was given it by her uncle, a collector. He told her it belonged to the Lincolns, and it meant a lot to her, especially in her last days. She was interested in what shaped Lincoln as a person, and my parents brought me up with those values of honesty and tolerance.' He rubbed the edge of his jaw ruefully. 'Can't say I've always lived up to them.'

'Oh, Al. How old were you when she died?'

'Nine. I was nine.'

'That's so young. The same age as Lincoln, right?'

'Yes.' Al turned his gaze on Sophie. He took the carved spoon back from her and tucked it away in his pocket. 'It didn't do Lincoln any harm.'

'How could it not have?' she asked incredulously.

Al walked to the perimeter of the churchyard where the grass in the margins was overgrown. He stopped suddenly and tucked his trousers into his socks.

'Snakes?'

'Ticks.'

Hidden in the long grass so well that he almost tripped over it was a rough semi-circular stone, the shape of a thumbnail, sticking out of the ground.

Cautiously but reverently, Al knelt and parted the yellow grass.

Sophie went to look at the letters; they were carved deeply enough by the stonemason to be perfectly legible: *Evan Thomas o Gyrmchwilfod 1781.*

'Mean anything to you?'

'Nope. Nothing.'

Sophie kicked around in the grass to look for other hidden treasures, and sure enough she found two similar grave markers, too worn to decipher.

They did a final circuit, but they didn't come across anything of relevance. The story about Al's mother had disturbed them both in their own ways. Sophie felt caught up in his sadness. She lay down on the warm grass and stared at the sky. A small white cloud stayed perfectly still above her while she turned slowly on the earth beneath.

Al sat down too.

She asked him the one question that had been bugging her. 'Why now, Al?'

'Why now? It's simple, really. It's a trip my wife and I have been thinking about taking for years.' He rubbed his hand over his jaw. 'And then, for my eighty-fifth birthday, my son, Charles, gave me two airline tickets. Gave them to me in a plain envelope, two return flights to Liverpool. He looked me in the eye and he was kind of lit up with passion. "Dad," he said, "just do it".'

Al took a deep breath and let it out slowly. He glanced at Sophie and smiled. 'It was the best gift! All those years we'd talked about it. So Virginia and I organised our Grand Tour, thanks to Charles.' His smile faded. 'A month later he died in the gym, of an aneurysm. Didn't expect it. He was coming up to fifty, but he was the fittest guy I ever knew. He looked after himself.'

'Oh, Al.'

He was silent for a few long moments against the distant background drone of bees. 'Nothing prepares you for the isolation of grief. Sorrow used to dwell in the deepest part of me, but after

Charles went, it lay just below the surface, the kind of pain that makes you into an animal, makes you want to hide away, alone. Virginia wanted us to cancel. But he'd given me the tickets and he'd said, "Just do it," as if it was important to him in the same way it was important to me. And I had the feeling that if I could come back here, I could, I don't know… reset my life, I guess. Make sense of it.'

Sophie plucked a blade of grass and chewed the sweet root. 'Yes,' she said. 'I know what that's like.'

Al shook his head hopelessly. 'But now that I'm here, I don't know how to unravel my feelings any more, not for Elin, for the Quaker grave, for the relic of my mother's, for Charles and my wife. All of it is knotted together in one big mess. It feels like a job I've left unfinished.' He gave her a crooked grin.

His eyes were very blue, and very sad.

'This is my last deployment,' he said.

Back at Mountain Ash, Sophie went to sit at her desk. She only had one lead to go on, so she started with the obvious: Quakers in North Wales. There were forty locations that had regular meetings, way more than she'd expected, including Llandudno, Dolobran, Bala, Colwyn Bay, Ruthin, Bangor, Machynlleth, Wrexham, and all across South Wales and the Southern Marches. She started to scroll down them, checking the names and contact details, knowing at the back of her mind that if Elin was still alive, she could be anywhere in the world.

When she came across the name Elin Jenkins at a meeting house a couple of miles outside the market town of Llangollen, she almost missed it – as Sophie knew from Google, Elin Jenkins was a fairly common name. She felt belatedly excited, and there was a meeting the following day, Sunday, at ten. She sat back and wondered whether to phone her in advance, or not to phone her.

Was it better to surprise her? It seemed the kind of thing that she should do in person, where she could see her expression and adjust her approach as she went along.

Obviously, Elin hadn't got married – Sophie considered the idea she'd married someone else called Jenkins, but it was a bit of a stretch.

Early evening, Al went outside into the fresh air.

Sophie clicked on her home screen and joined him in the clear evening light. She stretched out her arms to the blue sky to ease the tightness in her shoulders.

Al was looking towards the mountains, shielding his eyes from the sun.

He looked drained of enthusiasm, as though the anti-climax of being disappointed had taken away his purpose.

At that moment, Sophie nearly told Al that she had found Elin – or at least, that she might actually know where to find her, but something stopped her. She thought about it from Elin's point of view.

She didn't know what the other woman's circumstances were. Maybe Elin would think it was quite a stalkerish act to come all the way from Philadelphia to find a distant ex-girlfriend. Maybe she wouldn't want to see him. For both their sakes, it was best to warn Elin in advance, and then, all being well, they could surprise Al with the good news.

Al reached out to the hills with both hands, as if he could touch them. 'Somewhere out there, Greg is climbing a rock face.'

'Or descending it. He'll be on his way down by now.'

'He's one of the good guys,' Al said, turning to face her. He rolled his sleeves up his forearms. 'He thinks a lot of you.'

'Yes,' she said, non-committally.

'You're going to tell me it's none of my business, aren't you?'

'No.' Sophie laughed. 'I agree with you, actually. He is one of the good guys.'

'Do you mind me asking, have you ever been married?'

'No to both questions.' She walked over to the cold fire pit and kicked a half-blackened log back into the centre, feeling hideously embarrassed without really knowing why. 'I don't even know if I've ever been in love. I thought I was once, but looking back, I'm not sure. I never looked too hard at the relationship. It's better that way, if you don't look too hard at things.'

Recognising her discomfort, Al said, 'I didn't mean to pry.'

'It's fine. Greg – yes, he's a nice guy. We speak the same language, but that's all.' She said it instinctively and it sounded a cliché, but what she meant was that they communicated in the same way and it attracted them to each other.

She appreciated Greg for bringing up the idea of them climbing together, and then for not trying to talk her into it. He'd put the idea out there for her to take up or leave, whichever she preferred. He didn't keep on about things – he was happy to let the conversation drop and for her to pick up on it, or not, either way. He was easy to be with and he didn't make her feel he was judging her in any way. He didn't mention how she looked, he didn't offer her advice, he didn't show her how to do things, all things she found annoying in a relationship.

That wasn't to say that the language they used was all one-sided.

When she spoke to him, she never made him commit to dates he was staying, and she'd never asked him about his previous relationships, or how long he would carry on living his free and easy life for, or whether he had any plans for the future. And the thing that interested her intellectually was that it didn't matter that she hardly knew anything about him. When he turned up, she was pleased to see him, he gave her a sweet jolt of energy, and the day took on an effervescent multisensory sparkle, like snow falling in sunshine.

And when Greg left, that was okay too. She'd never felt any angst about it because she knew he would come back. So what seemed on the surface like a lack of commitment on both their parts was actually founded on their own unique version of reliability.

Al was looking at his watch. 'Owen said he was going to join Greg this afternoon on Arenig, to do some bouldering,'

'Really? They've probably stopped for a drink on the way back. I'll start on the supper. I can always reheat it for them.'

'Can't you call him?' Al said, looking at his watch again, visibly concerned.

Sophie scooped her hair away from her face and considered it. 'It wouldn't feel right,' she said. 'He comes and goes as he wants. Anyway, if there's a problem, they'll call us.'

'But isn't it part of courtship, to ask questions about each other?'

He looked so earnest that Sophie laughed out loud. 'Courtship!' she exclaimed with a snort and added, 'Al! We're not *courting*. Where did you get that idea? He's a guest.'

'A guest.' Al looked faintly disgruntled. 'I suppose you think of me as a guest too, do you?'

'Well yes.' Sophie stopped herself from adding *because you are*. 'I mean – it's a good thing! My happiest times are when the place is quiet and everyone is safely tucked up in bed, all their energy going into sleep, and I'm the one who watches over them, who locks up, and switches out the main lights. I love that feeling. I get up early too, for the same reason. The sun comes through the curtains, and I open up again and listen to the birds and look out to see which of its many faces the hill is showing. And the guests come into the dining room and I'm waiting for them, I can look after them, they're mine while they're here.'

Al shrugged.

She had the feeling she'd offended him in some way.

'Each to his own, I guess,' he said with a frown.

After supper, Sophie made a fire and they sat and stared into the flames, a beacon in the thick dark. They weren't talking much because there was only one thought in both their minds now. Al's concern was rubbing off on her, but she knew that it was easy to meet up with people and have a change of plan, without thinking much of it. If there was a serious problem, Greg would do the sensible thing and call mountain rescue. In conclusion: there wasn't a serious problem.

When they got bored of staring at the fire, they went to The Lamb.

Dai greeted them and automatically made Al a Bloody Mary.

'Have Greg and Owen been in?' Sophie asked him.

'Haven't seen them,' Dai said.

'Any sign of Eric and Jane?'

He growled. 'Don't talk to me about Eric and Jane! They're busy with some moneymaking scheme. Like two kids they are, all secretive and bursting to tell, and giving each other little nudges and conspiratorial winks. Very annoying.'

While this was intriguing, Dai couldn't shed any more light on it. Sophie and Al found they couldn't settle at The Lamb either, so after their drink they headed back again and Greg's car still wasn't there. She unlocked the door and felt the emptiness of the place echoing around them.

Al got himself a glass of water, and she went back outside and stood listening for the sound of his car with her hands on her hips.

Rustlings, quiverings, whispering of leaves. There was a faint red glow amongst the grey ash in the fire pit and she kicked a log over in a shower of sparks. She could feel the heat on her face, and the cool of the night on her back. She sat on one of the railway sleepers and looked across at the mountains, black against the navy sky. *Where were they?*

She hadn't appreciated Greg enough, that was the problem. She should have gone climbing with him while she had the chance. Her solar plexus was tight from tension. *He'll be fine*, she thought.

A few moments later, Al came back out. He sighed deeply and sat down in silence, his hands on his knees, staring at the fire.

When his eyes met hers, she knew what he was thinking.

We should do something.

'Yes, okay.' She took her phone out of her pocket and called Greg's number, but it went straight to voicemail. 'Hi, Greg, it's Sophie and Al here, if you get this message let us know if you're okay.'

She put her phone back in her pocket and went over to the wood store, unhooked the canvas from the woodpile and threw a couple more logs on the fire. Grey smoke billowed and curled around them. 'I used to go into the hills with Eric in the summer holidays, to check on Bert's sheep, and we'd come down as it was getting dark, and I was usually tired and cold, and a sprinkling of lights would appear in the distance and I got a lot of comfort knowing that one of them was ours. I loved that feeling.'

'Sounds good.' Al was shifting his weight from the balls of his feet to his heels, his shadow dodging behind him. He scratched the back of his neck and sat down again.

She knew how he felt – it was hard to keep still. 'Al, what would you eat now, if you could eat anything at all?'

He thought about it for a moment. 'Rice pudding, with brown sugar on top, and a sprinkling of nutmeg, the way Jane used to make it. Cooked long enough for the rice to get sticky, so you can eat it cold with a fork if you want to.'

'With brown sugar almost turned to caramel.' She laughed.

'I once had porridge with a jug of cream and a jug of whisky. You ever had that? It's a good way to start the day. My wife prefers a Bucks Fizz, which these days is her breakfast drink of choice. Certainly less fattening than cream and whisky. Is that traditional here, to have whisky on your porridge for breakfast?'

'I don't think so, I've never heard of it, but we can have it tomorrow,' Sophie said, as if tomorrow was going to be another ordinary day, something they could take for granted. She looked at her phone to see what the time was. In the blue glow, she could see that it was almost midnight. It had been fully dark for two hours. An owl hooted over the lake and the sound echoed across the water. 'Imagine doing this all the time, worrying about someone you love.'

'You always worry when you love someone,' Al said. He sounded depressed about it.

Sophie looked at him, because there was something heartfelt in the way he said it. 'Do you worry about your wife?'

'Yes. We've grown apart since Charles died. She feels it, too. She's decided to redecorate the basement while I'm away. She wants to paint over the Lincoln family tree.'

Sophie looked from the flames to Al, eyebrows raised. 'Keen on decorating, is she?'

Al threw his head back and laughed out loud. 'You sound just like Greg.'

'Mmm.' She laughed too, knowing that they were passing time, talking for the sake of it, because it was better than sitting in silence, but now they'd stopped talking and the silence was back again.

She looked across at the black hulk of Arenig Fawr against the navy sky. Something caught her eye, and as her focus adjusted, she blocked out the glare of the fire with her hand. She could see something moving, a small dot of white, a head torch bobbing in the dark, traversing the mountain.

Standing up to get a better look, she pointed it out to Al. 'See that light, Al? Kind of, at one o'clock? And look, there's another one behind it, I can see them both now!'

Al pressed his hands against his thighs stifling a groan and got slowly to his feet. He looked in the direction Sophie was pointing, and after a few moments he said, 'Yeah, I see it. What the hell are they doing up there in the dark?'

She followed their painfully slow progress for a few minutes, and then lost sight of them. 'I can't see anything now, can you?'

'Nope. Maybe they're hunkering down for the night.'

'Why would they do that?' Sophie went back to the old argument she was having with herself. 'If they need help, they'll ask for it.' Unless they couldn't. Or they were determined to get down under their own steam. It would be a major thing to Greg to ask for help, a last resort. 'They're heading in the right direction, anyway. There's no reason we have to stand here and wait for them, Al. We'll hear them come in. They'll get here when they get here.'

But despite that, neither of them moved.

Sophie couldn't take her eyes off the mountain. She was looking for those two head torches, smudges of light, waiting for them to reappear in the dark. She knew they wouldn't go to bed, the same way she knew they weren't going to have a whisky breakfast. Minutes passed and then suddenly Al pointed, 'There they are! To the right, you see them?'

Sophie focused on them with renewed relief.

Suddenly, one of the white lights dropped away from the other, falling vertically down the hill at speed.

Sophie let out a yelp and she and Al looked at each other sharply, wide-eyed with shock.

'Al, did you see that?'

'Yes,' he said curtly.

She shivered, and it felt like all this had happened before, as if it was a visceral experience that she had a deep knowledge of. It wasn't panic or fear, it was a hard, cold feeling, of bleakness, of acceptance. 'Do you fancy coming with me for a drive?'

He nodded. 'Let's go.'

Sophie went inside to get the keys, and she locked up and they got into the car.

They drove down the road, parallel to the reservoir, and took a left turn along the narrow lane where she guessed they would park. Sure enough, her headlights picked out Greg's four-wheel drive parked up on the side of the track. She pulled up alongside it and took a flashlight out of the boot of the car and shone the cone of light up at Arenig Fawr.

'Hey!' Al shouted into the darkness. 'Greg! Owen!'

One of the head torches reappeared near the ruins of Amnodd-wen, and Greg called back to them out of the darkness from some distance, 'We're okay! Stay where you are!'

The rush of relief at hearing his voice made her light-headed.

'What was that?' Al asked.

'Greg. He said stay where we are.'

They were silent for a moment. 'Is Owen with him?'

'Yes, they're okay. It's a bit boggy where they are now, but they're not that far from the quarry. From there, they just have to follow the track down.' Standing close to Al, she saw two shapes coming out of the darkness, and the light of one man flashing behind the other showed him as being impossibly square, monstrous, unfamiliar.

'Is that them?'

'Could you give me a hand?' Greg sounded close to exhaustion.

She realised that he was carrying Owen's backpack as well as his own, and Owen was groaning in pain.

They hurried up to help them the final few yards to the car park.

'Owen's dislocated his shoulder,' Greg said as they relieved him of the backpacks. 'I'm going to take him to A&E. He's in a lot of pain.'

Owen groaned weakly, nursing his arm. 'I so am.'

'Which hospital? You're going to drive him to Wrexham now?' Sophie asked, blinking against the brightness of the lamp. 'Switch that off, will you?'

He did, and they were once again lost in the darkness, but as her eyes adjusted she saw the angle of his jaw, the curve of his cheek.

'What happened?' Al asked.

'I slid on loose ground and kind of lost my head torch.'

'We saw it fall. It was a heart-stopper, I can tell you. I mean, why were you climbing so late?'

'It took longer than we thought, and my phone went dead on me. Sorry, guys.'

Greg opened the boot and she helped him put the bags in. In the little glow of the boot light his skin was tight, and his eyes were weary.

He looked pretty awful and it distressed her. She wanted to kiss him better. 'Do you want me to drive? We'll go back to Mountain Ash together and drop your car off. I can get the four of us in mine easily.'

He hesitated long enough for her to know he was tempted. 'You've got better things to do than hang around A&E all night. You've got a business to run.'

'Can you stop the talking?' Owen said through gritted teeth, leaning on the car. 'I just need my shoulder sorting out and I don't care who does it.'

'Greg, you're tired.'

'And you've been drinking.'

'Yeah.' She'd forgotten about that. 'We went to the pub.'

'I mean – what's the point of taking the risk? In twenty minutes you could be in bed. We brought this on ourselves. We're not your responsibility.'

This was exactly what she'd been saying to Al. 'Fine,' she said, but it hurt, and for a moment she wanted to argue. She felt irrationally annoyed. 'Okay, let's go, Al.' They got into the car. The night felt strange, unearthly; Sophie knew it was a combination of tiredness and stress. Now that she wasn't going to drive to

Wrexham, she felt drained of energy and desperate for bed. 'See?' she said to Al irritably, 'I told you they didn't need us.'

'That's what you're angry about, that they didn't need us?'

She reversed and drove back along the track the way they'd come. Behind her, Greg reversed too, and the light from his headlights washed across them.

'It's great they're all right,' Al said. 'Relatively speaking. That's a blessing, right?'

'Yeah.'

'This hospital they're going to, is it far?'

'About forty miles.'

'One way?'

'Yes.'

'You wanted to go with him,' Al said.

'And he didn't want me to. See? I told you!'

'He was thinking of you.'

'And I was thinking of him.'

'He knows that,' Al said. 'And like he said, you've got a business to run. It's important to you.'

He's important to me, Sophie thought. *And it's your fault*, she wanted to say.

The journey back seemed longer than she remembered, and the road unfamiliar, even though she'd driven along it countless times.

When they got back to the hostel, the fire had died down again, the embers glowing red, woodsmoke billowing around them. They stood by it in silence.

It was as if they'd been away for a long time and come back different people.

'Thanks for coming with me tonight,' she said to Al. 'It's not much of a holiday for you, is it?'

'It never was a holiday,' he said.

'Shall we have that nightcap now? To help us sleep.'

Al looked at her steadily and nodded.

Sophie went to the bar and poured them a measure of Scotch each.

'Bottoms up,' Al said. 'You know, watching that flashlight fall, it didn't look like it would be a happy ending.'

The weight of watching it fall suddenly lifted off her. She hadn't realised how heavy it was and she felt a sudden euphoria. 'I do like a happy ending,' she said.

*

Al didn't hear the boys come in. He had his earplugs in and he slept right through.

When he woke up in the morning, Greg's arm was dangling down in his field of vision, his fingers curved towards his palm.

Across the room, Owen was propped up on pillows in the bottom bunk, lying on his back.

His breath caught in his throat and he woke up and turned his head and looked at Al. 'Are you awake, Al?'

'Yes. How are you feeling?'

'Not too bad,' he said softly. 'Sorry about last night, mate, about the cursing and things. It hurt like hell, but once they got it back into place, I was fine. Good as new.'

Al guessed they had given him painkillers. 'You're entirely forgiven,' he said. 'Have they strapped you up?'

'I've got a sling. The doc thinks it shouldn't come back out but this guy who plays rugby, his used to come out all the time. It was a standing joke. Poor sod.' He closed his eyes and Al did, too.

He decided he would lie-in a bit longer, but then Owen said, 'The rugby guy gave up playing in the end. I don't know how I'm going to work, though. Seren is going to kill me.' He stared up at the bunk above him. 'Sophie didn't look too happy last night, either.'

'She thought…' Al began, but he changed his mind. He thought about her saying that the happiest times are when everyone is tucked in bed, safe and warm, and he wondered if that was the right reason to keep this place running.

As Greg said last night, he wasn't her responsibility, and Al saw how she took it when he said that, how hurt she looked. 'We guessed something had happened when you didn't make it for supper. And of course, we couldn't get in touch with you.'

'Greg said he had a full charge on his phone when we left. It was only when we came to use his phone that we saw it hardly had any power left, and he switched it off to save it. And then he couldn't switch it on again. We didn't expect you to worry. It didn't occur to us.'

Al believed him. And he thought about the way Sophie thanked him, and he tried to imagine her sitting on that railway sleeper alone, staring into the dark alone, seeing the light falling, alone, driving to the quarry, alone. But she was a strong woman. Alone, she would have reacted the same way, he had no doubt about that; she would have got into her car to see if she could help.

Sophie ran the bunkhouse for emotional reasons. It was a way of being with people and looking after them without commitment.

Eric and Jane had kept the place for a completely different purpose: financial. It was the only way to run a business, really. But then, they were married.

He wouldn't say that he and Virginia had a perfect marriage. He knew for sure that she'd spent a lot of time worrying about him over the years when he was away at sea, but they both made sure that they never parted on an argument, so that if the worst happened, she'd have no reason to blame herself. In the main his doubts were small and fleeting and he believed hers were too. He hoped so, anyway.

He assumed Owen had fallen back to sleep, but his eyes were open and he was still looking at Al. 'Hey, Al, about the snorkelling—'

'Yes?'

'We would never have lived it down if we'd got caught swimming in the reservoir. We'd have been the two idiots they talk about in the pub.'

Al suspected he was right.

He gave up on the idea of going back to sleep and he got out of bed, dodging Greg's dangling arm, took his washbag from the footlocker and went for a shower.

Sophie was in the kitchen, reading the news on her phone. She was wearing an orange midi dress and orange strappy sandals. 'Porridge?' she asked Al cheerfully.

She served it with cream and plenty of brown sugar that slowly dissolved in a puddle of sweetness on the oatmeal. With a flourish, she put a jug of whisky in front of him.

Al could imagine Virginia recoiling in horror at the sight. He added a splash of whisky, not too much; he was running out of days and suddenly he felt a deep pang of longing for this place, as if he had already left his heart behind. He tried to explain the feeling.

'You know what that is? That's *hiraeth*,' Sophie said. She was as bright as always, but her face was puffy, as if she hadn't slept. 'It means a kind of heartfelt yearning for somewhere. It's an emotion as much as a word.'

'You've put your finger on it.' He tried the word out. '*Here*—'

'—*Eyeth*. As if you're saying eyes, but with a lisp.'

'*Here-eyeth!*'

'Spoken like a Welshman,' she said, laughing. 'You've got a new word in your Welsh vocabulary. Any signs of life from the lads?'

'Greg's flat out. Owen's awake. He's got a sling for his arm.'

She considered this information. 'Okay. Al – I'm going out shortly to see a friend.'

'You are?' He looked so surprised it was almost an insult. 'You're perfectly dressed for the occasion,' he added gallantly.

'Thanks! I'll be back by lunchtime. Please could you tell them to help themselves to porridge?'

CHAPTER TWENTY-FIVE

Driving to the Quaker Friends' Meeting House, Sophie thought about Elin who had, as Mary put it, 'seen the light'.

She was going to have to be tactful about the past – not everybody wanted to be reminded about it.

The meeting house was up in the hills above Trefor. It was a mock-Tudor-style building with a wooden sign: MEETING THIS WAY. An arrow directed her to a grassy lawn in the garden. Beyond the garden was brown bracken, crisped in the heat, and beyond the bracken, miles of heathland covered in heather, dense enough to turn the hills purple.

A circle of twenty wooden chairs were arranged on the grass. A dark-haired guy was sitting in one of them, wearing dark jeans and a black T-shirt, his legs outstretched, his eyes closed. Which was convenient because it meant she could stare at him. He was good-looking, about her own age, maybe a little older.

There was no altar and no lectern, so she sat next to the man in an act of solidarity. He sensed her presence, opened his eyes and smiled a greeting. 'Good morning.'

'Hi! Are you the priest?'

He laughed. 'No, it's not that kind of service. Is this your first time here?'

'That's right. I'm here because of a friend,' she said. 'Elin Jenkins.'

'Ah, okay.'

Sophie felt two emotions at the same time – triumph, followed by dismay because it was a dumb thing to say. It was going to be perfectly obvious that Elin had no idea who she was – and vice versa. 'I mean, I've come through my mother, who knows her. Knew her, I should say. She was a friend of my aunt, actually. Anyway, I thought I'd give it a go. It sounds interesting.'

'Fair enough,' he said.

He looked amused.

He'd probably come here early to enjoy the peace, and she wasn't letting him have any. He closed his eyes again.

'Um, I haven't got a hymn book,' Sophie said.

'You don't need one. We have prayer and waiting.'

'Waiting? Waiting for what?'

He put his hands behind his head and considered his words before he spoke them. 'For the spirit to move us,' he said.

'Oh.' She hadn't reckoned on audience participation. 'What if I don't get moved?'

He grinned. 'You can sit quietly and enjoy the peace.'

'Okay.' She took the hint.

Sitting quietly, staring at the wispy clouds, the open air seemed the obvious place for prayer when the weather was like this, she thought; with the choir of sheep, bees and birdsong, and the occasional circling drone of a fly.

She wondered what Elin looked like in her old age. She only knew her through a handful of adjectives as a dark-haired, lively girl; a rebel. She probably had white hair now and was cosily plump.

Sophie checked her phone. *Five minutes to go.* People were coming across the grass, chatting, laughing, smiling at her, filling the circle of chairs.

There were three elderly ladies, *distinct possibilities*, she thought, a couple of families, a woman pushing a man in a wheelchair, and two women in their twenties wearing torn jeans who ran past the building and slowed to a halt when they saw they weren't late.

The white-haired ladies smiled at Sophie and closed their eyes in prayer while she stared at them and tried to imagine any one of them dancing naked on a grave and being reunited with their lost lovers. Who wouldn't want that? Who wouldn't be delighted to know that they were still wanted passionately after all these years?

After a few minutes silence, the guy in black said a few words about something unknown emerging on the horizon of their lives, and Sophie closed her eyes, too. Her thoughts veered off in all directions; she wondered whether Elin was here, and about the three girls – Lydia, Belle and Molly – continuing on their walk to Bala, and if Greg was going to climb today, and whether she would go home and make Al's day a time for celebration.

And then her thoughts settled and stilled. Time went by unmeasured. It was so deeply quiet that she opened her eyes and blinked in the bright greenness of the day. She looked at the faces of everyone in the circle, sitting relaxed – some faintly smiling, and she felt a sudden unexpected burst of happiness, as sweet and physical as the spray of juice from a fresh orange. She recognised it instantly, and she also realised with some wonder that she'd never felt it before.

A man's voice said from close by, 'Thank you for the peace of this space, and the company of friends.'

Sophie took a deep breath and breathed it out slowly, looking through her eyelashes at the people in the circle, wondering which of the men had spoken and who would speak next. They all seemed content with the silence. It felt buoyant, relaxing, like the sensation of lying on an inflatable in a pool in the sun.

She closed her eyes tight again and the time passed and the grasshoppers chirped. She jerked out of sleep when after some time, people around her started to move.

She sat up and glanced at the guy next to her in a sudden panic that she was going to miss Elin. 'Excuse me, which one is Elin?'

He looked around. 'She's there, right behind you. The lady with the guy in the wheelchair.'

'Thanks.' Sophie felt a thrill of satisfaction at finding Al's first love.

Elin Jenkins was wearing a deep blue and white striped shirt dress, with a belt tied in a knot around her slim waist. Her dark hair was short, flecked with grey, her tanned, veined hands resting lightly on the wheelchair handles. She was laughing with the three elderly ladies who had come early.

In contrast, the man in the wheelchair looked physically broken. He was strapped into it, his head held up by a padded collar around his neck. He was stylish in a light-coloured linen suit and a straw trilby with a black hatband. The three ladies said something to him, and his reply made them laugh.

The man in black had begun to stack the chairs. 'Who is the guy Elin's with?' Sophie asked him.

'That's Rob Johnson. Her husband.'

'Really? She's married?'

If he was surprised at how very little she knew about this friend of her mother's, he didn't say. He smiled. 'We're serving tea and coffee in the meeting house,' he said, 'if you're not in a rush.'

Sophie looked at the way Elin was bent forward over her husband, laughing affectionately, her face above his. She felt rather resentful, as if they'd tricked her in some way. This was not the story she was expecting.

Still, she was here now.

She moved closer to them, hovering patiently on the outskirts of the little group until the three women moved away and she introduced herself. 'Hello! I'm Eric and Jane Oswald Hughes's niece, Sophie,' she said. 'You're Elin, aren't you?'

The woman's blue eyes widened in surprise. 'Well! There are some names from the past,' she said. 'So, you'll be Mary's daughter!'

'That's right.'

'This is Rob, my husband.'

'Hi!' Sophie greeted him. She wiped her sweaty hands on her orange dress and shook his hand. It was crooked and hard with scar tissue. She met his watery hazel eyes, submerged by tears, magnified by his glasses.

'I won't get up,' he joked, tilting the brim of his trilby.

Sophie laughed, but Elin didn't. She was looking at Sophie curiously, her eyes a deep blue, almost navy under her angled eyebrows. Her skin was cobwebbed with lines, tight over her cheekbones, and she had dark purple smudges under her eyes. She was attractive and held herself like the kind of women you see shopping in Harvey Nicholls and visiting the Royal Academy; intelligent and astute. 'What brings you here?' she asked, getting to the point.

Sophie hooked her hair behind her ear. 'I've taken over Mountain Ash since Eric and Jane retired and I've got a visitor who remembers you from years back.'

'What visitor?' Elin asked.

'His name's Al Locke.'

'Al Locke,' Elin repeated. She frowned, as if she was trying to place him, and then she touched her finger lightly to her upper lip. 'What's he doing here?'

Sophie glanced down at Rob – behind his glasses his gaze had grown distant.

'He's researching Abraham Lincoln's family tree. The Welsh branch.'

'Is he?' Elin gave a little smile.

'You showed him where Lincoln's great-great-great grandmother's grave was. He's come back to find it.'

Elin raised her eyebrows in surprise. 'But it's all submerged. There's nothing of Hafod Fadog to be seen now.'

'Yeah. He didn't know.'

'Didn't he?' Elin pursed her lips in thought. 'No, obviously he didn't.' Then she gave a brief laugh. 'It was a long time ago,' she said. 'And he's had a wasted journey. It was such a long time ago,' she repeated, more to herself than to Sophie. Her words seemed to melt with yearning as she spoke them.

Her husband heard the way she said it, as if the words were painful to her, and he raised a trembling hand in the air like a pupil wanting attention.

Straight away Elin caught it in hers, steadied it and pressed her lips against his scarred and crooked fingers.

As she did it, her eyes met Sophie's for a moment and their gaze locked. There was something in that look that Sophie couldn't place. And then she recognised it. *Defiance.*

Elin's eyes reddened and she looked away, towards the meeting house. 'I'm so sorry, we must go. Give Jane and Eric our best regards, won't you? And your mother.'

It was a dismissal, and Sophie said quickly, 'Actually, I came to invite you to a barbecue, if you'd like to come? Tomorrow's Al's last night and we're giving him a good send-off.'

Elin raised her eyebrows. 'Who's inviting us, him or you?'

'I am. I didn't know if I'd find you here or not, so I haven't mentioned it to him yet. I didn't want to have to disappoint him.'

'Ah,' Elin said mischievously, 'you were going to surprise him with me, were you? Tah-dah!' She rested a warm hand on Sophie's arm. 'Don't tell him you met me,' she said, with her sweet, knowing smile. 'I'd really appreciate it if you didn't.'

She turned the wheelchair abruptly and wheeled it over the grass as Rob raised his straw trilby and shimmied it in farewell.

Sophie watched them go up the ramp into the meeting house. She looked around. She was alone, the last person left in the garden. All the chairs had been put away and as she passed the open door she could hear the warm hum of conversation from inside the room.

'So that's that,' she said to herself.

When she got into her car, the heat was stifling.

She sat back and went over the conversation in her head, feeling sweat roll slowly down her chest and pool in her cleavage. Tears of frustration leaked from her eyes.

She was still exhausted from the night before, because for a while that panic she felt when she saw the light drop down the mountain gave her a flash of insight into her feelings about Greg, a sudden painful despair over missed opportunities, and all the possibilities that she'd turned her back on.

She had invested a lot, too much, in Al's love story, acting as if it was some kind of relationship template she should aspire to. It was like the early reckless days of love, when the other person and all the feelings they stirred up were still an exciting novelty. They were the best times, when she felt truly alive, and then at the end, she supposed, at the end of life, love held the same urgency, everything had to be said before it was too late, when people realised the enormity of what they had had and were about to lose.

And in between those times, there was the long period of sanity and insanity of getting along on a daily basis, the awareness of permanence that tipped into boredom sometimes.

Sophie yawned and wiped the tears from her chin. She hadn't for a moment considered the search for Elin would end like this, in a dismissal. She knew where she'd gone wrong. She'd made a mistake, coming here herself, making herself the go-between.

She should have told Al where to find Elin and let him come himself.

It might have been different; and now she'd gone and spoilt it.

CHAPTER TWENTY-SIX

'Captain, I've come to offer you an apology,' Eric told Al at the bunkhouse, his hands in his pockets, squinting against the sun. 'I'm the kind of man with a vivid memory of being wronged, whilst readily forgetting the wrong I've done to others.'

'That goes for all of us,' Al said with a dry laugh. 'Anyway, you were only telling the facts. About the wedding invitation, I mean.' He put his sunglasses on. 'Was it true that Elin waited for a letter from me, day after day?'

Eric puffed out his cheeks regretfully. 'Yes, it was true enough. And I had little enough sympathy for her at the time, I'm ashamed to say. I hope you find her, Al, before you go, for your sake, and for mine, too. Jane and I, we'd like to make things right as best we can. Believe it or not, I was a bit of a prig in those days, it might surprise you to know.'

Al was so astonished at Eric's statement that he laughed out loud. 'No! Were you? I didn't notice.'

Eric looked at him speculatively, rocking onto the balls of his feet. 'Take my advice, Captain. Never play poker. You're a terrible liar.' He glanced at his watch. 'I haven't got long because there's a man coming to insulate my loft at three. It doesn't need insulating, mind, because it's carpeted, but he's phoned me a few times now and I like to have a little sport. What are your plans?'

'I'm going to the National Whitewater Centre to watch the kayakers.'

'Very soothing. I'll walk with you, stretch my legs,' Eric said.

They made their way from the bunkhouse to the road across the top of the dam to see the release of water. The grass was green on the topsoil, curving down into the valley. The transverse drainage channels led to a churning outfall; Al admired the engineering.

It was half a mile to the entrance of the National Whitewater Centre. At the cafe with its striped sunshades, Eric told Al to sit down and allow him to treat him to a coffee.

'I've bought you a ham and salad sandwich,' he said a few minutes later, raising his voice over the noise of the water. He put the tray in the middle of the table. 'I feel that low blood sugar might be contributing to your sudden introspection.' He said it with the utmost seriousness, looking at Al from under his dark bushy eyebrows.

Al laughed. 'You know, you could be right. It's been a while since breakfast.'

'I recognise the symptoms. As soon as I begin to feel that life's not worth living and I've run my course and I might as well check my will, lie down and say my goodbyes, I ask myself one simple question, when did I last eat? And once I remedy the lack of food in my life, I am immeasurably cheered and feel I'm good for another ten years at least.'

They watched the kayakers manoeuvring in the tumbling water. Al was glad he was with Eric. He was a resourceful man and basically decent. He liked to imagine they would keep in touch.

A sudden flash of yellow on the river, and a lone kayaker tumbled down the foaming water, struggling to keep his craft upright. Al felt some sympathy for him, and he watched him for some moments until he was swept out of sight.

*

'Hello, Mountain Ash.'

'Who am I speaking to?'

'Sophie.'

'It's Elin here, Elin Jenkins.'

Sophie was suddenly wide awake. 'Hi! Do you want to speak to Al?'

'No,' Elin said quickly, 'don't do that. I wondered if you and I could meet up some time when you're free.'

'Okay! I'm free now. Did you have a place in mind?'

'I was thinking of Bala Lake.'

'In the cafe?'

'No, let's meet in the car park. Go to the far end and I'll see you there. Shall we say in about an hour?'

The lake at Bala was busy with holidaymakers, but there was only one vehicle parked at the far end of the car park, a red Honda. Sophie drove up, parked alongside it and got out of the car, fanning herself with her white baseball cap.

Elin was sitting by the water's edge in one of two yellow picnic chairs. Her eyes were hidden behind large sunglasses. Her dress was rippling in the breeze. As Sophie approached her, she could smell her perfume like an aura.

'Hi,' she greeted her.

'Come and sit down.'

'Thanks.' Sophie sat in the picnic chair and stretched her legs out in the sun. It was a good call, to come up this end, where the silver lake whispered against the shingle and reflected the green hills, and they were away from the busy sailing club, the cafe, the lively children and the barking dogs.

Elin reached down and took a small red flask out of her white tote bag, the lenses of her sunglasses flashing in the sun. 'I've made us coffee. It's better than tea, isn't it, for a flask?'

'Yes. I love coffee.' Sophie tossed her hair away from her face, happy to go along with the small talk. She had a pretty good idea that Elin wanted to talk about Al, and the conversation was probably going to be one you wouldn't necessarily want to have in front of your husband.

Elin poured the coffee into two cups. 'You took me by surprise this morning at the Friends' meeting. You stirred up all sorts of memories I thought I'd laid to rest.'

It could have been an accusation; it was hard to tell. 'I thought you'd want to know Al was back.'

'I wasn't sure how I felt about it,' Elin said and gave a wry laugh. 'What made you think of looking for me there?'

'My mother said you'd become a Quaker and I googled all the websites until I found your name.'

'Clever girl.' Elin's voice softened. 'Tell me, how is Al?'

'Fine. I mean – he's got white hair, but he always looks good, and he's got that unquenchable enthusiasm, you know, that people have when they're passionate about something. Like Abraham Lincoln, I mean.'

'Yes, he was keen on Lincoln when I knew him. It bonded us,' Elin said with obvious tenderness. She appealed to Sophie suddenly, as if her opinion mattered, 'You only need one thing in common, really, don't you?'

'I suppose, yes, I've never thought of it like that before.' A red sailing boat tacked against the breeze.

'Is he still married?'

'Yes.'

'Good.'

A large fluffy black poodle dashed into the water, doggy-paddled in a frantic circle, and came back out transformed into something wet and skinny. 'He was really keen to find you.'

Elin lowered her sunglasses. Her eyes were very blue. 'Is that what he told you?'

'He didn't have to. He turned up after a long flight and a long taxi ride. He got showered and changed, filled his water bottle and off he went to Capel Celyn, all dressed up, smart, smelling of aftershave, wearing a jacket despite this heat. I thought, who puts on aftershave to go for a walk? I mean, he's eighty-five and he didn't even have a rest before he went out.'

It seemed important to give Elin the full picture, so that she would know how important it was to Al to meet her again. 'When he came back, he was like a different man. I thought something terrible had happened to him, but it was just the shock – he hadn't known about the drowning.'

'Eighty-five, is he? Of course, he would be.' Elin pursed her lips and exhaled slowly. She shook her head in disbelief at the passing of time. 'He was a good-looking young man, a head-turner.' Elin smiled faintly, pressing her fingers against her lips. 'Look, I'll be straight with you, I'm not going to see him. I've thought about him a lot and you must think I'm an awful coward, but it just stirs things up in me that I'd rather forget. Has he met Jane and Eric?'

'Yes. I got the feeling from Eric that you had some kind of falling out.'

'Falling out?' She gave a dry laugh. 'You could call it that, I suppose.'

It was hard to tell what she was thinking behind the sunglasses. Sophie waited for her to pick up the conversation again, but the silence dragged.

'I didn't realise you were married. You didn't take your husband's name.'

'No. I had a reputation to repair. I wanted to make Elin Jenkins a name to be proud of.' Her hand shook, spilling her coffee.

Sophie watched the coffee glisten and run like quicksilver across the dry earth. 'And have you?'

Elin smiled. 'I hope so. Rob and I don't have a conventional marriage. You've met him. His injuries were all my doing,' she said, a hint of bitterness in her voice. 'Being young is like being in dreamland. Al and I lived in the moment and I suppose you could say we suspended our critical faculties, but everything we did seemed to make perfect sense at the time. But as a result, I had a lot of stored-up emotions which I directed towards Rob. I ended up hating him. I was awful to him. He was working up in the quarry. I wanted to hurt him.' Her words were soft against the whisper of the water rolling the shingle. 'He smiled at me, walked up to the edge of the quarry, spread out his arms and looked down. I can't say he jumped; it implies energy. Rob was passive. It was like the life had already gone out of him. He just let himself fall.'

'Oh.' Elin's story was so bleak and pointless, so incomprehensible, she couldn't bear it. Sophie pulled her cap lower over her eyes. Despite the sunshine and the view, she felt miserable and desolate, as if she was coming down with something. She wished that they'd stayed by the Loch Café and the boathouse, distracted by the noise and laughter. She thought of Rob in the wheelchair, bent and broken, and his jaunty wave as Elin wheeled him inside, and suddenly she felt a surge of anger, against him, against life. *Emotional blackmail*, that's what it was.

Elin turned to face her. 'To attempt suicide was a criminal offence back then. So I swore on oath in court that it was an accident and that, no, he had no reason to jump, that we were going to get married. And eventually, we did. I owed him that, at least. We moved in with my parents who had relocated to Corwen, to a nice big house on the outskirts of the town. I'd been a nurse, and it made sense for me to look after him, to be his carer, and theirs, too, towards the end.'

'That's messed up.' Sophie had the urge to leave now, get in the car and get Al here, reunite them, make things right before it was too late. 'You don't love Rob, and yet you've looked after him all these years?'

Elin frowned. She took off her sunglasses, perched them on her head and turned her startling blue gaze towards Sophie. 'I do love him. You can't look after someone for this long without loving them.'

'But you've had no life of your own.'

'Why do you say that?'

'Because – oh, I don't know.' Sophie slumped back in the picnic chair and looked out across the water, winding her hair around her hand. 'Don't ask me. I don't get it.'

'I've been *needed*,' Elin said, looking almost amused. 'I know I've disappointed you, after all the trouble you've gone to to reunite me with Al. The truth is, Sophie,' Elin said, putting her hand on Sophie's arm, 'those weeks with Al were the best and happiest time of my life. Nothing can dull them or tarnish them. We were happy and young, and it was gorgeous, being so close in every way. We were soulmates. We had that perfect time together. Life was pure joy. I know the wonder of being in love, because I've experienced it.'

'If you feel like that,' Sophie said in frustration, 'why won't you meet him, just for old times' sake?'

'I'm old now,' Elin said wryly, and she laughed. 'It's ridiculous. You can't get that feeling back.' She turned up the collar of her striped shirt dress where the sun was reddening the side of her neck and she studied her hands for a moment. Her nails were pearly pink. 'Look at me! I've grown claws in my old age,' she said. 'All spots and tendons. I hope Al finds what he's looking for.'

He's looking for you, Sophie thought. She gave it one last try. 'Is there anything I can say to change your mind about coming to the barbecue, just so you can say hello to him on his last night in Wales?'

Elin got to her feet abruptly and folded up her picnic chair with a snap. She put the lid on her flask and put the flask back in the tote bag; each action was deliberate. 'No,' she said briskly. 'Let him remember me as he remembers me.'

Sophie gave Elin her cup back and folded up her chair. She took her white baseball cap off and fanned herself with it. The sweat was making her forehead itch. So much for returning in glory with

Elin as the trophy. It was disappointing and frustrating, but she could understand why she didn't want to meet him; sometimes in life you had to let things go.

She was about to walk round to her car when Elin called her back. She was waving at her with a faded red document wallet. 'Could you give him this before he leaves? He'll find it interesting.'

The document wallet was old and well used. Sophie weighed it in her hands. 'What shall I tell him? Can I say it's from you?'

Elin gave her an amused half-smile. 'He'll know. Somehow, despite the distance between us, we seem to have been travelling the same path.'

CHAPTER TWENTY-SEVEN

Al was in a weird place in his head when he reached the lake. The water was glittering so brightly it was blinding him, and he felt a strong feeling of hatred towards it, a surge of rage. 'What?' he shouted at it. 'What the hell do you want of me?' He cursed it loudly, the words carrying on the breeze.

Suddenly he could see something dark breaking the surface of the water and he was filled with dread. He shut up and stood still, watching, a prickling rush of adrenaline rushing through him as he stood waiting for something to happen. Nothing happened, but he carried on watching and waiting with his heart drumming so fast that it skipped beats and he banged his breastbone with his knuckles to steady it.

The dark shape wasn't getting any closer and neither was it getting any further away.

Debris, he concluded, blinking away the purple after-image, and shielding his eyes from the dazzle. He watched for the shape for a few minutes, until it was lost in the choppy water. It had seemed to be drifting towards the north shore.

Moments later, though, it reappeared, and he fixed its position against the mountains until he became absolutely certain that it was an illusion. It wasn't actually moving at all.

He squinted at the sparkling, alive and whimsical water, which was moody, not to be trusted. Over the past few days, it seemed to reveal a little more of what lay beneath it, like a veil being slowly pulled away, a bride's veil, or a widow's veil. Each day the features of the village became clearer in his mind. He imagined he could now see part of the wall of the farm close to the surface. He wondered if the water level was dropping in the drought. He remembered the night he'd gone for a swim and the feel of his foot touching something dark and deep down under. He wondered if the village was emerging from the waters. He altered the focus of his gaze and looked up at the scrubbed brown mountains, their colours fading out slowly as the cloud shadows moved across them and then he scanned the water again.

*

When Sophie got back to the bunkhouse the place was empty. She guessed where Al would be, and she went down the lane to find him.

He was sitting on the rock by the water's edge, staring at the lake.

Sophie squealed as she staggered down the bank, grabbing a branch to steady himself, and it broke off in her hand. 'Look out!' she shouted, sidestepping down, and she threw the branch in the lake and patted her heart dramatically. 'I thought I was going to go in for a minute.' She put the folder down and sat on the rock next to him, took her shoes off and scraped the dried earth off the heels with her thumbnail.

He looked amused. 'Did you have a good time with your friend?'

'Yeah, it was okay, I suppose.' She frowned, stretched out her legs and studied them critically. 'Look at that! For some reason that I've never understood, my shins don't tan. It's as if I'm wearing socks or something.' She was babbling, putting off the moment of telling him.

Al looked at her quizzically.

Okay. Here goes, get it over with, she thought. 'Al, I've got some news. I've seen Elin, but she doesn't want to meet you. I'm so sorry,' she said in a rush.

'Ah.' A breeze ruffled the lake, throwing reflections across him like confetti. His face was unreadable.

Ah? She wondered. *What did that mean?* 'It wasn't – she doesn't think badly of you or anything. In fact, she said being with you was the best time of her life.'

Al winced, bowed his head and rubbed his face with his hands. He straightened again and turned to Sophie urgently. 'Do you get the impression she's happy?'

'Yes, I do. She's a Quaker now.'

Unexpectedly, Al threw his head back and laughed. 'Oh, Elin,' he said.

Sophie laughed along with him, mostly from relief. She picked up the document wallet and held it out to Al. 'Also – she wants you to have this.'

He took it from her and looked at it doubtfully. 'What's in it?'

'I don't know, I didn't look,' Sophie said virtuously, leaning back on the rock and shaking her hair free of her face. 'It might be private, mightn't it?'

Al opened the document wallet. 'Papers,' he said.

'Yeah?'

Al flicked through them and Sophie glanced over. Some of them were yellow with age, handwritten, the ink faded. Others were neatly typed, and some were just scraps of paper that had been scrawled on.

Al put on his reading glasses and took a sheet out at random which fluttered in his hand in the warm breeze. '"History of the early Quakers",' he said. 'Listen to this: "Amongst many people of substance attending the meetings at Fron Goch was Margaret Evans".' He looked up at her over the glasses. 'Does the name ring a bell?'

Sophie shrugged. 'No.'

'"There she met John Morris of Bryn Gwyn, Denbighshire, and his wife Ellin, daughter of Ellis Williams, Caifadog, who was of royal descent. One of his daughters, Ellin, married Margaret's son Cadwallader Evans from Fron Goch, 1664 to 1745, son of Evan ap Evan. They had a daughter named Sarah." Look! She's underlined the name.'

'Nice,' Sophie said.

'"Consent of parents being obtained, they are left to their liberty to consummate their said intentions to see their marriage orderly accomplished".' Al chuckled to himself. 'This is exactly the kind of stuff I keep. You never know when you're going to come across treasure, some bit of information that if it's not written down you somehow can never find again.'

'Elin said that you and she had been travelling the same path.'

'Did she?' he asked eagerly. 'That's funny.' He seemed pleased at the thought. 'Tell me, did she ever marry?'

'Yes, she did.' She added, 'Her husband's been in a wheelchair all their married life.'

'Is he the reason she doesn't want to see me?'

'She said she wants you to remember her as you remembered her.'

Al raised his eyebrows and didn't comment. He was suddenly riveted by another bit of information he'd come across. 'Listen to this. "Eight years after Evan ap Evan, Cadwallader's father died, the family of five brothers and a sister, Mary, sailed the perilous journey to America from Liverpool, on the 18th April 1698. Cadwallader and Ellin were accompanied by their three children including Sarah, their eight-year-old daughter, and their servants." Where was I? "They sailed via Dublin and departed from Dublin on the 1st May on a vessel named the *Robert and Elizabeth*, belonging to Robert Haydock, with Ralph Williams in charge. During the eleven-week voyage to the New Jerusalem, forty-five passengers and three of the sailors died of dysentery, including their sister, Mary. Every day a couple more bodies were dropped into the sea".'

'Grim.'

'Yeah. "But Cadwallader, Ellin and Sarah survived to be 'kindly received' by the settlers who had already made their homes there. They owned 609 acres of land. In Pennsylvania, Cadwallader, who had not been a Quaker at home, joined the Friends and received a gift of ministry; his testimony though short, was 'instructive, lively and manifestly attended with divine sweetness'".'

'That's nice.' Sophie was glad it was making Al happy. She wondered whether one day she might get all excited over her ancestry. She also wondered what she was going to cook for supper. She rested her weight back on her elbows and squinted up at the sky. It was hazy, oppressive in the heat.

Al had fallen silent beside her.

When he next spoke, his voice was tremulous. 'This is interesting,' he said. 'In Pennsylvania they had these sort of date nights at the Gwynedd Meetings for young people to get to know each other and maybe get married.'

'Like a kind of youth club,' Sophie said helpfully.

'At one of these meetings, Sarah Evans married John Hank from White Marsh.'

'Hank? Where have I heard that name before?'

'Wait! Okay! Sarah and John had a son, John Hank Jr. He married Catherine and had a daughter named Nancy. Oh, Sophie!' he said urgently.

'What?'

'I don't believe it.' Al's voice was hoarse with emotion. '"Moving to Fayette County, Kentucky, Nancy married a man named Thomas Lincoln".' He looked at her, his blue eyes bright with excitement. 'Brace yourself. "And a son to them was Abraham Lincoln".'

Now she really was interested. 'No way! Really?'

Al looked at her. 'Our ideas have been vindicated, justified. It's all wrapped up,' he said incredulously. 'Sophie, this is what I've been looking for. I've been searching for this information for a long time.'

She nudged him with her shoulder, teasing him. 'No kidding, Al. Seriously? You don't say!'

'Hold this for a moment.' Al thrust the folder at her and took the carved Welsh love spoon out of his pocket. He ran his thumb fondly over the carved key, the lock, the chain, the cross. 'See these letters in the heart? CE? I bet you a hundred bucks Cadwallader carved it for Ellin. Take a look.'

The letters were worn to a deep, rich patina. 'CE,' she said, 'can't argue with that.' It was smooth and tactile, warm with ancestral memory. She closed her fingers around it and thought of the hands that had held it over the generations, valuing it as a symbol of love and integrity. She imagined a young man painstakingly carving it over long winter nights in the hills of Wales, and maybe it was Cadwallader for his beloved Ellin, who was she to argue? And it made sense that Ellin took the precious gift with her to Liverpool and kept it safe on that dangerous sea voyage to Pennsylvania.

Al's gaze was distant, settling on the heat-hazy hills. 'Ellin's granddaughter, Nancy, would have taken it to her new home in Kentucky, one day to be treasured by my mother in Philadelphia who gave it to me along with her insight and values. You know, Sophie, I feel as if Elin and I between us have pointed a beam of light into the darkness.'

Sophie agreed. Elin had told her how their interest in Lincoln bonded them. Maybe for both of them, this had been their way of keeping the connection going over the years.

Al patted her shoulder fondly. 'Come on, let's go back. You know what time it is?'

'Yes,' she said with a grin as she gave back the spoon. 'It's time for a beer.'

CHAPTER TWENTY-EIGHT

The following morning, Eric was sitting at the kitchen table with his laptop and Halifax passbook open in front of him. 'Jane!'

'What is it now?'

'I've had a new email from Mr Ai Wong. He wants to know if you've mentioned this financial transaction to anyone, anyone at all.' He looked sternly at his wife over his reading glasses.

She met his gaze indignantly. 'Of course I haven't! And I'm not going to. Apart from anything else, Eric, I'm not sure it's legal.'

'Of course it's not legal, Jane,' he said, lowering his voice. 'Financial institutions are very cautious these days. Anyway, the good news is that Mr Wong has instructed that the money is all ready to be transferred to us. Less his share, of course.'

Jane shook her head. 'And a big share, it is too, at fifty per cent!'

'It's his commission. We mustn't be greedy, Jane. Five-and-a-half million US dollars is still plenty for us, and he's a family man, remember.'

Jane went into the kitchen and filled the kettle. 'To be honest, when you think about it, it's more than our scratch card win.'

The scratch card win had come at the perfect time for them, just when they'd been resigned to working into their eighties and never having any time for themselves – or each other, come to that. And it was hard in the winter, physically and financially, when the weather was cold and damp, and the snow stayed on the hills for months and nobody in their right mind would want to climb, kayak or even walk to the pub.

They used some of the money to do the guest house up to sell it, and it was Dai who suggested having it as a bunkhouse. 'Cheap and cheerful,' was how he put it. 'Get with it, Eric! A bunkhouse is the way to go! If they want en suites, they can come to me.'

Telling Sophie they were selling was the hard part. She had spent most summers with them there as a child. She loved the place. It was home from home for her, and although they agreed that they couldn't keep Mountain Ash on for Sophie's sake, it wasn't an easy thing to tell her, either. They'd put it off for so long that Mary told her instead, casually, in passing, thinking that she already knew.

And they were right, Sophie was upset.

Eric reassured Jane she just needed the time to get used to the idea. Nobody liked change. They would still live in the area, and she would always be welcome.

They didn't hear from Sophie for quite a few days after that and they concluded she was vexed with them. Jane wrote her a warm letter explaining that old age had caught up with them and while they were fighting it off as best they could, they had other things they were keen to spend their remaining energy on such as Nordic walking and knitting with dog hair.

But before they could send the letter, Sophie had arrived at Mountain Ash unexpectedly, looking thin and pale, as if she needed some brisk mountain air. She turned up with her phone in her hand and a spreadsheet and six months of bank statements, and said she wanted to buy the bunkhouse herself – she wouldn't change a thing. And Eric and Jane believed her when she said she wasn't doing it for them. She was totally doing this for herself, she said. She was making a new start. It was a wonderful, heart-warming thing to hear. And she seemed to be doing all right, too.

Following this train of thought, Jane said to her husband, 'People don't realise that money isn't everything. Let's face it, Eric, no ordinary person needs $11 million, do they?'

'I agree but it's still nice to have,' Eric said. 'I have given Mr Wong our bank details. He wants us to get a move on, because of the risks. I must say, he is quite bossy at times.'

'He probably doesn't realise how he comes across.'

'And as he says, in life you have to take any available chance to succeed.'

'*He's* certainly taken a chance.'

Jane poured the water into the mugs, stirred, and fished out the tea bags. She added milk and put one on the table next to her husband.

'Thank you, *cariad*,' he said. 'I'm just letting him know we've struck a hitch though. But only a minor one.'

'What's the hitch?'

'I've told him our bank wants a transaction from his bank first: £50, to prove he's on the level. Dew, there's no honour even amongst bank managers these days. He's going to let me know when he's transferred it.'

While he waited for the transaction to take place, Eric got up and looked in the cupboard for a biscuit to have with his tea. He found the digestives, and dunked one, keeping his eye on the screen. 'He's done it. Fifty pounds.'

Eric finished his biscuit and promptly transferred Mr Wong's fifty pounds from the Halifax account into their current account. 'And there we are! It's done.'

He sat back, folded his arms and looked at his wife with immense satisfaction. '"Nor thieves, nor the greedy, nor drunkards, nor revilers, nor swindlers will inherit the kingdom of God." Corinthians. We've scammed the scammer and we're fifty pounds up on the deal. Don't look at me like that, Jane. I have left the sum of £9.06 for Mr Ai Wong, the manager of the CTBC Shengjing Bank, to spend as he pleases.'

'I'm sure he'll appreciate that,' Jane said.

*

Al's last night at Mountain Ash was a celebration of friendship.

The fire was burning, the food was cooking, and the kayakers, a father and his two teenage sons, were still standing shyly on the outskirts of the fire with their hands in their pockets.

'Come on, lads, help yourselves,' Greg said, leading them to the Tuff Tub full of ice where the beers and soft drinks were chilling.

Sophie was grilling the sausages and burgers on the barbecue. 'You think there's always going to be enough,' she said over her shoulder, 'but I like to make sure. Fresh air's good for the appetite.'

'Do you know, Al,' Eric said seriously, 'you can't get tinfoil for baked potatoes any more only aluminium foil, which is not the same at all and lacks durability?'

'That's a fact I'll take home with me,' Al said with a grin.

He sat next to Eric on the railway sleeper and Al watched the flames eating into the logs. He drank his beer, and over the beat of the music, the sky slowly darkened to turquoise and the night closed in on them, black shapes in the firelight. He looked across at Sophie.

She was sitting on the other side next to Greg, her ankle resting on her knee, holding a can by the rim.

They were talking about climbing, about the way they experienced it in their guts, in their soul.

These were things she'd never talked about before.

'When you're there on a route, it feels spiritual, transcendental,' Greg said.

She nodded. She had understood it in that exact same way. She knew what it was to come alive, to have total focus, to feel the flow of the climb, to know the mountain intimately through her fingertips, to rest her cheek against the warmth of the rock.

'Authentic Desire,' she said, looking into his dark eyes. It was the name of a climb, and also what she was feeling.

He clinked his beer against hers and smiled. 'You got it.'

She could very easily imagine them climbing together, coming back buzzing, desperate for beer and hard adrenaline sex. It would be a good day, a worthwhile day.

Jane was searching in her bag and she took out a package wrapped in white tissue paper and handed it to Al.

He was surprised, but they were both looking at him expectantly, so he felt obliged to open it. Inside the tissue were two grey woolly cuffs. He looked at Jane quizzically.

'They're wrist warmers,' she said. 'There's nothing like them for rheumatism.'

Eric tapped him on the knee. 'Remember that dog, Keith, who chased us from Bryn Mawr?'

Al shuddered. 'Trust me, I'll never forget him.'

'Well, Captain, Jane knitted these wrist warmers from his dog hair,' Eric said. 'As a memento. They'll be more use to you than a snow globe.'

Al put them on his wrists and held them up to the light of the flames. 'They're warm, all right. I feel like a werewolf,' he said.

'Aye, just to be on the safe side, don't go wearing them on a full moon.'

Al laughed. 'Thank you, Eric. And thank you, Jane.' Uncharacteristically, he reached across and kissed her hand.

'There's a charmer!'

The kayakers were talking to Owen about the route they would be taking the following day. They were stoked to be here for the release of water from the dam, which meant they would be doing the legendary Graveyard, part of their white-water route along the River Tryweryn to Bala.

Jane passed the burgers to them, mightily impressed by their healthy appetites.

After they finished eating, Owen got to his feet and sang a hymn in the silence, making room for God on that lovely night.

Above them the dark-blue star-pricked sky was smudged with cloud.

'You're getting out just in time, Al,' Owen said, sitting down again. 'It's going to rain tomorrow.'

'He's taking the weather with him.'

'Aye, by tomorrow evening those hills will all have greened up again.'

'We'll get wet,' one of the kayakers said, and laughed.

CHAPTER TWENTY-NINE

Next morning, Al sat on the edge of his bunk with his kitbag on his knee, looking round the room for the last time. He took his bag into reception, left it by the desk and went outside.

A chill breeze was coming from the mountains, tugging at his shirt and stripping the parched leaves from the trees, sending them swirling around the yard like whirlpools.

The bare, distant hills were slowly being blotted out by a bank of black storm clouds. Arenig Fawr was fading in the mist, dark, brooding, without definition. It was true, it was going to rain.

He was feeling that last-day aimlessness of the traveller, the waiting, the hiatus, the gap between separate worlds. There was nothing to do until the taxi arrived. He'd had his last breakfast at the big wooden table, he had emptied his locker. Looking at his watch he realised he had time to take a final walk down to the lake.

In the green tunnel the leaves rustled and shivered, and he passed the dead badger with hardly a glance, walking to the sweetness of birdsong, humming a tune that had come to him at the barbecue the night before, until he came out onto the road.

A red car was parked up in the lay-by, and he descended the steep mossy bank, steadying himself with his hands, until he reached the rocks that edged the lake.

He whistled in surprise at what he saw.

The lake was nearly empty. He stared at the remains of the village emerging glistening from the muddy landscape. He could see the bend in the road where the school was, and the bridge, with the river running under it unhindered. He could make out the foundations of the post office, the chapel with the remains of its walls, and he could see the chapel cemetery, too, visible against the hills.

A flash of red caught his eye. A woman was walking purposefully through the mud with her back to him, her red dress fluttering against her black wellingtons. She was brisk and purposeful, with a bounce in her step, heading towards Hafod Fadog. He suddenly felt very alert and full of energy, because the culmination of all that he'd hoped for was closer now than it had ever been.

He clambered and slid over the red rocks, his heart pounding, wanting to get close to her. He eased himself down onto the wet, shifting gravel, always watching her, breathless but saying her name to himself. For a long time as he walked cautiously and laboriously through the sucking mud, like a man in a dream or in a nightmare, he got no nearer to her.

She was heading to the Quaker cemetery. She made her way slowly, respectfully around the remains of the wall, as if she could still see it as it used to be, with the gate half open and the farmhouse below.

He was not too far away from her now. She was studying the ground with her hands on her hips, looking for something.

Then she stopped, bunched her dress up and crouched by something in the mud, pausing to push her hair out of her eyes with the back of her wrist.

She straightened, stretched, looked up at the dark sky.

He watched her with excitement and joy, and with longing.

With *hiraeth*.

It was so much what he'd hoped for that he didn't dare call her name.

If this was it; if he took away this final image of her like a gift, this would be enough to last him, he told himself.

But it wasn't true. He had been imagining her for the past six days and the last sixty years, and she was still too far away from him. Here and there, glistening in the dim light, rippling pools reflected the purple clouds. 'Elin!' he called in desperation.

She turned towards him, flicking the mud off her hands.

He couldn't see her expression, just the tilt of her head as she looked at him. She showed no sign of recognition, and she didn't raise her hand or shout a greeting. She stood very still, her arms dangling by her sides, and the only movement was the fluttering of her muddy dress.

For a moment, that's how they remained.

She went back to her task, tugging at a white stone half buried in the mud, the kind of stone you find on a beach, a stone he'd seen before.

Tentatively, he approached her. She was grunting softly under her breath with the effort and he crouched next to her, and they pulled it together. Despite that it seemed impossibly stuck in the embrace of the silt, and then without warning the mud slurped and the stone came free. They laid it down, and with her foot, she filled the indentation with gravel and put the stone back, rinsing the mud off her hands in a puddle. She straightened, shook her hands off to dry them and looked up at him triumphantly, sharply angled eyebrows raised above blue eyes, mud in her hair.

'Hello.' She raised her dark, curved eyebrows, smiled, and then she held her arms out to him.

When Elin smiled like that, right at you… it was like stepping into sunlight.

He wrapped his arms tightly around her with a groan and felt her cheek hot against his. She rested her warm, damp head on his shoulder, their clothes blowing in the gusty west wind. It was just as he'd always remembered, the feel of Elin's slender body against his, her warmth.

He pressed his mouth against her hair and raised his eyes to the summit of the mountains lost in black clouds to say a prayer of thanks for finding her again.

'You okay, Elin?' he asked her when he could speak again. 'Everything all right with you?'

'Yes, Al.' She laughed and raised her eyebrows as if it was a long-held joke between them. 'Everything all right with you?'

It was the same between them now as it had been in the beginning. Time was slipping away. 'Tell me what your life's been like,' he said. 'Have you been happy?'

'Yes, it's been a good life.'

'Do you have a husband? Children?'

'A husband.' She looked down at the white stone and looked up at him, her gaze locked on his. 'I was going to have a baby, but she died.'

Despite not being a perceptive man, she didn't need to say any more. He understood the gesture and the pain in her eyes, and he guessed how it had happened, and the part he'd played in it. He rubbed his wet cheek against hers, feeling as if his heart would break.

'She's next to Margaret Evans,' Elin said.

'Margaret Evans. That's it. I couldn't remember.' He repeated the name on the modest memorial that looked like a stepping stone in the mud. He would never forget it again as long as he lived. 'I'm sorry, Elin, I'm so sorry,' he said into her hair.

'Don't be. It's the same between us as it used to be, isn't it, Al?' she said. 'The feeling that there is everything to look forward to. We have this miraculous ability to make the very best of things.' She raised her face to his, and, submerged in her blue gaze, he felt his spirit lift and soar, the joyful pounding of his heart. Huddled together, her warm mouth on his, the mouth that fitted his perfectly, they kissed and held each other tight. Presently, reluctantly, she let him go.

A gust was blowing the storm clouds over them and the sky darkened. 'It's going to rain,' she said softly.

There was a low, growling rumble of thunder, and the rain was immediate and heavy, a deluge. Together they made their way back to the rocks on the shore; Al looked up the familiar route of the steep and mossy bank and in a sudden burst of strength he lifted Elin up in his arms and carried her to the tree-line, his head humming with effort, his heart pounding wildly, his breath tearing in his throat.

They were laughing as he put her down. They grabbed each other's hands and ran together towards her red car and he doubled over on the bumper to catch his breath in the noise of the rain.

Don't go, he wanted to say as she got into the driver's seat.

He saw the blue disabled badge on the windscreen, and a straw trilby with a black band on the passenger seat. He wondered about it for a moment, and then he crossed the road to the track and stood in the green tunnel of branches and watched her driving away, tyres splashing, wipers squeaking.

When he got back to the yard of the bunkhouse, the taxi was idling in the yard.

Sophie was waiting for him under a rainbow-coloured golfing umbrella. 'Here he is!' she shouted, twirling the umbrella, her words muffled by the rain.

The driver was checking the time – he had already stowed his bags in the car. 'I've got some newspapers you can put your feet on,' he said gloomily, looking at the mud on Al's sodden shoes.

'Give me a minute. I just want a last look round.' Al went inside, breathing in the familiar smoky smell of the bunkhouse for the final time.

Sophie brought him a yellow towel, warm from the drying room, and she looped it round his neck. 'You can dry yourself off in the cab,' she said.

Al gripped her hands, the rain dripping down his face. He looked transformed.

'Sophie, I saw her! The lake was empty, all the water had gone, and she was just there, the way I remembered her.'

For a moment she wondered if it was his imagination. 'Did you talk to her?'

'I did.' His smile faded, and for a moment he seemed full of regret.

'Is everything okay?' she asked him.

'Yes,' he said. 'Everything's okay.' He nodded, as if he was confirming it in his mind. 'Sophie, it's been a blast.'

'Hasn't it!' She looked towards the window, untangled a strand of hair caught in her eyelashes and raked her hair away from her face. Then she turned back to him. 'I'm going to miss you.'

The taxi driver came in. 'Are you ready? Got everything? Passport, phone, keys?'

Al patted himself down. 'Yup. Got 'em.'

The driver rubbed his hands together. 'Right then. Let's be off.'

'So how was it?' the taxi driver asked, looking at Al in the rear-view mirror.

'Wonderful!'

'Did you find Abraham Lincoln's ancestor?'

'Actually, yes. Her name was Margaret Evans.'

'Good for you! And you've given his mother – what was her name, now?'

'Nancy Hank.'

'Yeah, that's it, Nancy. You've given her a Welsh pedigree?'

'I have.'

'And you're putting it on Wikipedia?'

'Maybe.' Al wiped the condensation from the window with the edge of his hand. 'Yeah,' he said, 'I could do that.'

'And was your girl waiting for you in the village?'

Al thought about this for a few long moments.

'Yes,' he said at last. 'I think she was. I think she was waiting for me.'

The driver chuckled to himself. 'Who says the art of conversation is dead?'

Al was reflecting that he'd spent a long period of time losing himself in the past. When he got to the airport, he would call in at the duty-free shop, and buy Virginia something nice.

But what he was really taking back to her was something very different – it was the miraculous human ability to make the very best of things.

He would look to the future and give her that, so that together they could carry on going with a fierce joy and love of life.

And should he, one day, meet Charles again, he could stand before his son with his head held high and, in his presence, return with equal fervour the lit-up passion of his gaze. *Just do it.*

'Still,' the driver said, 'I expect you're glad to be going home, now that the weather's broken.'

Through the window the landscape was pixelated by the rain: green, yellow, grey, brown. For the first time in many years, Al felt grief building up in him, like a hard, unyielding lump in his heart.

'I *was* home,' he said.

*

Long after the taxi disappeared from view, Sophie stayed in the porch with her arms crossed, watching the rain splash up off the yard, ruffling puddles, turning dust to mud, covering the leaves, bending the trees.

The village of Capel Celyn would soon be covered over again after its brief reappearance, submerged but not lost.

She realised with a sudden surge of gratitude how happy she was to be here in this place, doing what she did and living the life she had chosen for herself.

Hers was the light on the side of the hill, welcoming walkers, climbers and ramblers as they faced their challenges and kept their pilgrimages, telling their stories as they passed through on their trudging, bone-aching, triumphant journeys.

Some of them, like Al, held it in their dreams and would return.

A LETTER FROM NORMA

Dear Reader,

I hope you have enjoyed the story of *The Drowned Village*. If you want to keep up to date with my latest releases, just sign up at the following link. I can promise that your email address will never be shared and you can unsubscribe at any time.

www.bookouture.com/norma-curtis

There is nothing quite as intriguing as coming across a lake that covers a drowned village. They are to be found all over the world, but the one I know best covers the village of Capel Celyn in North Wales. It is a beautiful, clear stretch of water encircled by green hills, and the grassy dam has a gracious majesty, sweeping down into the valley like a bridal train and enabling an impressive lacy release of water down river for rafters and kayakers.

It is only during a rare, long hot summer that the lost village puts in an appearance, gradually disturbing the surface, and then one day you can see the curve of the bridge, and the road, and the foundations of the school, and the walls of the cemetery. The grave marker of Lincoln's ancestor lies peacefully under the water most of the time, undisturbed but unforgotten. These are the remains of the small, lively community that lived and farmed and loved there over generations.

There are many things in our lives that get covered over as time passes but which nevertheless leave a permanent legacy. There was fierce opposition to the flooding of the village of Capel Celyn which ultimately led to Wales having its own parliament and in 2005, Liverpool City Council finally issued a formal apology for the drowning. That's the bigger picture, and a different narrative.

This story is about the lives that it affected, especially that of the handsome American hero who fell in love with a Welsh girl from a green valley and came back to find her.

It's always fabulous to hear from my readers – please feel free to get in touch directly on my Facebook page, or through Twitter, Instagram, Goodreads or my website. If you have a moment, and if you enjoyed *The Drowned Village*, a review would be very much appreciated. I'd dearly love to hear what you thought, and positive reviews help to get our stories out to more people.

Warmest wishes,
Norma Curtis

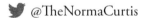 @TheNormaCurtis

ACKNOWLEDGEMENTS

The characters in this story started off like new acquaintances. My husband, Paul, initially gave me his keen perspective on them over a glass of wine, and my inspiring agent, Judith Murdoch, with her professional talent for knowing what makes a good story, cut and refined it until the happy result was that it led to Bookouture being interested in the novel.

Kathryn Taussig, with her editor's insight and instinct, showed me that I'd only just skimmed the surface of the story. She went deep, and I'm so grateful because the book is all the better for it.

Printed in Great Britain
by Amazon

87878817R00150